THANK GOD FOR MR. CHANEY

Rudy Gray

iUniverse, Inc.
Bloomington

Thank God for Mr. Chaney

This is a work of fiction. All of the characters, names, incidents, organizations, and dialogue in this novel are either the products of the author's imagination or are used fictitiously.

iUniverse books may be ordered through booksellers or by contacting:

iUniverse
1663 Liberty Drive
Bloomington, IN 47403
www.iuniverse.com
1-800-Authors (1-800-288-4677)

Because of the dynamic nature of the Internet, any Web addresses or links contained in this book may have changed since publication and may no longer be valid. The views expressed in this work are solely those of the author and do not necessarily reflect the views of the publisher, and the publisher hereby disclaims any responsibility for them.

Any people depicted in stock imagery provided by Thinkstock are models, and such images are being used for illustrative purposes only.

Certain stock imagery © Thinkstock.

ISBN: 978-1-4620-3469-7 (sc)
ISBN: 978-1-4620-3471-0 (hc)
ISBN: 978-1-4620-3470-3 (e)

Printed in the United States of America

iUniverse rev. date: 7/27/2011

CHAPTER 1

The awakened sparrows and blue jays gibbered insistently. He looked out into the shadow-filled street past tree branches and limbs, buds newly forming. Birds were buildng their nests now and fresh warmth teased the air.

It signalled a beginning of the day, of early spring, of life. Still, he couldn't contain the rancor lingering inside him. The pure joy from beginnings would have to embrace him another day.

Dionne stirred in bed behind him. He sucked his teeth quietly, though with partial apology. Once again, it had been anger, contrition, and a poignant impotence in relating to her. Was peace to be forever beyond him? How tired he was of wrangling with her, being constantly on the rack, struggling to prove himself worthy of his place in her universe. The great struggle was over, the marches in this or that great American city, and they'd gained little. The great passion over noble causes, diverted elsewhere or at rest. In fact, things were getting worse. So what had been the point?

He did love her dearly, treasured her presence in his life, her dynamism, her beauty, her fascinating neuroticism, and her soul. But the fact was that their relationship had come to a fatiguing impasse. For months now, he'd been restless, inattentive to her, acrid in his responses. Resilient, she'd ridden his various moods and rhythms like a seasoned downhill racer, but this did not assuage him. Nor did her doting on him and his handsome, brown-skinned, moustachioed figure, his smoldering eyes and aquiline nose, calm the restiveness of his spirit.

She did not swallow everything with equanimity, however.

"These pedagogic hacks!" he had raged the night before as he was wiping the dishes. "They strut about the halls like they own the universe. 'I'm on the fourth salary step! What step're you on?' Or they sit around the teacher's cafeteria table—one finger tucked into the handle of their third or fourth cup of coffee, which they seem to need more than oxygen, and in the other hand a cigarette, smoke wafting off through the air—and talk about what great teachers they are, how they teach dynamic, scintillating lessons and how the kids're spurred on to seek the Holy Grail. If they really meant it, I wouldn't mind so much, even if they failed in their efforts. But they don't mean one word of it. Worse, they don't care. After all, what difference does it make? These little brown animals they call the students and their brown mothers and their brown fathers, if they're around. And their brown smells—it's all immaterial to them anyhow. What do they know about ejumication?

"And the mediocrity and cant get traded back and forth, and nothing changes because nothing is supposed to change. The whole thing's a travesty that insults the kids, the world, and makes a mockery of my life, because I have to be drenched in it!"

Dionne slammed the washrag down on the edge of the sink, stared at the faucets for a few moments, turned off the water, and pulled off her rubber gloves. Her nails, always neat, polished, ruby red, and not too long, were one of the sexier parts of her.

"Sweetheart. Sugar," she said in a low voice that always portended conflagration. "I love you dearly. You work a taste in bed, and I need you … always. But sometimes you give me a swift pain in the ass. Listen, why don't you quit. Tell Ida she's on her own, and I'll gladly support you. You stay home, take a little part-time job, and you can spend the rest of your time contemplating your navel and the universe's imperfections—perhaps even map out a cosmic plan to revolutionize the educational system. Dedicate it to me and Ida."

"Why do you have to be sarcastic?" he snapped, staring at a soap bubble in the sink.

"I mean it. You think I'm just blowing hot air like your teacher friends? I'll put my money where my mouth is. Can you?"

"Don't be ridiculous."

"Then shut up!" She stormed into the living room. "Christ, how you drive me up the wall with your pissing and moaning about the goddamned teachers!" she said, pacing back and forth. "You're a civil servant, for goodness sakes! Not the curator of the Museum of Highest Art. You're hobnobbing with people who barely scraped through college with Cs and maybe Bs. Who came from homes where you read books to pass exams and advance on the job, not for pleasure or culture. You make me crazy with this naive horsehooey about some higher mission. You been listening to too many public service announcements, brother man. You don't really expect exaltation, candid truth, and brilliance, do you? From the sons of tie salesmen and garage mechanics in these post-Viet Nam times? Give people a break. Give the way things are a break. If you're well past them, hey, tough noogies. You're black and erudite and full of those sparkling diamonds of thought. Fine! Sue City Hall. It's the pie that's been served to you, and you'd better sink your golden ivories into it and be thankful. Because, honey baby, it's the only grit in town. Period. End of speech."

He was still in the kitchen, putting away the dishes, so he had to raise his voice a little to her. "When you were a little girl, you must've wanted to be a rodeo rider, didn't you?"

She lit a cigarette. "Okay, let's have it."

"You like to ride broncos all the time. Crack your whip, hurl invectives, give me what for to a fare-thee-well. You don't try to listen to what somebody says."

"I do listen," she said, blowing a quick puff of smoke into the air. "I've been listening too much."

"You don't listen. You just sit back and pass judgment. You wait for your opportunity to jab with your indignation sword and twist it and destroy the scaffolding of anyone's argument. That's your thing."

"Oh, yeah. Maybe I wouldn't have to do that if you would just be a man! Instead of a scholar and self-pitying, goddamned gentleman."

Stung, he carefully, gingerly hung the dishrag on the rack over the sink. Then he started for his jacket to leave but stopped. Instead, he flopped down in her blue vinyl beanbag chair and glared at her.

She, of course, stared back, not wavering with her bold eyes.

"Wanna watch some TV?" she said finally.

He shook his head and looked away.

"How about a drink?" she uttered, apology in her voice.

"Knock it off!"

She jerked and then started for the bedroom.

"I'm going to bed," she said, her back to him.

"Good night." He didn't move.

"You coming?" There was sensuality to her anger now.

"I may go to my own place tonight."

"No, nigger," she shot back at him, "which is it? You here? Or there?" She folded her arms.

"I'm there," he said, getting up and putting his things together. "I need to straighten some things out in my place. Change clothes."

"Okay, if that's what you want." He caught a slight tremor in her voice. "The poor booby is pouting."

This set his teeth on edge, but he was not going to explode. He held fire. "You looking for a new argument to start now? One harangue wasn't enough?"

"Okay. Okay. I'm sorry," she said, her voice lower.

"Don't do me any favors."

"Why do you pay me so much mind? You know how I like to run my mouth. I love you, baby. And when I see you jerking yourself off, it hurts me, and it scares me. You're the issue. Not the teachers. I couldn't care less about them or their mediocrity or phoniness. You're the house I live in."

In the ensuing silence, the kitchen sink drain sucked the last liter of dishwater into it—an ugly yet sensuous sound.

"Well," she said after a pause. "You going? Staying? What?"

His perverse pride propelled him toward the front door where he met her blocking figure, jaws tense, anxious eyes fixed on him.

"Those were rhetorical questions," she said.

Later, when she wrapped her unripe-peach-fuzz legs around his naked haunches and took him in with what was at once insouciance and hunger, his unabated anger choked his performance, and though she thrashed about a little and moaned, he knew her passion was not altogether sincere and that he was really striking out in bed. Still, she clung to him after, begging him to forgive her mouth and somehow find himself, until he finally fell asleep after first pretending to.

The urge to escape still in him reminded him to button his shirt quickly as he noted the accusatory numbness of his privates.

"Off to school?" he heard behind him. The voice was drowsy, muffled, and feminine. "Bestow our erudition on the eager little kiddies. Magic in the classroom."

"No magic last night," he commented with surprising courage. "Sorry."

"I'm a big girl now," she offered, the faint mustiness of her breath managing to float to him, stinging him with more guilt. She was upset. "I don't expect flashing lights and 'Stars and Stripes Forever' every night. Besides, you weren't that bad."

"Go back to sleep," he said, unassuaged.

"Aye, aye, sir."

He touched the skin covering his pectorals, now softer, sagging. He was slowly sinking like the Titanic into an ocean of midlife flab. A handsome ship still but taking on water fast.

His irrationality somehow connected this to all his failures, setbacks, craven behaviour, and disasters. Part of a long, ongoing process, entropy masked by pseudo-productive energy. When would he ever be able to see through all this, through the opaque shell that encased him, so that he could apprehend answers, dynamics, and solutions more easily and make the right judgments?

He depended too much on the opinions of others, even those unexpressed. Words hurled at him wielded too much power, struck blows to his guts much too devastatingly. A disapproving eye or disdainful face smoldered in his brain long after the action causing them should have been forgotten. And he dwelled too long on actions he took that he shouldn't have or actions he didn't take that he should have.

Dionne's words the evening before had not only stung him but set off a knee-jerk string of tortured remembrances. The unanswered calumny spraying onto him from contemptuous fellow teachers down through the years. The patronizing he'd endured from "his lessers." The lapses in inner strength, resolve, and wisdom on his part.

What better instance than that time he'd arrived at his erstwhile home unexpectedly early and found Ida, still in her light blue housecoat, uneasy, frightened, uncharacteristically silent, clutching the kitchen stove, avoiding his eyes? He stared at her and thought he detected a slight tremble underneath her housecoat. The finer details of her he'd come both to ignore and notice more in the year they'd been separated from each other.

The school had been closed because of a fire in the ceramics shop whose fumes, mostly from plastic, could cause respiratory problems or even asphyxiation for many people there. It was an unplanned mishap he'd welcomed.

Still puzzled by her strange behavior as she hastily placed a grocery list into his hand and asked him to buy the listed items, as she "needed them immediately," he glanced around for his son, whose absence he'd begun to sense.

"Where's Anthony?" he asked her, looking into his bedroom. "Hey, Anthony! Where are you?"

"My mother has'm," she answered a little too quickly.

"She came by this morning to pick'm up?"

"Yes." Ida scraped a smudge from the stovetop.

"Must've been real early," he asserted as his eyes looked around the house. "Unless she had'm all night."

"You wanna call her, if you don't believe me?"

"That's a strange thing to say," he said as he stared at her. Then his eyes snapped to their bedroom door, closed. He marched to it and opened it.

"Who asked you to go in there?" she said.

Inside was Ray, tall, light-skinned, wiry, handsome, with deep-set greenish eyes, his close cut 'fro mussed, sweater on, zipping up his fly. They looked at each other briefly, and then Earl slammed the door.

The interloper in the bedroom walked to the door and opened it just as Earl had returned his glare to Ida's now-bold, staring eyes.

"Look here, brother," said Ray. "Don't be slamming any door in my face like—"

"Get back in the room!" Ida ordered.

"Say what?" Ray said, trying to look outraged and menacing.

"I said, *'Get back in the room and close the door!'*"

An edge had come to her voice that was beyond divining by either man.

Without another word, Ray complied. Her eyes returned to Earl's, and the two stared at each other for a few moments.

"Well," she said finally. "Don't tell me you didn't see this coming."

"Your wrong and strong righteousness is touching," he growled.

"I'm not gonna get into this kinda conversation with you, hear."

His only response was to continue staring at her until he stared her down. "Just remember," she continued, "it wasn't me who went cold on us! Wasn't me who cried about the terrible world day in day out till I wanted to scream."

He merely bolted from the house.

His rage at himself for this grand cowardice, masked as "civility," turned to rage at Ray, the interloper in his space zipping himself up, an air of nervous triumph about him, and then spread from Ray to "the brothers" and their ways before it spiked. The slave who arrived home after a day's labor to find the master's shoes in front of his shack had an excuse. Earl had no excuse, a fact that boiled in the pit of his gut for years after. The seeds for this had been planted in him early in his life by his upwardly mobile background and bourgie values, but now, turning his self-loathing outward, his disapprobation had gone to a new level.

He developed a contempt for various things about "the brothers" he observed—their special language and culture, which he'd always felt outside of, their competitive interactions with each other, the issues that concerned them that never concerned him. Moreover, their swagger, their loudness when speaking to each other, especially their laughter he'd often felt was at him rather than the absurdities of the surrounding universe that should have been their target, were objects of his never-ending scorn. With their situation in American society being what it was, how could they afford so much time and energy at physical movement and show, along with the corresponding neglect of their minds, their complacency in the face of their untapped potential, their lack of sophistication about politics—a lack yet covered by pungent cynicism—and the general way of the outside world that contrasted with their acuity on the everyday vicissitudes of life, so much general superficiality, so many glib and unnecessary word games, and so much redundant insubstantial banter?

Still, intellectually, he understood many of the reasons.

Not unmindful of the other side of this coin, he deeply admired their strength in the face of unconscionable adversity, their far-reaching wisdom about the American way of life, their existential grasp of human motivations and complexities, their charisma, their electric and unspoken communications with each other, their overwhelming sexiness, and, most important, that they were he and he was they.

At the center of this entire conflicted inner rancor, still, stood Ray, surreptitiously mocking him, arrogant, triumphant in his indiscretion. This grated Earl's insides, and his self-reproach from his enmity dominated his spirit.

To offset all this, he involved himself in The Civil Rights Movement, where he met Washington and became close friends with him (though more from the efforts of the latter) despite his disturbing resemblance to Ray. Yes, Washington and Ray were the same physical and facial types—there was no doubt—but Washington's likability put him in another class of people in Earl's personal hierarchy, and he had ignored that until months after their friendship had begun. Ironically, it happened when they both found themselves in fierce competition for the attentions of a very attractive young officer in one of the black nationalist organizations they'd become loosely affiliated with in their search for one that would fit their political needs.

It turned out that the young woman had chosen neither of them, but the damage had been done, the incident generating a growing inner resentment and hostility in Earl, which became a wall between the two, not unnoticed by Washington. No matter how Earl tried to ignore it, conceal it, or rationalize it to himself, it never abated throughout their association.

The culmination of their situation was the march for voter rights in that small southern city whose physical beauty contrasted with its internal ugliness, in human interactions. Anxious, he felt his heart pounding as he looked at his friend, large discs of water under his armpits, war paintlike tension lines on his face. They exchanged smiles as they joined the other marchers preparing to trek through an otherworldly gauntlet of people flanking the sunlit street and riot-helmeted policemen scattered among them. Most ominous of all was the figure of Sheriff Jordan and a few of his deputies, standing in front of the two-story city hall steps, their military-creased shirts, gleaming badges pinned to them, menacing reflector sunglasses, seeming nonseeing, an army of extraterrestrials, and most terrifying, the hands gripping taut leashes holding teeth baring German Police dogs that were wagging their tails as if in eager anticipation of an imminent opportunity to maul.

He watched himself lock arms with a small black woman and a teenager as the twenty-one college students, lawyers, teachers on vacation, and mostly local black citizens—clerks, domestics, handymen—began their march toward the city hall steps. He was near the rear of the parade. Washington was at the front.

When the marchers were seventy feet away from the steps, Earl thought he caught a glimpse of the mayor looking timorously around a curtain on the second floor.

"Stop right there," snapped Sheriff Jordan with a deep, menacing drawl. "You don't have a permit to participate in this criminal march, so I'm asking you people to stop now before there're any consequences."

"We have a permit," said Washington.

"Your permit's been revoked." The sheriff looked around at his deputies.

"We were not informed of this," said Washington calmly. No one else in the parade was allowed to say anything.

"I'm informing you now."

"Who revoked it?" Washington fixed his glare on Jordan.

"Boy, I'm not here to be interviewed by you or any of you. I'm here to enforce the law."

"We have a right to know who revoked our permit," stated Washington firmly. The other demonstrators readied themselves.

The sheriff looked around again at his deputies. "Y'know, I don't think these people're accustomed to our warm climate. Makes 'em teched upstairs. So they do all these outlandish things against our municipality, make things unpleasant for everybody, sort of like the way things are in that garbage dump called New York."

The deputies grunted low-key assent as the dogs stirred and the cattle prods and nightsticks came into view. Worse, fire engines were cruising up to position.

"Now why don't y'all just turn yourselves right around and go back to where you started, and we'll just forget the whole thing."

Washington gestured with his head, and the parade moved forward.

Somehow, in the madness that broke out, Earl became disengaged from his two companions and caught a glancing blow from a nightstick that sent him to the ground. He crawled quickly to the side of the street amid screams and hose spray, voices thick with mania and clicking cameras.

He scrambled between two parked cars, stood up, scanning the many livid faces in the spray mist and dust, and lurched behind the milling crowd to a faded-red brick building. He ducked into the shade from the merciless, insistent sun.

It was then that he saw Washington. One of the water hoses was aimed full blast at him on the ground in the middle of the street. His hands were in front of him in an effort to stave off the steel rod of water ramming him, the spray rainbow filling the air. Then he was rolling about, trying to escape it, but the hose did not relent. Instead, another joined it, and the two intensified their forces.

Suddenly, the rods snapped to another victim and, for Washington, were replaced by jabbing and searching cattle prods and clubbing and crashing nightsticks aimed mainly at his head and shoulders. He covered his head with his arms and jerked about in a prone Saint Vitus's dance as the prods found his privates and solar plexus, poking relentlessly.

His eyes glued to the nightmare, Earl ducked deeper into the shade. He wanted to turn away but couldn't, his revulsion equalled by his fascination. Why was faint glee mixed with his horror? Then, amidst this turbulence, he steeled himself for facing an unpleasant truth about himself.

Washington had morphed into Ray in Earl's frenzied heart bouncing around in torment on that ground, now writhing on his back, his legs pulled to his chest, his shirt sleeve in the grip of savage teeth, his other hand weakly, jerkily trying to push away the prods.

Earl shut his eyes to press the image from his mind and turned away before opening them again. Then the self-reproach from the pinprick of satisfaction deep inside him suddenly lurched from the center of his consciousness.

Three white faces were before him, leering with beer-glazed eyes, their cheeks and necks flushed. "Lookit what we got here," one said, some of his teeth missing. "One a' them piss-ass civil righters." He'd obviously begun chewing tobacco too early in life.

"Doin' his own little demonstratin' back in here," said another, with a scrawny neck.

"You gettin' what you want, boy?" said the third, freckle-faced with red hair partially covering his eyes.

They laughed.

The bony-necked one glanced over his shoulder. "Anybody takin' pictures?"

Earl crawled back against the wall.

"Nah," the freckle-faced one said. "He's one a' them good ole nigrahs. Knows his proper place. Don'tcha, boy? Ain't botherin' nobody. Waste a' energy. Let's go get us one of them ones got sand in'm."

They walked away. The neckless one spat on Earl's shoe.

And their laughing faces joined the other flames in his brain.

The bus ride back had been longer, it seemed, than the night they'd spent in jail, listening to derisive laughter and imprecations among the turnkeys. Some perfunctory medical attention had been given to the injured among them, Washington certainly, and there were the gracious invitations from the townsfolk to leave and not come back or "stay and enjoy their hospitality." It was possible for the demonstrators to derive some middling victory from that; but they still felt their collective tails between their legs, and the companions they left there had terrible fear on their faces. In addition, even when the bus crossed that Mason-Dixon Line, the sense of relief in its passengers was minimal.

There was little conversation among them. Some demonstrators tried to sleep away their pain and outrage all the way back. A few read. Others stared ahead or, like Washington, his head and hands bandaged, gazed out the window at the passing countryside with its lush, many-hued greens and voluptuous oaks. There were some tears whose suppression was discouraged and some vituperation. Earl, not sitting with Washington, leaned back on his headrest and focused on the blue tinted sky view. Even the passing treetops and the still-seeming clouds above appeared to mock him.

At the Port Authority Bus Terminal, the demonstrators parted, embraced each other, voicing determination to start anew at the earliest opportunity. All had the feeling they were sneaking into town.

Washington walked over to Earl and gave him a light punch on his arm. "Say, good professor," he said. "What say we jump to a waterhole and cop us some beers or something with more character if you want?"

Earl stared at him. For a terrible moment, he wanted to escape. The desire, however, turned to rage, not from Washington's likeness to Ray but from the self-revulsion the events in that southern city had caused. Still, he stood rooted in his spot.

At the bus terminal bar, Washington ordered a double scotch for himself and a rum and coke for Earl, who now felt everything moving outside of his grasp. They toasted the good ole U.S. of A. and sipped quietly, gazing at the military array of bottles and glasses behind the bartender. A brief silence fell between them during which neither touched his drink.

An attractive black woman, very dark, 'fro cut so short and neat that it looked artificial, passed by in the main concourse outside. Her ample behind seemed to shimmer in her mauve skirt, its contour lines rhythmically playing with the bright yellow bus terminal light.

With a deadpan face, Washington eyed her through the window and grunted. "Man, I'm gonna gobble me up some serious trim tonight," he said, following her until she was out of sight. "She's gonna be so busy gasping for breath, ain't gonna be nothing left for conversation."

Earl snorted and took a sip.

"You quiet, but I don't see you telling me to do something else." Washington said, emptying his glass and gesturing to the bartender.

Earl offered his palm, and Washington brought his swathed paw down on it.

Another silence.

Washington began to chuckle to himself.

"Craziest things come to you at the craziest times. I'm on the ground, see, doing my horizontal boogaloo, this peckerwood poking me with his prod like he's one of the Three Musketeers. Well, I happen to look toward the sidewalk front where the dry cleaners was, and I see this white lady—fifty, fifty-five—standing there, watching me get it. She's got this wide-eyed, crazy look like the others, and her face is all flushed. And each time they poke me, she's jerking with her fist, like she's punching some invisible person. And her pocketbook's on her forearm swinging back and forth. And I'm thinking to myself, 'Wonder if she's got a Coke in that pocketbook. 'Cause if she does—in this hot sun and swinging back and forth like that—and opens it to take a swig, she's gonna get a spray just like we getting.'"

He laughed at the idea for a few moments more. Earl could negotiate only a tense wan smile as he studied his glass.

"Yes, sir," Washington went on, his chuckle subsiding. "She's gonna get sprayed just like us."

Earl reached for a small dish of peanuts and tossed a handful into his mouth, chewing distantly.

"D'ya think she'da begun to see our position?" the former asked and then laughed ruefully at his question.

"Damn peanuts're stale," Earl growled. "Taste like rabbit shit."

"How d'you know what rabbit shit taste like?"

"You'd think with the money they charge in here for this watered down piss, they'd put some of it toward fresh goddamn peanuts!"

"Hey, check you out," said Washington, straightening himself up in his seat.

Earl drained his glass, gulping, letting the warmth sink, and a tiny unheard buzz began to touch his ears.

"It's just that I'm fed up with all the bullshit. Seeping through the cracks in the walls. This whole stinking thing is bullshit."

"You done forgot to say the word right man. Bu'shit."

Earl stiffened and glared at his friend. "Hey, don't throw any saddle on my back."

"Brother, you talking to the newest member of the retired class. I'm putting my sword up for the duration."

"What's that supposed to mean?"

"Hey, take it easy. This's your ol' buddy, Wash."

Earl mellowed. "Look, right now you're talking to an asshole. What I'd better do is go home to bed. Catch you on the rebound."

"I hear you, brother. Look here. We all came away from there feeling like assholes. But lemme tell you something—proud assholes. Y'hear what I'm saying? I'm not ashamed of one thing we did. I know you ain't. We made those crackers lose their cool. And that says something about them. We tooted a loud horn."

Earl nodded, bid his companion good-bye. He went home, lay on his sofa, and lost himself in the ceiling. He'd lied before, consciously. But this was a lie he told by omission, and he felt more deeply ashamed of his cowardice here than anywhere else except that moment in that southern city.

He never went back to the organization, never called Washington. When Washington called him, he was cool and distant on the phone. He dropped out of all activity and resigned himself to just schoolteaching, representing the very value system that he considered an ally to those forces he'd gone up against in the South. This added to his contempt for himself and everything about him.

His jacket on now, he picked up his attaché case, gave himself the once over in the mirror, and turned to the drowsing figure of Dionne in bed. He looked at her now-quiet breathing, feeling once more the sting of her words the previous night.

Her eyes opened. "Leaving?"

"Long trip up to the Bronx," he said with feigned nonchalance.

"Do you have time to give us a good-bye kiss?"

He did, a few stretched moments ending with her sigh.

"Know what I wish?" she said. "That you could crawl right back in here with me and just hold me."

"Me too." And he half meant it.

"Go to work," she said, turning over. "Gotta ration our fantasies."

He'd never rationed his. That was one of his troubles. He'd once let them gallop out of their restricted corral, wander too far a field, and now they were out of control, stumbling obtrusively into his consciousness and out almost involuntarily. His only control over them was in his restricted revelation of them to others.

He looked regretfully back at the apartment house as his car pulled away. Surely, his childish behavior had been uncalled for. But had she been right? No, he couldn't accept that, because if all that she had said of him was right, maybe what he dare not face about himself.

CHAPTER 2

"You sure the science lab's down here?" Fox asked.

"Shh," responded Kaseem.

For Kaseem Abdullah (Rodney Wilson), "cool" meant being an ice pop in a heat wave. To stay inside his rhythm, he had to have control of himself and everything around him. Less than that was unbearable. Rodney had become Kaseem because something deep inside him didn't care for Rodney very much. He wore a small earring on his left earlobe, showing a need to be what he thought was "with it". Along with this, his tall-for-thirteen appearance concealed a coiled spring.

His friend Fox (Oscar Roach) fidgeted by the staircase doors, periodically glancing out through them and down the empty hall, tapping a quiet rhythm with his fingers against the jamb. He stopped when Kaseem fanned his hand at him. A dark, small, wiry youth of fourteen, he seemed like a young man for whom standing still meant looking like he had to go to the bathroom.

Kaseem pressed his body against the faded and rusty tiled wall that faced the area underneath the stairs descending from the first floor. As he controlled his breathing, he regarded his small companion with some annoyance. No control. People with no control got on his nerves.

He glanced up, studying the graffiti-filled walls, the peeling staircase banisters, large pink wads of dried bubble gum lined along their undersides like tiny camp bunkers. *Cheap school*, he thought. *Glad I don't go here.*

He tensed and signalled to Fox, who, stoatlike, slipped to the other side of the stairs. He inhaled, flexed his fingers, and measured his breathing as the swinging door on the landing above swung closed and the staccato sound of heels of too-soon-worn pumps descended toward them.

A full key ring jingled almost in Kaseem's ear as he moved slowly toward the foot of the stairs. Then she was in full view, her shapely back to him, holding what seemed like three voluminous textbooks, a large number of keys, a small canister, and, around her long brown neck, a gold necklace.

In a flash, he was on her, both arms around her chest, clamping her arms to their sides, her armful crashing to the floor. Fox lurched to her, tucked his fingers under the necklace strand and yanked it from her neck.

Kaseem pushed her violently against the wall and then followed Fox through the stairwell doors, sharply to the left, out through a poorly secured basement exit door, through which they had entered the school, and across a shortcut in the adjacent woods. On its far side, they retrieved their notebooks and textbooks hidden under a lightning-struck, fallen tree. They ogled their contraband and then, after they had regained their breath, calmly boarded a nearby bus to their school. They used stolen bus passes.

Randolph Junior High School was a fairly modern building some twenty years old, built during a brief school construction boom during the late fifties. From above, it looked like a large square "U," one of the arms being for the gymnasiums and cafeterias and the other arm for the industrial arts department, library, and the science labs.

The inside base of the "U" faced the main thoroughfare—Baychester Avenue—and a nicely kept front lawn littered with a few candy wrappers and balled up notebook pages. The underside of the base faced the schoolyard with its handball and basketball courts—a few rims missing—all connected to a small playground with broken swings, almost enclosed by woods. Part of this playground ran around the left arm and halfway up the block.

The bus stopped a block away from the school on the same side of the street, across from a small low-rent housing project, Winship Houses, a scatter site housing remnant. The neighborhood was primarily suburban, residential, where the splendor of Christmas decorations was often belied by continuous penny-pinching and privation. Kaseem and Fox got off the bus with the other school passengers who, mixed with other strollers to Randolph Junior High and nearby schools, engulfed them, making him feel safe.

They passed a row of benches on the edge of the playground that looked out toward the thoroughfare. In front of the benches, there was a small row of asphalt tables on which checkerboards had been painted, now somewhat faded. Michellene was sitting on the bench talking to her friend, Elva.

Both girls were eye catchers and drew the attention of the passing students but it was the very neatly dressed Michellene who poked Kaseem's inner itch. It took an effort on his part to take his eyes off her and this always bothered him.

She was approaching the peak of her beauty at thirteen, teasing tan, large provoking eyes that seemed to challenge and penetrate at the same time. Despite two renegade pimples, her skin always drew attention from the boys in the school. Kaseem liked her, and she knew it, often not bothering to hide her awareness from him. Also, they were in the same official class.

She waved at him with walking fingers and he nodded to her as he and Fox passed.

"Boy, I'd sure like to cut me a piece of that," he said to Fox who leered at Elva winking back at him.

"Why don't you?" returned Fox, almost licking his chops. "She look like she like you enough. And we got bread now. Take her out and then cop you some."

"Might do just that." Kaseem enjoyed the idea.

"Speaking of which, what do we do with this?" asked Fox.

"I'll hold it," Kaseem answered as if surprised by the question.

"Yeah, right," snapped Fox, wagging his head. "You hold it."

"Yeah, right? *Yeah, right?* Will you listen to this? Like I'm gonna go somewhere with it. What's your problem, man? Wasn't it you who brought me into this?"

"Don't go all hyper on me. Chill. Don'tcha see Dirty Harry standing at the damn door? We gotta get our shit together now."

The contour lines on Kaseem's face sharpened as he snapped his gaze ahead toward the school's entranceway. Spriggs, the school's policeman, was standing at the door, eyeing the entering students.

He was a large, muscular, brown-skinned man with jet-black eyes and a Genghis Khan mustache. His piercing gaze often made people nervous and most often was on Kaseem and Fox, as if he knew something.

"Shit," Kaseem said. "What a time for that motherfucker to be there."

Though they were still a half block away and buried in a throng of students, they seemed almost on top of the policeman and walking along an empty deserted road. Kaseem stopped short and pulled on Fox's jacket sleeve. "Gimme the thing," he said. "I'll duck around the side entrance. You go 'head on in the front by the nigger, book to the side, and let me in."

Fox, slightly put off, jammed his hand into his jacket pocket and brought out his fist, which he moved to Kaseem's nose at first, brandishing it, and then to his open palm, releasing its contents. Kaseem dashed away along an adjacent path that led to the side of the building, which was hidden from the front, where there was a door that wasn't supposed to be opened but often served as an exit for class cutters and school escapees as well as an entrance for intruders.

Fox proceeded uneasily toward the main entrance and Spriggs. If ever there was a menacing figure in the consciousness of all school outlaws, this policeman was that man. He seemed made for his uniform, its badge reflecting the morning light. Smiles were strangers to his round, lined face when he was on duty.

He looked at Fox as the youth tried to slide by him into the building.

"Where'd your homeboy go?" he asked. "I saw y'all thick as thieves up the block."

"He been went by you already," returned Fox. "You didn't see'm?"

"I look like I need a Seeing Eye dog to you?" said Spriggs, regarding the uneasy youth. "He didn't come by here. I'd've seen the turkey if he'd come by here. He musta ducked off somewhere. I dunno. Y'all're into something very wrong."

A few passing students snickered and covered their mouths.

"Why you gotta be on my case alla time? What I do?" Fox pleaded, thrusting both palms upward in fake supplication.

"Man, I'm not even thinking about you. No need to get paranoid now. By the way, you happen to hear anything in your travels?"

"About what?" Fox became aggressively attentive.

"Like a mugging in this other school 'cross town," said the officer. "These two dudes took off this girl, messed up her neck, took her gold necklace. Tell you, y'all kids getting outrageous."

"And you got to tell me this?" said Fox, trying to inch away. "What would make you think I would hear something? You trying to say I keep that kind of company? Hey, terrible world. Way it be's."

"Yeah, you right. Making idle conversation, I guess. Taking up your time with the woes of the world."

"Well, what're friends for, am I right or wrong?" said Fox as he entered the building. He wasted no time getting to the side entrance. Glancing around, he let Kaseem in and told him of his conversation with Spriggs.

Kaseem's jaws tightened. "I just wish the nigger would mind his own damn business," he said through his teeth.

"You forgettin' *that* is his business," commented Fox, thrusting his head forward. "Just make sure he don't know something."

Earl had entered the school earlier and, doling out a few mumbled greetings to the general office staff and a few people in the hallway, started for his room on the second floor. He bumped into Spriggs coming upstairs from the basement. The officer punched him lightly on his shoulder and then told him of the mugging of a girl in another school by two black youths. The teacher shook his head and the two men bemoaned the kinds of evil youths were now committing.

"Something we're doing wrong, man," the officer said as he headed outside the school.

We have to stay at the gate until we find out, thought the teacher as he continued to his classroom.

He opened his window and looked down at the small groups of children beginning to gather in front of the school.

He sensed someone behind him at his doorway. An annoyance swept through him, because he knew who it would be. He put on a wan smile-mask and turned.

Ingram, prematurely balding, ashen white face, jowls beginning too soon to sag, stared at him with the faint suggestion of a grin Earl was sure had mockery in it. Earl's eyes dropped to the intruder's paunch, and he forced a bigger smile in return.

"Cheer up, kid," said Ingram. "Another day at the hole's begun. Can't run back out. Can't escape. We have our great magnificent exalted role to play in this grateful world."

Irritation writhed around inside Earl. He hated the idea that this mediocrity felt free to infer his thoughts and feelings. It meant that he thought they were the same, an idea totally abhorrent to him.

"Once more, the great struggle with the uneducable little animals," the former continued. "Soldiers on the front of a losing war. Come on. Buck up. Fire yourself up. After all, there're the measly little bimonthly emoluments that await you, which is really what it's all about, isn't it?"

"Excuse me," said Earl, walking by Ingram and starting down the hall. "Something I meant to look up in the library."

"Aha!" he heard behind him. "Scholarly pursuits in the wasteland! Give my regards to the books but don't get your hands too dusty!"

He escaped around a corner. If he could browse around for a short while, have congress with good ideas, get the taste of Ingram's nihilistic idiocy out of his mouth, he could face the day better.

The library was closed. Damn! He stood in the middle of the hall for a while, dreading the return to his classroom and Ingram's lurking figure, and then turned on his heels. Through the empty halls, he could hear the gathering children's din from outside. The morning bell opening the school's doors was minutes away.

He passed Ingram's classroom. Its occupant was standing near the rear door. "Hey, come here," he said. "Wanna show you something."

He entered Ingram's classroom, with its sparse, meager order, its unimaginative bulletin board displays, its hackneyed ambiance. His idea of acknowledgment to black progress was a picture of Booker T. Washington juxtaposed to one of Chubby Checker and Wilt Chamberlain standing side by side at some fund-raising affair for needy children.

"Lookit this," he said, pointing to a couple of neatly written compositions displayed on the side bulletin boards. He then pointed to one in particular.

"Denzel Jones," he said. "Class clown. Nobody can do anything with him. But I could. Look at this. Betty Williams. I think she's a hooker myself. But look at that writing, willya? Yeah, there're a coupla spelling errors here and there, but these're the students nobody's supposed to be able to do anything with. I did, though. Not bad, huh?"

Earl nodded his head and pressed his lips together as if to say "not bad," though, inside, he was not overly impressed.

The bell rang.

Ingram's face continued to be a smug mask. "Just takes a little teaching, y'know?"

The approaching rumbling in the nearby staircase and the hallway below began, but Ingram continued, impervious to it and Earl's desire to return to his own classroom. He looked at other similar compositions, nodded at them, and fought the rising annoyance. Children were now rushing by the door to their classrooms.

Kaseem went by.

"Do you know how long it took me to get this one to bring his notebook and pen to school? It was a battle, I tell you. A battle."

"The Pledge of Allegiance" had come onto the loudspeakers. Everyone froze and pledged. The hallway was now packed with milling children, most of whom conformed. "The Star-Spangled Banner" followed.

He had been polite long enough. "Excuse me," he said to Ingram through the intrusive morning announcements. "Have to make sure my lions aren't wrecking my classroom."

He started out of Ingram's classroom and back toward his own, but the commotion down the hall, involving Kaseem, Mr. Devonshire, Mr. Rako, and Officer Spriggs stopped him. He stood at his front doorway and watched. His class president, Marie, was taking the daily attendance.

Ingram came up to behind him, "That is one bad article," said the latter. "Send the creep to a school where they can tend to his special antisocial needs. Me? I wouldn't come within ten million miles of him for all the tea in China."

"Why would you want all that tea anyhow?" returned Earl. "You'd only have to take a sabbatical and spend it at the urinal."

He entered his classroom but not before first glancing at Spriggs taking Kaseem into the teachers' restroom.

Earlier, Kaseem had raced up the stairs to the second floor. He didn't want to deal with "Dirty Harry". Spriggs made him nervous because he knew the officer didn't like him. Still, the young man began to feel safe as he started toward his homeroom, though the hostility toward his official teacher squirmed around in his gut.

He stopped, his stomach catching.

Spriggs was walking in his direction from the far end of the hall. Knowing he would never reach his official classroom before the policeman, he slipped through the nearest rear door.

It was Earl Chaney's room, now with only a few loitering students in it. Mr. Chaney was not present, but his briefcase was on his desk. This not being Kaseem's official classroom made him even more uneasy. Suppose Spriggs decided to come in and search him? Any second now, the officer would walk by the door. Panicked, Kaseem moved to the rear bulletin board.

His eyes quickly scanned the yellow construction paper with its pictures of famous black writers from the past up to the present. He fingered the necklace.

An inspiration struck him.

He strode to a corner of the bulletin board and, turning his back to the class, quickly picked at the staples with a small key, holding the paper to the cork background with his index finger. He pulled five staples partially out, making sure they stayed in the paper, shoved the necklace underneath, scratching himself slightly, and replaced the staples in the cork background, pressing the paper down, leaving only the faintest bulge. He pressed hard on the staples and then stepped back to inspect them.

He exhaled with relief just as Spriggs strode by the rear door, glancing at him.

"Get outa my classroom!" shouted one boy in the room who was staring at him with a smile laced with hostility. It was Vinny Ford, an archrival of Kaseem's, a medium-sized young man, brown-skinned, close-cropped Afro, whose smoothness and sarcastic eyes seemed both to contrast with and mock Kaseem's rough-hewn edginess.

Kaseem threw both his hands up and shook his head as he inched toward the rear door. The young man peeked out into the hallway and saw Mr. Chaney talking to Mr. Ingram. Spriggs was a few doors down the hall, talking to a female teacher.

Suddenly, "The Pledge of Allegiance" came over the loudspeaker, which meant everybody had to freeze in their movements. Kaseem slipped back into the classroom, just far enough that the rear clothing closet would conceal him from Mr. Chaney, who had been pulled into Mr. Ingram's room anyway. Out in the hall, he would have to move to avoid Spriggs.

"The Star-Spangled Banner" followed the pledge, and then everyone took their seats as Mr. Chaney glanced into the classroom from the hall. A few students began hastily copying other people's homework.

Kaseem slipped out of the room and moved toward his own official classroom. The halls were full now, so it was easy for him to lose himself amidst the throng, though he continued to glance toward the officer still talking to the teacher.

He froze again.

Mr. Rako, the assistant principal of the grade and the supervisor of the floor, was walking toward him, though he didn't appear to see him. "Damn," Kaseem growled to himself as he made a smooth lateral movement through the rear door of another classroom.

Mr. Devonshire, the official teacher of that room, was standing by one of the rear closets. He was a large, extremely dark man, balding at the top, and he wore glasses. His large nostrils flared as he looked at Kaseem.

"You're gonna come in here?" he said. "Where do you belong?"

Kaseem tried to slip back into the hall.

"Hey, mister," the teacher said, following him. "I asked you a question."

"I'm going to my class, all right?" Kaseem snapped.

"You're gonna give me lip now?"

"I don't listen to Oreo cookies."

Mr. Devonshire lunged at Kaseem, seizing his arm.

"Get your hand offa me," the youth sang, his voice in high register.

"I'm about sick of your mouth."

"Get your fuckin' hand offa me!" Kaseem jerked his arm free.

The enraged teacher shoved Kaseem against the wall, the youth's hand shooting to the teacher's wrists. "You piece of garbage," the teacher said. "I'll make wallpaper outa you, you talk to me like that."

Mr. Rako rushed up to them and pulled them apart.

Spriggs had heard the commotion and was walking toward them now. Earl Chaney came out of Ingram's room and looked on. Every face in the surrounding universe—inside and outside the classrooms—enclosed them.

When Kaseem saw with a sideways glance that Spriggs was coming toward him, he felt suddenly separated from himself. Everything was now out of control. He glared into the black face of Mr. Devonshire and then the white face of Mr. Rako and felt the growing impulse to increase his abuse, as if his mouth had taken on a will of its own. Why not? He was clearly in the soup now.

"Get to Mr. Hanley's office," ordered Mr. Rako with a deadly calm.

Kaseem started to swagger toward the nearest staircase.

"Wait," said Spriggs. "Can I have a word with'm please?"

"Be my guest," said Mr. Rako.

"Just keep that fool outa my face," said Mr. Devonshire over his shoulder as he returned to his classroom.

The officer pulled the youth into the teacher's restroom, chasing a teacher out who'd been catching a quick smoke. The disturbed teacher had been looking forlornly out the window at the woods behind the school building. He quickly jammed his cigarette butt into a metallic ashtray, nodded to Spriggs, glanced disapprovingly at Kaseem, and left.

Kaseem inhaled and readied himself for the worst.

CHAPTER 3

The room was sparsely furnished with a dilapidated table on which teachers often did clerical work. Its legendary splintered chairs were scattered about. There was a blank bulletin board on whose bare corked base was tacked a month-old announcement about plans for a field trip that had not taken place because of a lack of funds. In one corner, a broken rexograph machine took up space.

Spriggs turned to the young man. "Alone at last, chump. You know the position."

"Shall I hum a tune?" said Kaseem as he turned his back on the policeman, spread his hands on the faded wall, and leaned against it.

"Uh-oh. My man quick with the comeback," returned Spriggs as he proceeded to pat Kaseem down. "Using that cool sophistication to cover his usual stupidity. I'm impressed."

"You impressed? Wow. Hey, can I tell my teacher about how I impressed you? You know, like show and tell."

"You'd better be careful who you fooling with, young fella. I got the bush to boil your tea in from the giddyup," said Spriggs.

"You hurt my feelings, putting me through all this embarrassment."

"Ain't another soul in the room. Don't game me, okay? Not after that performance out in the hall. You clean. Hey, you hear anything about a gold chain snatching at Wilson, you clue me, hear?"

"Why you like to hassle me?" asked Kaseem.

"You have to go to the principal now."

Kaseem glared at Spriggs.

"And don't be cutting no eyes at me, if you know what's good for you. You'd better go ahead on now."

Mr. Rako entered the room. He made a "what's going on?" face at Spriggs, who then told him.

"I guess I'm the dude did it, huh!" exploded Kaseem. "Me! Good ole me!"

"Getting all dramatic like Joan Crawford," said Spriggs. "Nobody's blaming you for anything. Just a routine search, that's all. He's clean."

"I should say he's clean. No pen. Hardly any textbooks. Sloppy notebook. I don't know. Get down to Mr. Hanley's office."

"I'm going, all right," sneered the agitated young man as he bopped out of the room with his belongings.

"Lose the attitude!" snapped Mr. Rako,

As Kaseem walked past Mr. Chaney's room, he glanced at the rear bulletin board.

Mr. Hanley, the principal, frowned as he looked at the intercom, slowly placed its receiver back on its cradle, and momentarily tapped his fingers on the earpiece.

He appeared to have stolen his nose from Sherlock Holmes, and he used his eyebrows accordingly, raising one while the other remained in place, whenever he was puzzled about something or was confronted with any contretemps. The youthfulness of his face contrasted with his prematurely graying hair, though overall he seemed to have preserved himself well.

He was a man on the rise. The district powers-that-be looked upon him favorably. He had, after all, taken a fairly difficult junior high school and turned it into a fair junior high school. That in itself was a major accomplishment. Faculty and students admired him for that.

The administrators, on the other hand, were somewhat envious and belittling, not that it mattered.

Thus, for the first time in his career, he could eye a desirable goal with eager confidence. There was a possible prestigious opening in special education administration and supervision, perhaps a welcome mat to district superintendent itself. He had long ago given up entertaining such ambitions but now....

For this reason, he had reacted with great discomfort to Mr. Rako's tirade over the intercom. Kaseem had had it: *Get rid of him. Suspend him, and while he's out, start expulsion proceedings. A guy like that doesn't deserve the privilege of going to school with decent kids.*

He felt such great contempt for this mediocre satrap, pushing papers around his desk for some imagined purpose or other, disappearing at needed times, always maintaining a certain distance from the kids, pretending to have a power and authority he sorely lacked. Thus, the principal hesitated to answer him at any great length, for fear that he might say more than he had planned and invite possibilities for a camaraderie he didn't want.

In fifteen years as an administrator, Rako had not grown to even a minimal understanding of the limitations of his role. He'd just seemed content to ignore his mediocrity like a pile of rags tossed into a corner. This irked and puzzled the principal

Furthermore, a report Hanley had read at the beginning of the year deeply disturbed him, one criticizing the disproportionate numbers of black and Latino children being suspended and/or expelled from the city schools, with the NAACP, The Urban League, the ACLU, and CORE looking into it. Worse yet, before his tenure, entirely too many of these children had been suspended and/or expelled from his school for various reasons. Still, he wasn't always sure they were good enough reasons, so there remained in him a continuous overlay of qualm. Consequently, he had now become somewhat gun-shy.

Mr. Rako, flashing a dirty look at Kaseem more to impress the general office staff than anything else, strode into the office.

"Let's not go off half-cocked," said Mr. Hanley, his hands going up in front of him and then reaching for the intercom again.

"Yes?"

"Mrs. Reinking? Mr. Hanley. I'd like to ask you something." *What good is calling this woman going to do*, the principal mused to himself, searching desperately for some kind of out. "I'd like you to give me a brief, off-the-cuff evaluation of Kaseem Wilson."

"Rodney?" she asked, clearing her throat.

"Rodney."

"Well, he seems to be absent today."

"No, he's here in my office."

"Oh, he's in school."

Nice to know she takes attendance, Hanley thought.

"Yes, he got himself into a bit of trouble this morning."

"Dreadful boy. Just dreadful. Impossible. So-so work. I mean, if he's done something that will cause you to get rid of'm, I certainly won't come up with any arguments against it," said Mrs. Reinking.

A few regret-filled moments later, he called Kaseem into his office. As he watched the boy do a hippy-dippy walk toward his desk, he felt a perverse kind of sympathy for him and at the same time a smoldering rage a trapped bear must have felt for the trapper.

Chapter 4

Julia was a beautiful woman, not pretty but striking. She had large oval-shaped eyes with piercing black irises and an ample nose and mouth, all set pleasingly on a longish skull. She kept her hair in a pageboy that, though it hadn't been cut in some time, complemented her face well and brought out the stately look of her neck. Her figure, despite her autumn years, was still good, her legs, though thinner, well-tapered.

Yet there was no man in her life. True, when she walked through the streets, her eyes determinedly straight ahead, she drew male looks and occasional entreaties from them to join them in some imagined rendezvous. Her forbidding stern look and manner, however, usually discouraged any further propositioning.

This hadn't always been true of her. In fact, she was pregnant with Rodney when she married his father, Kevin.

Though Kevin's Viet Nam experiences had embittered him, he never let this spill over onto his relationship with her, and she couldn't have been more deeply in love. He was going to give her the world, his compensation for the self-diminutions and waking nightmares he'd endured in that war.

Little thought in either of them had been given to his prospects for work and the support of his family. True, he'd had two years of college before he was drafted at twenty into the army, but his academic work had been only mediocre; even if it had not been, he would have found these post-Viet Nam times very tough.

Three years in Viet Nam, being wounded once in the arm, how prepared could he be for supporting a family already starting before the nuptials?

The elements for disaster were already firmly implanted in the weft of their circumstances. It didn't take long for them to surface.

The wound, though not serious, and the three years gave Kevin the idea that the world to which he'd returned owed him. It didn't agree. Still, he hung on.

He tried night school while he worked as a machinist during the day. It had been in a modern literature class that he'd met Julia, who was then a nursing major. They had dated and grew close until one night, in a surge of passion, Rodney had been conceived.

It'd been a wonderful moment, and she'd felt everything would be fine as long as the magic of that first night remained, which, in her ecstasy, she'd assumed would be forever.

Even when she had missed her period and the slight pangs of worry began to take hold of her, she had managed to hold onto her optimism. She had refused to press marriage onto Kevin; she had too much pride for that. Not even the urging of her straitlaced mother, Mrs. MacNeil, could persuade her. Instead, it was he who took the initiative that enhanced her good feelings.

Even after Rodney's birth, the Shangri-la continued. He would enthusiastically take the baby out for long walks in the park, lugging the bulky carriage down the stairs like a young Hercules, bring her flowers whenever he could, and do it with a flourish; and he worked like a horse on his job. Even the initially disapproving Mrs. MacNeil was eventually won over.

Then things went wrong.

The faltering economy began to squeeze workers out of jobs, and Kevin found himself one of them. First, there was shock—that this should happen to him, a wounded Viet Nam War veteran. Then the shock turned to outrage before it finally hardened to bitterness.

Julia was already aware of this. Seemingly bland and nonchalant, she was also strong enough to face facts. There was no mistaking the tension in her stomach and the deep silences that had begun to creep into their conversations. There was no mistaking the petulance that was suddenly there in his manner toward her. And worse, she had had to go on maternity leave from her job, and Mrs. MacNeil became the reluctant sole support of the whole family when Julia and Kevin moved in with her. This, of course, did not assuage his spirit.

"Why the eggs always overdone?" he snapped to her one morning. "Eggs always hard and powdery. I like 'em loose and up—you know that!"

"Cook 'em yourself if you don't like the way I do 'em," she answered.

"I know you ain't talking to me." He straightened up in his chair.

"You know wrong. I'm talking to you." She glared at him.

"I bet I put something on you, you open your mouth again."

"Then you'd better make your peace with your maker, 'cause, nigger, you lay one finger on me, and you'n He're gonna have an early meeting."

Silence. He knew she said little that was bluff.

"All I want is for you to do the damn eggs right, okay."

"Well, I'm sorry, okay? I'm sorry!" she said, storming out of the kitchen. "I'm doing the best I can!"

Later, she came out of the bedroom and saw him staring out of the living room window, his hands in his pockets, a forlorn droop on his shoulders. She stared at his back and wanted to go up to him, but helpless paralysis and anxiety seized her. Then she knew things were worse than she had thought.

It continued. The coffee was always grainy; he was tired of chewing on nasty tasting roach doo-doo. When's she gonna learn to make the damn coffee right? Or on any given instance of the diminishing occasions he was home in the evening: "TV picture's too blurry! I can't tell whether that's a gun in his hand or a handkerchief!" Or "You watching that crap again? Don't you ever get tired of it? Same ol' corny shit every damn week. Like us."

"Here, here's three dollars!" she would sometimes return, handing him the money, smarting inside from the vitriolic truth of his shafts. "Take yourself to a movie so that Rodney and my mother don't have to listen to your garbage mouth!"

And why was there never enough food in the fridge? That, too, became just one more affront to him.

Never, though, was Rodney ever the recipient of Kevin's rancor. Even when he dragged home from the two minimum wage jobs he now had—washing dishes in an all-night diner and pumping gas across town—he would go to the baby's bed and stare at him, a love and pride glowing in his face. There were even those times he would try to be the old Kevin to Julia, occasions that grew fewer and farther between. Ultimately, a freeze settled into their bed, relieved only by sporadic explosions of desperate passion.

Things worsened.

Kevin was laid off from both his jobs. Prices continued their climb. Julia was forced to return to work as a dental assistant, scarcely having completed the weaning of Rodney.

The two working women made sure that Rodney would seldom be left with a nonfamily member. Kevin grabbed at whatever pickup jobs he could get. Thus, a scattering and fragmenting of the family resulted, and Kevin's patriarchal position weakened even more. Decisions, mainly financial, were made above and around him. He seemed to have very little say and didn't venture any opinions. He merely withdrew into himself and distanced himself farther from Julia, Mrs. MacNeil, and even himself. Only Rodney, by now four, brought out vestiges of Kevin's old self.

Mainly, there was his ever-present smoldering resentment, a resentment of the world, of Mrs. MacNeil, of himself for allowing all this to happen to him, finally of Julia. Eventually, the streets in a neighborhood already deep in disarray became his sanctuary.

"Where you going?" Mrs. MacNeil asked him one day as he was primping in front of the mirror, smoothing out his newly cleaned jacket.

"To London to visit the Queen," he said, and he was out the door.

"You don't have no respect for nothing!" she shouted at the door as the distant sound of his descending steps faded. "That's what's wrong with you!"

"Hope he gives the Queen my regards," said Julia, entering the living room, awakened from a much needed nap.

One day, Kevin had been trying to listen to some jazz while he was minding his son. Mrs. MacNeil had just come home from her job as a nurse's aide at the nearby Workmen's Circle Home for the Aged.

Rodney had been making too much noise around the apartment, drowning out the finer subtleties of Thelonius Monk's riffs. In frustration, Kevin called the boy over to him and smacked him on the back of his head.

"Now you chill, hear," he said to his son, whose eyes began tearing. "I wanna hear this music. Lemme at least have this!"

The four-year-old exploded in wails of rage, backing away from his father.

Knowing his wife would be home shortly, the father stood up and began to advance balefully toward him. "Knock it off now before I give you something to cry for," he growled, his eyes glancing toward the clicking lock.

Mrs. MacNeil ran out of her bedroom as Julia burst through the front door and placed herself between man and boy. "What is wrong with you, Kevin? You chastise the boy because he done something wrong! Not because he's interfering with something you want!"

Kevin gaped at her and the now-screaming Rodney, turned, and stormed out of the house, snapping off what was the beginning of a particularly electric Monk riff.

Later, when he returned to the apartment, now dark and full of the sonorous sounds of sleep-induced breathing, he sneaked into Rodney's room and gently placed a kiss on his temple. He also placed next to his pillow a small Popeye doll.

Julia pretended to be asleep.

One day, Julia came home earlier than usual to discover that neither Rodney nor her mother was there. Kevin was usually out in the street somewhere; she expected this. But her mother not being home with the child at this time of the day? That was strange.

She went next door to the house of Mrs. Johnstone, who sometimes babysat, and sure enough, found Rodney there sitting on the sofa and reading a Spiderman comic book.

"Where's my mother?" she asked the genial woman, who shrugged her shoulders and averted her eyes.

"On the street somewhere," Mrs. Johnstone softly answered.

For almost an hour, Julia walked around the streets, sometimes cruising in a cab, searching for Mrs. MacNeil. An anxiety was beginning to grip her, because there had been something portentous in Mrs. Johnstone's manner that she couldn't put her finger on. So she had left Rodney with her neighbor, because she wanted him out of range should she stumble across anything unpleasant. There was, swelling inside her, a combat soldierlike toughness she always kept in reserve for hospital traumas and events in her life that demanded it.

Moreover, there had been an indiscernible malaise in her for the last month, and it seemed to her that every time her thoughts touched on Kevin, the malaise would crystallize. Now, as the search for her mother lengthened, thoughts of Kevin, what their relationship had become, what had happened to her love for him—had it slipped to some junk memory back room?—crowded her head. That it could have been teetering on the edge of a precipice was a thought she never allowed herself to entertain.

Something told her to walk toward Morningside Park, and there, sure enough, was her mother sitting on a bench facing a building across the street.

Strange, she thought as she rushed up to her. "Momma! What're you doing here?"

Mrs. MacNeil turned to her, her brown face taut, revealing a slight pallor. Her eyes widened as she looked at her daughter, and then she appeared to force a smile onto her face.

"Just sitting here, taking in some air, resting my knees."

"But why so far from home?"

"Never mind. C'mon, let's go home." She got up and straightened out her dress.

"Momma, I wish you would tell me what is going on." Julia regarded her mother.

"You gonna stand here running your mouth all day? Let's go. We got a dinner to fix."

Her mother had never spoken to her like this before, and there was a new tension in her voice. She knew that her normally placid, phlegmatic mind had been stabbed by something so devastating that it had caused this strange uncharacteristic behavior and the tautness in her jaws. She noted also how eagerly her mother appeared to be trying to rush her away from this spot.

Her attention was drawn again to the building across the street, the one her mother had been staring at when she came up to her, the third-floor area. Her eyes now flashing, her mother took her hand, something she hadn't done in almost a quarter century of their lives together, and tried to pull her away. "You one hard-headed something. Always been. Like your father."

They stared at each other for a few moments, Julia trying to fathom the uneasiness in this dignified woman who had raised her.

"You go ahead on home, Momma," she said finally. "There's something I wanna pick up at this store around the corner."

"What?"

"Momma!"

"I'll go with you."

"No, you go on home. Pick up Rodney," Julia said.

"You getting rid of me?"

"No."

"You are," her mother said. "You're getting rid of me so that—"

"So that what? What?" The two women gaped at each other. "Look, this's silly. I'll be right home."

This last remark was said almost between her teeth as Mrs. MacNeil, now teary-eyed, said, "Hmmmmph. I hope you find what you want," as she walked away toward home.

Julia crossed the street toward the building of their concern, walked around the corner, stopped, and peered back around it at the receding figure of her mother, the picture of abashed indignation, which soon disappeared around another corner. She waited a few moments and then stepped out into the block and looked up at the building. What had her mother been looking at? Something was happening inside this building, which had riveted her attention.

She studied the building, feeling slightly foolish, occasionally glancing self-consciously around her at passersby who scarcely noticed her. She stepped out toward the curb to get a better view of the building's face.

She strained her brain to come up with a reason she should walk away from this. No reason took. At length, she readied herself for giving this obsession up and going home, making sure to bring with her a small bottle of cheap white wine from a nearby liquor store.

Something caught her attention.

She noticed that all the windows which opened out to the fire escape and naturally had bars on them had their window shades open to half-mast. This was to fool burglars into thinking that someone was home. Any possession there to burgle would not be worth the possible confrontation.

There was an exception to this. One window had its shades pulled all the way down. In fact, two windows to its left, on the same floor—no doubt belonging to the same apartment—had shades pulled down, too.

She went upstairs to that apartment, hesitated, pushed the bell, and waited. Perhaps nobody was home. She started away.

Suddenly, she heard muffled voices and what seemed to be bare feet paddling toward the door. She noted the peephole and stepped to the side. The peephole made a slight scraping sound.

"Yes," came a female voice from inside.

"Excuse me. Could you help me?"

"What do you want?" the woman said.

"I'm looking for a number which I can't seem to read."

"Go talk to the super downstairs."

"He doesn't seem to be around," Julia said. "Please."

"Lemme see you."

Julia stepped closely into the peephole's view, making sure her face wasn't seen too clearly.

"It's a lady," she said to somebody inside. "It's all right."

The door opened a slit, wide enough to reveal a scantily clad, brown-skinned, pretty young woman with partially faded lipstick and wide, bold eyes that widened more when they beheld Julia. Julia had occasionally seen this woman in the neighborhood.

But Julia's attention was not on her.

She was looking over the woman's jet black Cleopatra wig through her bedroom door to a full-length mirror on an open closet door, in which she saw the reflection of a pair of man's trousers and a striped shirt hanging on a bedpost. She knew them well. She'd purchased them for Kevin at Alexander's only the previous week.

Worse, despite the loss of intimacy in their marriage, her memories still enabled her to recognize the bare feet next to the bedpost.

She found herself pushing past the young woman, who exclaimed, "Hey, wait a minute! What the hell is this?" and marched to the bedroom door, a sickening stone in her stomach. What she faced as she stood in the doorway was a truth she'd, for some weeks now, in her darkest thoughts, sensed, expected. Still, there was the sight of Kevin naked to the sheet pulled over his stomach, his feet bicycling to hide under the rumpled sheets near them, as if that act itself would recapture the trust now forever shattered, which his staring, frightened, self-reproachful, saddened eyes acknowledged. Still, the sight staggered her.

Their eyes held, it seemed, an eternity, in the special bond of betrayer and betrayed. The young woman rushed up to her. "Say, listen, whaddya call this?"

Julia grabbed a fistful of the woman's unwigged hair and shoved her against the doorjamb, her rage making the woman gasp and become silent.

"Don't take it out on her," said Kevin quietly, his voice quavering. "It ain't her. You know that."

Julia held her for a few seconds more before she thrusted her away, looked at Kevin, and left.

As she descended the stairs, she heard the woman's now-emboldened voice: "What the fuck you call this, Kevin? I oughta call the police on that crazy bitch!"

Kevin came home late that evening. Mrs. MacNeil was stonily silent, nightgowned. The dinner dishes were put away, and Julia was congenial. There was no trace of dried tears around her eyes, and she even had kept his dinner warm.

But Rodney was still up, and that was unusual. As Kevin sat down to pick at his food, the boy sat at the table, watching him. Julia leaned against the wall with her arms folded. Not in any state of mind to try to fathom the silence, Kevin focused on his son, who seemed to glow in his presence.

"What you doing up so late, Rodney? You wanna get bags under your eyes so big you have to lean forward?" he asked. "And you can't fall asleep because you can't lift your bottom eyelid up?"

Rodney rolled with laughter, almost falling off his chair.

"Shh," said Kevin. "You'll wake up your grandmother. Besides, I think I saw the sandman looking very annoyed at you and checking out his watch. And he got him a Omega digital."

Julia shifted her weight to her other foot.

"Now, all kidding aside. You gonna be starting school soon. You don't wanna be lugging a half-asleep brain there."

"What's a brain?" Rodney leaned his chin on Kevin's hand.

"That's what's inside your head, where all your dreams and most of what you say comes from."

Julia nodded slowly.

"Hey. Pretty soon, whaddya say we go to the park? Play some ball."

"Yeah!" Grinning excitedly, Rodney leaned forward on his two fists.

Kevin glanced at Julia.

"We'll see," she said.

"Off to bed with you now," ordered Kevin as he lightly poked the child's nose.

Rodney jumped off his chair and gave Kevin a kiss on his cheek. "Goo'night, Daddy."

"Sweet dreams, little brother."

Julia followed the boy into his bedroom, tucked him in, and then returned to the kitchen. For a few seconds, she stood in the doorway, staring at him. Then she carefully sat down at the table, her eyes never wavering.

"Look, about that mess before," he said, averting his eyes. "Don't mean nothing. Just filling up holes."

"Your bags're packed," she said, somewhat matter-of-factly. "I want you out of this house tonight."

He gaped at her. "Just like that," he said finally.

"Just like that."

"Just like that," he repeated, as if he was trying to beat down her resolve, using that phrase like a hammer.

"You hopped in the bed with that slut, didn't you? Just like that. You bailed out on our marriage just like that."

He looked down at his uneaten dinner. "And Rodney?"

"Look, don't ... all right?"

She went into their bedroom, returned with the two suitcases, and dropped them next to him. "We were going to go to the islands with these for the honeymoon we never had. Now they're my parting gift to you." Her face had become stone.

"You're gonna chase me away from the boy? I'll be goddamned. Suppose I don't wanna go."

She stepped back out of his way and folded her arms.

"What'd you want from me?" Kevin pleaded. "You became the man of the house, not me. Me? I was nothing but a bread crumb in the sink waiting to be washed down the drain!"

A faint hint of moisture appeared in his eyes.

"Think of what you're doing, Julia. You're removing me from our son's life!"

"You think you were the only one having a bad time of it? You think I was having fun? Sure, you got some bad breaks, and it was not all your fault. But you coulda been more of a man about it and handled it better. Now if you don't mind, I've had a horrendous day, as you well know. I'm tired. I wanna go to bed."

"And you'll sleep sweet like a baby. Maybe that's what you wanted all along."

"Look," she said, "if you don't want me to go see your wench friend—and I'll do it—you get your sneaky, no-good, worthless behind outa here now!"

Kevin lunged at her and slapped her on her head.

She quickly grabbed a carving knife, stepped toward him, and stopped, struggling for a few moments to bring herself under control. Kevin had taken a step back and readied himself for an attack. Finally, she placed the knife in the sink behind her and smiled sardonically. "Fair trade. You go upside my head. Then you go."

She watched him pick up the luggage and walk out of the kitchen and then out of the apartment. A purged triumph came over her as she wearily turned to her bedroom. Her breath caught in a short gasp. In the half-blocked kitchen light, she could make out the small figure of Rodney standing by his bedroom door, glaring at her.

She rushed him back to his bed and then got into her own, where she quietly wept for almost an hour before she fell asleep.

Now she was alone. There certainly was no calling Kevin back or encouraging him in any way on the phone. This was not in her. She would have to bring the boy up by herself and deal with his continual unanswered questions about his daddy.

Now a private duty RN with training in dental technology, she worked hard, practiced the most Spartan frugality, and, with the help of her mother, managed to save enough money to rent a two-family house in the North Bronx. It was a nice bricked house with a small garden in the front and an adequate backyard for occasional *al fresco* get-togethers, nicely situated on a quiet block far from the deteriorating neighborhood and, hopefully, its memories they had escaped. The young couple who shared the two-family house downstairs were professional people who were seldom home.

Rodney, however, was another matter. He grew surlier. He laughed derisively at things he should not have found funny—a starving animal on the street, a tragedy on a TV newscast.

"What's so funny about what you just seen?" asked Mrs. MacNeil of him one evening.

"Aw, y'all're just square," he returned, bolting from the room.

After a while, it became apparent that they had not escaped the old streets, that the old streets had begun to catch up to them. Worse, Rodney began to become involved in these new neighborhood changes, and before Julia had fully realized it, a strange new language and style had seeped into Rodney and their house. He began to walk in that hippy-dippy style that Julia so loathed and that bewildered Mrs. MacNeil. How could her precious grandson adopt such ways? How could something like this contaminate someone with the MacNeil blood coursing through his veins?

One day, Rodney entered the house and, without greeting anybody, swaggered toward the stairs to his bedroom. Julia, having had a particularly rough day at the medical building, was resting her aching body on the couch, a small cup of scotch-laced tea on the coffee table next to her.

His arrogant bop irritated her.

She rocketed out of the sofa and whipped her hand across the top of his head, knocking his head forward and causing him to stumble against the banister.

"Hey, what's up with you?" responded the beleaguered twelve-year-old.

She whacked him again. "I told you to keep that hoodlum walk outa this house."

"What's your problem?"

She swung at him again, but this time, with the lightning reflexes of youth, he deflected it with his arm and ducked. He went backward up two steps to move himself out of her reach.

"You got hand trouble, you know that?" he said.

She started after him again, saying, "You must think I'm playing with you or something," and thrust her hand at his face again, but he grabbed her wrist and then the other wrist when she swung that around.

"Okay, okay," he said as they engaged in a tug-of-war for a few seconds. "You win. I won't bop anymore."

"Let go of my wrists, Rodney," she said through her teeth. She waited a few moments. "I said let go of my wrists."

"You gonna hit me anymore?"

"Would it do any good?"

When he felt her relax her muscles, he released his grip and dropped his hands to his side.

Her shoulders drooped, and she lowered her gaze.

Then she whacked him again, this time hard. "Let that be a lesson to you. If you gonna be big'n bad, you'd better be ready for everything."

He rubbed his face, glared at her, almost burst into tears, and finally stormed upstairs.

His report card marks were a long series of red marks, dotted with occasional blue, always with a "U" in effort shown.

He would slouch in the recliner, looking off nonchalantly while she, waving his red-stained report card, as if it were a used sanitary napkin she was looking to throw away, scolded, threatened, and even tried to cajole him into putting forth some effort in his academic work.

"I can't watch you, baby. I got to stay on these pieces of jobs so we can meet the bills. It's your responsibility to help us out. Don't you understand that?"

His answer was a scowl off to the side.

"Sit up straight in that chair and look like a *human*!"

He didn't move. "That all, mom?"

"Yes," came the helpless reply.

One day, he entered the house wearing an earring on his left earlobe. She refused to speak to him for almost a week while Mrs. MacNeil continually asked him why he wore that ridiculous thing. He would answer in the typical street obfuscation that only frustrated the two women more.

Finally, after all the trips to school for his behavior and schoolwork, after all the talks she had given him, the punishments—some bordering on overkill—he "bopped" into the house one day and announced that hereafter he was not to be known as Rodney; he would be known as Kaseem Abdullah.

Though both women refused to call him anything but his "rightful name" of Rodney, Julia knew she had finally lost him, and something in her died. Still, she reacted with anger when she received that telephone call to come to the school for Rodney for what seemed like the billionth time. What also annoyed her was enduring the discomfort of asking her boss for time off. He never gave her a hard time about it, and he was always accommodating; but he also never failed to communicate to her the inconvenience her absence caused. His left eyebrow would go up, and he would sigh exasperatedly but then smile and accede. It had been, after all, the original agreement when she first signed on with him. Moreover, he knew that, for his accommodation of her, she would repay him with antlike, high quality work. The patients would be tended to with efficiency and tenderness. The appointments would never run into each other. The files would be kept up to date, and the medications would be organized to a tee. She was too valuable for him ever to consider releasing; in that, she was firmly confident. Still, she felt uneasy, and through her anger, she was sure that the end was at hand for her son.

She was not correct. Not just yet.

CHAPTER 5

Earl put the paper down on his desk and let an exasperated breath out. There was a class in front of him. He was just at that delicate point in the lesson—the transition from the motivation to the introduction—and the supercilious monitor was holding the request form in her hand and gazing anxiously at him. This was her second trip to his room, and the letters on the note requesting the monthly attendance form were larger now and underlined. The word "immediately" was underlined in red.

"I'm in the middle of a lesson," he said. "She'll have to wait till later."

The girl looked slightly pained. "But she said she had to have it right away."

"I appreciate your conscientiousness. But I am not going to stop in the middle of my lesson to do this. I'm free next period, and that's when I'll get to it."

She hesitated to leave the room. A low murmur was starting up in the room that ended at Earl's sharp glance.

"She said not to come back without it."

"Wait, let me write this note."

He hastily scribbled the note to the secretary, but the monitor was back in five minutes with another insistent note.

This time, he went next door to Ingram—the classroom on the other side, unfortunately, was unoccupied—and asked him to keep an eye on his class while he went downstairs and dealt with this pain-in-the-ass secretary.

Ingram looked at the form in Earl's hand and then at him, smiling wryly.

"Shame on you," he said. "Don't you realize that simply has to be done? Don't you realize that that form in your hand is the most important thing in this universe since the big bang? Yes, I know you want to educate the young'uns. Come on. Are you so naive as to think that a mere thing like education could even be considered of any importance downstairs? The form, my dear sir. The form. After all, you want that idle Ph.D at the board to be able to sip his coffee at his desk with peace of mind, don't you?"

Earl marched downstairs to the office. He hated those flights of ironic fancy Ingram indulged in. They always made him feel small and insignificant, a Lilliputian striving to be a Brobdingnagian.

After he jotted down some semi-improvised figures on the form while he descended the stairs, he walked into the office and up to a portly, bespectacled woman who had walked to the counter that separated the office staff from visitors.

They leaned close to each other like lovers amidst the surrounding hubbub.

"I'm sorry, Mr. Chaney," she said. "But I simply have to have that right away." The jet blackness of her hair seemed to complement her Donna Reed pretty face, notwithstanding her crow's feet and inchoate jowls. "They're on my back now about it. I was supposed to have it two days ago."

"I understand your position. But I was in the middle of a lesson. A very delicate point. Now the lesson's destroyed. I can't see how a half hour would have made that much difference."

A faint blush came to her cheeks.

"Believe me," she said, pushing her glasses up on her nose. "It would. They're jumping around here. We're moving toward the third quarter now, and Mr. Lassiter's been riding our tails like there's no tomorrow."

Earl glanced around the office and noted the frenetic way conversations were being held, forms were being typed, papers shifted around on desks, and various monitors rushed in and out. Also, sitting in a corner close to the principal's office was Kaseem, a still, moribund point amidst a swirling tempest of activity. The boy glanced at Earl out of the corner of his eye and then stared ahead.

Mr. Lassiter, a paunchy beanpole of a man, entered from another office, gave Earl and his polite antagonist a look, and walked over to another secretary to discuss a form that was in his hand.

Earl noticed that she hadn't flinched, seeing the administrator, as she took the attendance form from Mr. Chaney. Someone being ridden reacted with more tension than this.

"And the lesson I was teaching the children wouldn't?" he went on.

The secretary stiffened. "Mr. Chaney, don't do that to me," she said with a lowered voice. "I've got my job to do. You've got yours. What I'm doing—as insignificant as it may seem to you—makes what you do possible."

"Don't lecture me, please."

"The monies we get from the state come from *this*, and it's one of my jobs to see that it's down here on time so that I could get it in on time. Also, I don't particularly relish working with somebody on my neck, because somebody else is not meeting his responsibilities. It's not fair, and I'm not putting up with it."

Suddenly against the ropes, Earl let his eyes wander past her to outside the school where a handsome black woman in a nurse's uniform, clearly upset about something, got out of a '75 Dodge and started across the street toward the building.

"You teachers, for goodness sakes," she continued. "You sit up there in your classrooms and look down your noses at everybody else in this building. Well, let me tell you, you don't hold exclusive ownership of importance in this business. Yes, what you do is vitally important to our society. Nobody denies that. But what I do is important for the kids, too."

She strode back to her desk, and Earl turned on his heels. As he left the office, he glimpsed the nurse just entering. Too occupied with having just been told off and too angry at himself for having allowed it as he always seemed to do, he gave scant notice to her and marched upstairs to his classroom.

Julia entered the school, glanced at a good-looking black teacher who appeared to be storming out of the general office, and started toward it, a direction she had become all too familiar with. When one of the secretaries saw her, she picked up the intercom and spoke into its receiver.

The harried nurse glared at her son, who shrugged his shoulders at her and pressed his lips together. "I didn't do nothing," he said.

"Sit up in that chair," she said to him.

He didn't change his slouch.

She stared at him, the sense of helplessness coming over her again.

Mr. Hanley walked out of his office, a smile mask on. "Mrs. Wilson. How are you? Please. Come in."

She passed through the counter's swinging door and entered his office, where she nodded at Mr. Rako standing by the window.

"In here, ol' buddy," she heard behind her. "You're not out there to pose for animal crackers all morning."

Kaseem bopped in behind them.

"Mrs. Wilson," said Mr. Hanley solicitously, "could you take this young man here into my anteoffice while I confer with Mr. Rako for a few moments?"

"Of course," she said, ushering her son into the anteoffice, a spacious, windowless room with a large rectangular mahogany conference table as its centerpiece, ten chairs around it, one at each end. "Sit down," she said to her son, who, more slowly than necessary, sat at the head of the table. She sat catty-corner from him.

"When're you going to grow up and stop trying to kill me?" she said to him.

He didn't answer but merely stared off.

"Excuse me. Did I hear you answer my question?"

More silence.

"Look at me!"

He slowly turned his glare toward her. Her eyes did not waver.

"Who you cutting your eyes at?" she said balefully.

"You said to look at you. I'm looking at you."

"Stop being so smart."

"You believe them, right? You're on their side."

She didn't answer.

"Don't assume, Mom," he quipped with mock sternness. "When you *assume*, you make an ass out of you and me."

"What'd you say?" Her eyes shot flames at him.

"Why don't you go into the other office there and talk to them? I'm sure they won't come up with anything you won't agree with."

Mr. Hanley, Mr. Rako, and Mr. Devonshire entered the anteoffice and took seats around the table, Mr. Hanley dislodging Kaseem from his seat but making sure the boy was seated next to him. Julia remained in her seat. Mr. Devonshire, averting his eyes away from her, sat next to her, and Mr. Rako sat across from him.

"So," began Mr. Hanley. "Mrs. Wilson is a busy woman, so we don't want to drag this hearing out." He turned to Mr. Devonshire, who, more calm now, related the events of earlier that morning. Julia swallowed a mouthful of air and saliva as she listened.

"Can I give my side of it?" interjected Kaseem.

"No, you can't!" snapped Julia. "Just sit there and keep your mouth closed! Do that, for goodness sakes."

For the time being, Kaseem decided to do what his mother had told him. He sensed that he had pushed things to the edge and now had to begin exercising caution and restraint.

Mr. Hanley turned toward him and smiled. "You'll have your chance, son. We want to hear all sides here. Believe me, this's not a tribunal to crucify you. Just sit back and relax."

Mr. Rako started to voice an objection, but the principal's subtle head motion stopped him. Mr. Hanley turned back to the boy.

"I'm going to be brutally frank with you, Kaseem. After the incident this morning, I conferred with your official teacher, Mrs. Reinking. Her evaluation of you, I'm afraid, was not very encouraging. Your marks leave a lot to be desired. You're continually in trouble. You've been snotty to your teachers. You've got a serious attitude problem. There's nothing to stand on your side of the argument. Nothing we can use to find a way out for all of us. Look, here your mother has to pull herself away from her job to come here and deal with your inability or unwillingness to fulfill your end. Now doesn't that bother you? Doesn't it concern you—the disruptions you cause? Are you making some point to us?"

"Seems to me we've had this conversation before," said Mr. Rako, but Mr. Hanley gave him another look.

Julia looked at the assistant principal and noted that he was clenching his jaws. This puzzled her slightly, because one didn't clench one's jaws in a situation involving inevitability.

"Let's hear his side," said Mr. Hanley. "Speak your piece, son. Why are you your own worst enemy ... and your mother's ... and ours?"

Kaseem stared at Mr. Hanley.

"Please answer the man's question," Julia snapped.

"Well, he—"

"Who's he?" asked Mr. Hanley.

"Mr. Devonshire." Kaseem glanced down at his lap.

"Then please refer to him as Mr. Devonshire," suggested the principal. "And look up at us."

"Mr. Devonshire came outa his face wrong to me," said Kaseem, a slight tremble in his voice.

"I take that to mean you didn't like the way he talked to you."

"So what if you didn't like the way he addressed you," piped in Mr. Rako. "Too bad about you. He's a teacher."

"Doesn't give'm a right to treat somebody like a piece of garbage," Kaseem answered defensively.

"All right," interposed Mr. Devonshire. "Perhaps I came down on you a little too hard. For that, I apologize. But, one, you had no business in my room. Two, you refused to answer my question. Three, your general attitude was poor. Four, the language you used was not fitting for inside a school building or any other building for that matter. Correct?"

"You still didn't have to talk to me the way you did." Kaseem could feel his mother's outrage swelling.

Mr. Rako looked at the nurse. "Do you see, Mrs. Wilson, what we have to contend with?"

"It seems we're up against a concrete wall we can't crack through," said Mr. Hanley. "Is there anything we can do to change your attitude?"

Mr. Rako leaned back in his seat, obviously disconcerted by the direction Mr. Hanley was taking the discussion.

"It's the teachers," said Kaseem. "Prejudiced. Boring. Always coming outa their faces at me."

"Talk English!" snapped his mother.

Mr. Hanley looked down at a record in front of him. "Let's see. You've been in three fights, one in which you bloodied a boy's nose, one with a girl."

"A girl?!" Julia exclaimed.

"Yes, I'm afraid so, Mrs. Wilson," said Mr. Hanley regretfully. "Because he claimed she tried to make a fool out of him. On two occasions, you got into a shouting match with a teacher, one in the corridor, one in a classroom. You cut classes twice, pulled out once for talking during a fire drill, and you've been accused of theft. Now put yourself in a teacher's place. Do you blame teachers for taking a certain…attitude toward you?"

Kaseem looked down. Obviously, he didn't have a sharp, flip answer to that question so he became silent.

Mr. Hanley leaned back in his chair and stared at the boy. This would help him avoid Rako's eyes, sometimes on him and sometimes staring off. He did not want the assistant principal's expressed disapproval of his way of dealing with Kaseem to dilute his resolve.

"By all rights," Mr. Hanley went on, "I should have you put out of the school now. I have enough in front of me to more than back me up. But because your mother deserves much better than you're giving her and perhaps what we're giving her and because our philosophy here is to help and save rather than to throw away, I'm going to give you that one more *undeserved* chance. Now, the question is how're we going to do this when we're just about out of options? Tell me. Is there any teacher in this school it's possible for you to work with in anyway?"

The tension in the room made Mrs. Wilson drop her keys onto the table. Excusing herself, she snatched them up. She stared at her son. Mr. Hanley glanced at her. Did something reachable still exist somewhere inside the boy?

Kaseem looked up and peered into Mr. Hanley's face, searching for hints of insincerity and intrigue. "Mr. Chaney," he finally said, his memory still tied to the gold chain behind the poster paper.

The two administrators looked at each other. Mr. Devonshire looked at the boy with a faint knowing smile on the corners of his lips.

"Mr. Chaney," responded the principal, nodding in agreement. "Good choice. I'll tell you, son. You can't make it with him, you can't make it with anybody in this system."

"Amen to that," added Mr. Rako, unhappy.

Oh yeah, thought Earl as he looked at the note informing him that Mr. Hanley wanted to speak to him in his office. *So the bitch ratted to the principal, and now I'm going to get my third ass-chewing in two days … twice in one morning, the first reacted to in silence. No way.* This time he was going to open up his mouth and let some people have a piece of his mind. This was not the army, and he wasn't earning enough salary.

Still, he'd always hated confrontations.

He stood up as the teacher to cover his class and proceeded back down the stairs. Buttoning his jacket, he strode into the office, glancing at his secretary-adversary, who signalled him to the counter again. On her face was contrition.

"I'm sorry, Mr. Chaney, for my manner before. I'm under a great deal of pressure, and I guess I let it get to me. Could you forgive me?"

For a moment, he regarded her. Something happened here to turn things around, a very subtle power shift. He took her hand and squeezed it as Mr. Hanley opened the principal's office door and gestured for him to enter. He pulled Earl inside and immediately closed the door. Mr. Rako was leaning against the wall with his arms folded. Mr. Devonshire had left.

"Look, Mr. Chaney, I'm going to ask you a very important favor. An imposition, I know, but that's what happens to people who are top-notch in their professions. They have to take up the slack for some of the weaker teachers on the staff. I know you have a fairly sizable class now, and I know you have more than your share of problems in that class. And now I'm going to add to your burden and transfer Kaseem Wilson into it."

Something inside Earl crashed to the bottom of his soul. He let out a long silent groan.

"Yes, I know," the principal continued. "He's a royal pain in the behind. He's bad news to just about everybody, but you're a teacher who's not afraid of challenges, so I assumed you wouldn't mind. Do you have any objections?"

Earl glanced at Mr. Rako, who, expressionless, stared at him.

"I want to give'm every possible chance I can," the principal continued.

"And if I fail?"

"That doesn't even come into consideration here," Mr. Hanley said, shaking his head. "Doesn't factor in. A teacher like you? No, if it doesn't work out, it wasn't supposed to. The boy's used up all his chips already. You're an extra thrown in for good measure. Maybe the one he needs. Whatever, if he can't shape up with you, we all might as well pack it in. And it would have nothing to do with you."

Earl regarded the two administrators for a long time. Then he nodded.

The principal smiled and patted Earl's shoulder. "Good. Okay. Mrs. Wilson's in the anteoffice right now. Go in there and have a word with her. Reassure her. I think she needs it."

"You're a good man," added Mr. Rako, unfolding his arms and pushing himself off the wall. "I think when you die, they should make you a saint."

"Mr. Rako," said the principal, annoyed by the remark. "I would appreciate it if we could all think positively, okay?"

Chastened, Mr. Rako left the office.

Pretending to be oblivious to that, Earl walked into the anteoffice and noted the attractive nurse he had seen earlier.

Julia Wilson smiled and rose to shake his hand, but he gestured for her to remain seated and sat himself in the seat close to her. She looked at him with such great esteem that he was not quite able to gauge his response.

"Mr. Chaney, I'm at the end of my rope," she lamented. "I don't know what to do. I hate to put it on your shoulders, but you're Rodney's last chance. If he fails with you, it's the end. And he's all I got."

Her eyes quickly moistened, and she looked down, apologizing to him with a quavering voice and then struggling to pull herself back together. "Making a spectacle of myself."

"Cleans the bacteria out of the eyes," he responded, smiling. He hesitantly placed his hand on hers. "It'll be all right," he said quietly, an arrogance stirring in him. *He's saved, don't worry*, he thought, momentarily wondering what his life would have become if she'd been his wife with her dignity, aura, and sturdiness and then reminding himself that Ida had not been that bad at the beginning. And Dionne had his heart.

"See, it's necessary for me to work two jobs, sometimes three, to get us by, keep us in this neighborhood. This means I have to leave Rodney with my mother, and when she has to work, he's by himself, which I'm not crazy about. I took this dental assistant's job nearby so that I could be available to the school during the day should a problem come up. I know Rodney being left by himself so much is a problem. I wish there was some other way. His father and I split up years ago so there's been no real man in his life since then. He's very confused, hostile, and wilful, and I know a lot of it's toward me.

44

"Mr. Chaney, I'm told you're a great teacher and human being. And you're a black man, something Rodney needs badly. Please. Please stick with'm. For him to be thrown out of school—" She stopped then, beginning to lose control again, but this time caught herself.

He looked at her and, for a moment, felt the full power of what worth he was to society. Then he thought of all the events in his life that had seemed to diminish him. He could use a little healthy arrogance and egotism. And when he saw the moisture in her eyes, he knew he was hooked to the mission of Kaseem's redemption.

"Listen," she went on. "Do whatever you have to do. I'm behind you one hundred percent. Come by the house any time you think it's necessary. I'll even fix for you."

Earl's resolve solidified even more when Mr. Rako spoke to him later that day. "Mrs. Wilson's a very nice lady, a beautiful person. But take my word for it. The boy's a loser. Put up with'm until he finally hangs himself for good. It's all you can do."

How dare that man put limitations on him when he didn't have the faintest idea of what he was about as a teacher or a man? Still, that satrap wasn't of any importance now. Only Kaseem.

CHAPTER 6

He entered another empty office and found the young man sitting at the head of its conference table, his hands resting on the chair's arm. The youth turned to face the teacher and half smiled.

"Whaddya say?" said Earl.

"Nothing too much right now," the youth answered, averting his eyes.

"I hear that."

"Look, Mr. Chaney," Kaseem said as Earl sat down. "Before you say anything, I want you to know that I ain't gonna hassle you. I'll do my work. I'll cooperate with you in every way. I'll be a monitor for you even. I got myself in a mess. But, hey, I'm in it. And I'm gonna work my way outa it. Square business."

Slightly surprised, Earl regarded him. "Well, I guess no more needs be said. Let's go to my class."

"Everything's squared away I see," said Mr. Rako as they passed him on the way out of the office.

Now that you've hooked me, thought Earl, allowing himself some hubris.

When they entered Earl's empty classroom, Kaseem scanned the paper-free floor (unlike the floor of his former classroom), the desks, chalkboard, the bulletin board above it with its posted cutouts of great literary figures and stills from filmed versions of the classics, the closet doors, and windows, as if he was appraising a new home where he was determined to make it, no matter what. He also eyed the rear bulletin board, noting with some satisfaction that the practically invisible telltale lump was still there, undisturbed. He took an unassigned seat near that spot. Earl assured him that nobody occupied that seat.

When his official class entered his classroom, Earl was entering the information on Kaseem into the roll book. Mr. Rako would deliver the boy's record file to him later. Kaseem had been cleaning the desks of balled up paper.

Vinny entered and looked at Kaseem with a you've-invaded-my-turf-chump expression on his face and went to his seat.

"Class," Earl announced after he had stepped to the door briefly in order to supervise the between-classes traffic in the corridor. "I want to introduce you to the newest member of our family—Kaseem Wilson."

The students greeted him in low-key manner. Some rolled their eyes to the ceiling, or, a moue on their faces, looked out the window.

"There goes the neighborhood," quipped Vinny, not so much under his breath he couldn't be heard, eliciting chuckles.

Earl glanced at Vinny and then looked at Kaseem.

"Perhaps you'd like to say something to the class," he said to the latter.

Kaseem shrugged his shoulders and looked down. Then he inhaled and looked back up with a kind of boldness, absent of hostility.

"Look, class," he said. "I know I been a creep, acting like a hard rock and all. I got no excuses for that. All I can say is I'm gonna do my best to be good, to be good for the class and for Mr. Chaney to make my moms proud of me and to make everybody who said I was finished here wrong."

"I'll bet," said Vinny.

"Vinny," said Earl. "Not another word out of you unless it's something positive, understand?"

"Sorry, Mr. Chaney."

"I'd like to speak with you after class," he continued, still staring at Vinny.

The class ooooooohed and uh-ohed.

"That'll be quite enough!" Earl said, a slight edge to his voice. "Do you think I'm playing some kind of game here? I'm going to speak to Vinny and send him on to class. I won't have any dumb signifying side remarks and sounds from the peanut gallery! Have I made myself clear?"

"Yes, Mr. Chaney," everybody said.

"Now, since we have all this energy, let's turn our attention to the compound sentence and its elements!"

Which the class did noiselessly.

The next class had a warm-up on the chalkboard (a written exercise which would prepare the students for the lesson on figurative language) so Earl was able to speak to Vinny in the hallway. The backs of his official class students could be seen down the hall turning to the staircase. A few glanced back at them.

"You have to help me out, Vinny," he said. "We have a young man, obviously very troubled, who is on his last legs. We're going to try to give'm his last chance. I don't know whether we'll succeed or not, but we're going to try. That means all of us pitch in. *All* of us."

"I'm sorry, Mr. Chaney. I guess I came outa my face wrong. I won't do it again."

Earl stared at the young man. "Is there something going on between you two I don't know about?"

"No, Mr. Chaney."

"I don't want something jumping up in my face. If there is something, I want to know about it." Earl placed his hand on Vinny's shoulder.

"There's nothing. Square business."

"You're sure now?"

"Look, Mr. Chaney. We ain't exactly tight, but it's cool between us. You don't have to worry about nothing."

"Don't use double negatives," the teacher said as he wrote Vinny a pass and sent him to his next classroom. "And the use of 'ain't' ain't cool. Make folks around here think I'm not teaching you any English."

Now that everything was set, Earl was going to show the faculty what a good teacher could do. Beneath his self-doubts, there was a firm determination.

If he could save this kid, maybe that would somehow make up for his debacle in that southern town and the ugly inner response he'd had to Washington's victimization. Maybe by saving Kaseem, he could, in the deepest recesses of his own soul, save all the Kaseems around the country who had been lynched, physically, economically, psychologically, and morally—that included Washington, Ray, himself.

To add to this, Kaseem volunteered to be a monitor for him, to come in early in the morning and generally straighten out the classroom and mark any test papers. Also, he would make sure the bulletin boards were kept up.

Already, Earl was impressed with the "new Kaseem," but surely, his influence could not have been felt that soon. There had always been, inside him, that ever-present tendency to undervalue his powers. That also needed checking.

The pupil's cafeteria was an enclosure of adolescent Brownian movement. The eighth graders, those not on the lunch lines, rushed back and forth, table-hopping and visiting friends while a small cadre of harried teachers oversaw this, standing around, seeming lost, glazed of eye, yet ever alert for the first signs of a food fight or any other kind of fight. Paper plates and milk containers, full or empty, accumulated around the bottoms of the food receptacles, so the cafeteria staff had its work cut out for it. Many boys practiced their jump shots and finger rolls on these receptacles with the milk containers or oatmeal cookies wrappers, not always getting their baskets. Still, overall, there was a kind of order in the cafeteria one would not expect from a large chamber with smells (particularly those of overused cooking oil), incredible noise, and close to six hundred students already made restless by a half-completed day of school. Occasionally, Spriggs would pop in, converse with a few students, look around, and reconnoiter the few known outstanding behavior problems before he left.

Kaseem sought Fox out and pulled him to the rear part of the cafeteria, where there were fewer students and which drew the least amount of teacher attention.

"Man, your ass ain't in trouble?" asked Fox, flabbergasted.

"I been transferred to Mr. Chaney's class."

"Mr. Chaney's class! Oh, wow, you lucked out, bro! But you best be cool with'm. He's all right, but if you get on his shit list, he'll wipe you away with toilet paper and flush you down."

"I hear ya," Kaseem said. "But I intend to do that real chilly thing. See, we got a set up that just won't wait. I'm gonna be a monitor for'm. I come in early in the morning and straighten up his classroom. And while I'm doing that, I stash our booty from our earlier morning activities. So we can hit the bus stops, the streets, and occasionally the subways. Take them gold chains away from them fools to our hearts' content. After school, we tip on down to these dealers on Jackson Avenue or Prospect—no questions asked—and get us some bucks."

He slapped Fox five but suddenly stiffened.

Spriggs had entered the cafeteria and was headed toward them.

"So look," Kaseem went on to Fox in an exaggeratedly normal voice. "I think if we get there on time, we can get good seats. You know what I mean?"

"Huh?" asked Fox, turning around. "Oh."

"Well, well, well, well, well, look what we got here," greeted the policeman. "The two stooges."

"Now why you got to be that way, Spriggs?" asked Kaseem. "We ain't bothering nobody."

"Don't get all huffy," said Spriggs, patting Fox on his shoulder and looking at Kaseem. "You don't need to get your nose bent all out of shape when somebody's only joshing you. Learn to keep a sense of humor in your outlook. Know what I mean? It's a new day. Oh, and it's Officer Spriggs, if you please."

But his eyes said, *I don't like you two talking to each other—it's bad news. You got off on a hummer, Kaseem. But you best cool your role. Ol' Spriggs's eye is on y'all.*

Chapter 7

Later, while teachers were standing on hall duty during the between-classes passage of students, Ingram strolled over to Earl. His face was filled with crocodile melancholy, overwrought commiseration, and there was a melodramatic droop to his shoulders. He patted Earl on his shoulder, paused, and said, "Look at it this way. We have only a million more weeks to go, and then you can sleep all day, sit on the beach, recuperate, and collect your summer money."

Earl managed a faint smile that belied the gloating inside him. He liked those moments when he could feel superior to his colleagues, particularly when they were patronizing him. He would be the Pygmalion to a student nobody else in the school could handle. He pictured himself being honored at some NAACP ceremony with his father and mother looking on, tears of pride filling their eyes, and Washington asking his forgiveness for whatever he'd done to cause their relationship to end, Anthony bragging to his friends about his dad and Ida and Dionne clinging to each arm. Finally, there would be Julia Wilson bringing her clasped hands to her face, as if in prayer, and thankfully gazing upon him.

He went down to the teacher's cafeteria—something he rarely did—so that he could flaunt his new invisible trophy, so that he could implicitly lord it over his colleagues.

He caught the uneasy glances from some of the teachers. Others seemed totally unaware of him.

One came over to the table where he sat. It was Mr. Devonshire.

Earl, munching on a tuna fish on rye, gestured for him to sit.

"Look, man," the humbled teacher said. "I didn't mean to cause you to get stuck with that guy."

"Don't sweat it," returned Earl. "Kid's already voiced his determination to do right."

"Well, all right then. But he's treacherous. Watch'm. He's got arsenic behind his teeth."

"I know."

Devonshire regarded him for a moment. "Look," he said finally. "He called me an Oreo cookie. It sort of … stung. I'm not always thrilled with the dissolute ways of some of our folks, but I'm always in their corner. When Dr. King was shot, I walked around pretty pissed off. I even gave this white cop some lip when he gave me a parking ticket. Almost got my butt tossed in the slammer. And I was in the wrong and he was in the right. Eventually, I got my head back on straight and rejoined the human race. Then that kid…. Hey, that's all right. There was enough sense in me to realize that the young man was probably just talking trash, reaching for something to throw at me. Look, take this for what it's worth. If you can do it for the kid, go ahead and do it. More power to you. Straighten'm out. We don't want them saying, 'See, this kid's so bad not even a black teacher can handle'm.'"

Earl took another huge bite of his sandwich as another passing teacher patted him on his shoulder. He hoped his head hadn't really been the target.

The block had one- and two-family houses lined almost evenly with very little space between them. Most of the front lawns were neatly trimmed, and the bushes evidenced some attempts at maintenance. Sometimes the garages were in the front, next to the house, sometimes in the back. The driveways often were so narrow two seemed like one. Many of the tiny enclosed backyards were frequently used for outdoor get-togethers or elaborately improvised picnics.

Kaseem's house was one of the narrow two-family, four-story houses with a tiny attic and a basement section for the two continually absent tenants. The front yard was nicely maintained, its small surrounding bushes kept up diligently, although he did not always do his part in helping out, even when his mother asked him. Because of the increase in car thefts—not to mention the muggings and burglaries—in the neighborhood, she parked her '75 Dodge in the somewhat cluttered garage in the back.

He seldom felt good when he entered this block, because he always sensed his neighbors' disapproval of him, peering at him through their curtains and clucking. Thus, he would put a little more energy into his bop and, in his mind, render his surroundings invisible, nonexistent (so he thought) until he closed his front door. Then he would smell the dinner being prepared in the kitchen by his grandmother and hear her puttering about, and a deeper annoyance would grip him.

That night, she came to the kitchen doorway on her way to the broom and mop closet, saw him, stopped, and glared at him. She said nothing.

Sucking his teeth, he ran upstairs to his bedroom, knowing that his mother wouldn't be home from work for a while. Had she been, he either would have gone into the kitchen and attempted to talk to his grandmother while he picked at the food and got his hand slapped, a kind of digressive ingratiation, or locked himself and a kung fu comic book in the bathroom.

His room was messy. The week's used socks and jockey shorts were piled up on his desk chair, and the desk itself was piled with textbooks, magazines, and comic books. However, he did see evidence that his grandmother had attempted to straighten it up a little. He began to work on it. When his mother got home, he would need as many points as he could score with her. He was walking along the edge of the precipice now, but there was a chance he could back away from it if he did not mess up in any way.

The phone rang. He carefully lifted up the receiver in the upstairs hallway.

"Get off the phone, Rodney," stabbed his ears. It was his mother's voice. "I'm talking to your grandmother!" Quickly, he hung up and began to steal downstairs. His grandmother was at the dining room telephone, standing at the table and nodding grimly while she eyed Kaseem.

Then she hung up. "You're not going anyplace, Buster Brown," she said. "Your behind is in this house tonight and until further notice. Now you heard it."

She turned and went back into the kitchen. He followed her. "Aw, Grandmother," he said. "Why you wanna do something like that?"

"Reach the paprika for me," she said.

He knew that whenever she cut him off with an order or request, all lines for negotiation were down. He sensed also that this was because she really couldn't handle him if he decided to put pressure on her. He always knew the deep affection she felt for him, something he didn't always sense from his mother. Still, behind it all was the inexorable fact of his mother's firmness and unpredictable rage.

He decided, though, to push it further. As he handed her the paprika, he said, "Grams, don't you think your daughter's going too far? I mean, to expect a growing teenager to sit in a house and be deprived of healthy outside air. Wouldn't you agree?"

"She's your mother," his grandmother said firmly. "Refer to her as your mother."

"All right. Mom."

"Say it right, will you? When you gonna get some respect, boy?"

"People gotta give me reason," he said.

"What's that supposed to mean?"

Kaseem looked off. "C'mon, Grams. Please."

For a few moments, she didn't answer him but merely sprinkled the paprika on the salad she was preparing. She added a few sprinkles of pepper to the sliced tomatoes.

"You can put on all the airs you want," she said finally, now dicing a small section of onion. "You know what you did."

"But I didn't really do nothing." He gently placed his hand on her back.

"I know you heard what I said to you."

Stymied, he went back upstairs.

Later, his restlessness and anxiety overcame his discretion, and he decided to sneak out of the house. What the hell? He was in trouble anyway, so he might as well get his last licks in, have some fun. Perhaps he could fix this later. Right now, he needed fortification against what was coming.

He went to his dresser drawer, reminding himself that he would have to find a better place for his loot, and took out the Green Hornet ring case. He put it into his jacket pocket and then was carefully starting out of the bedroom when he heard the television being turned on in the living room downstairs.

Because the television was so positioned that anyone watching it would have the front door in her view, it being right next to the living room, getting to that door was now impossible. He stopped, cursing to himself. His grandmother would be watching the television momentarily, and the only other way out was through the back door, which was through the kitchen. He would have to cool his heels in his room.

Shortly, he heard what sounded like a car commercial and his grandmother stirring in the kitchen. He tossed the small box from one hand to the other and gnawed lightly on his top lip.

He made his move.

He slipped out of the room and started down the stairs. The problem would be to get out the front door without being seen or heard, and the lock's click was often loud. After he decided it wouldn't work, he backed up the stairs just as she was returning to the living room.

He didn't hear her sit down, however.

Suddenly, she came to the foot of the stairs, making him duck back against the upstairs hallway wall. For a short while, she stood there, probably looking upstairs. "Rodney," she said.

He didn't answer. She sucked her teeth and went downstairs to the basement. The basement toilet flushed. That was what he wanted! Like a cat, he tiptoed swiftly down the stairs, and then his fingers became a safecracker's as he turned the lock and opened the front door. Now outside, he closed the door almost completely to the jamb and then held it to soften the lock's sharp click.

He put his key into the lock, turned it slightly, and waited. The toilet flushed again. Quickly but carefully, he closed the door and turned his key to complete its rotation, the click stabbing his ear. Hopefully, the cellar toilet flushing would have drowned out the sound. Maybe not.

Whatever, now free, he turned to the street.

Fox was sitting on the stoop of the four-story housing project building—Sycamore Houses—he lived in with his mother, two older sisters, and occasional father as well as any supplementary adult male figures who happened to appear at the breakfast table.

He smiled at the approaching Kaseem. "Brother man," he sang, a capella style, "about to do up some serious business."

The jewellery store on Jackson Avenue faced a few condemned buildings and a large desolated lot where buildings used to be. Still, there were stores with Plexiglas separating proprietors from customers and complicated labyrinths for entrances. In most, customers had to be buzzed in. The jewellery store, certainly.

The proprietor studied the two youths through his storefront for a few seconds before he buzzed them in. He was a large bellied man who must have played halfback at one time. He wore a rust-colored necktie and a pencil mustache. The boys noticed that one hand was under the counter.

"How can I help you?" he asked, a little knowingly, slight recognition of Kaseem and Fox in his eyes.

Kaseem produced the Green Hornet ring box, opened it, and showed its contents to the proprietor, who pulled a small sliding door back with his other hand. Kaseem shoved the necklace through the opening. The jeweller closed the sliding door, removed his hand from under the counter, and examined the necklace with a magnifying glass.

"How much can we get for that?" Kaseem asked.

The jeweller didn't answer immediately as he studied the necklace. "Okay, fourteen karat, S-style, twenty-four inch."

Then he looked up at Kaseem. "Forty dollars."

Despite the deep feeling that he was being ripped off, Kaseem acknowledged the forty dollars as more than his expectations. Still, he allowed intense disappointment to cloud his face before he finally "accepted" the figure. Fox started to protest but was tapped on his shoe.

"You won't do any better than this," the proprietor said as he passed four tens to them. "Don't spend it all in one place. And come back again."

"You ever make twenty dollars this fast before?" asked Kaseem as he handed Fox his share. "Now, not to bring this up, but ain't I entitled to some special … consideration?"

"Aw, man," returned Fox. "I knew you were gonna run some shit like that down on me. Here." He reached into his pocket and produced a half-decimated dollar bill.

"You chumpin' me? What I went through today—that's what it's worth to you?"

"Aw, now you gonna try to play it off. What it have to do with our snatch today anyhow?"

Kaseem stared at him for a few moments before he fanned his hand in his face. "Forget it, man. Forget you!"

"Why you gonna catch an attitude?"

"All fulla questions, ain't you?" Kaseem said. "Maybe we should get Vanna White to come sit on your lap'n shit. Damn right I'm catching an attitude. My moms gonna put me *under* the house for the duration, and you gonna play big fucking businessman on me. Like you General Motors. Sitting on the cash register and counting the beans. That's what I get, I guess. Hey, fuck it. I ain't got no attitude no more. Everything's cool. No big thing. I'm a man, see. We gonna be making googobs of bucks. Ain't no use squabbling over a couple goddamned bills—chump change. I just don't like you downplaying all that shit I had to go through today."

"Ain't nobody downplaying nothing. Don't jump all paranoid on me."

Tips was a tall, brown-skinned eighth grader in one of the lower-track classes, lower even than the one Fox was in. Though nice looking, he had a personality like a rattlesnake, an animal that used its rattle so that it would never have to deal with any real challenges.

Moreover, he knew how to cover this with a certain kind of oily charm.

He was known as "the man" to the neighborhood kids and even to some kids from distant neighborhoods. Found usually hanging out in a corner candy and newspaper store, his "base of operations," Tips could easily be contacted despite his cautiousness. Most important though, he could be depended on for the highest quality "cheeba."

"What it is?" he sangsonged to the two youths. "Check out the wares, and it always be's a pleasure to do business with y'all."

They purchased two sticks each from Tips and then went into the store to buy some peppermint candy and a box of Clorets chewing gum.

"Y'all got it made," commented Tips as they parted from him. "Paaaaaarteeee time."

They went to the park benches facing the thoroughfare down the block from the school, sat on them, and smoked their "herb" as they half-consciously watched the cars drone by on the road—a few patrol cars on some more important mission than rousting two pot-smoking teenagers. Spriggs, of course, would be in another world, his evening life, Mr. Chaney, in another galaxy.

It was good stuff. The "buzz" started right away. Their tongues loosened, and they began to giggle a lot over trivial things. Everything on the earth became multicolored roller disco lights swirling in the park on a cool evening.

"Whooooee!" exclaimed Fox. "Ol' Tips can come up with some prime shit."

"I hear that," returned Kaseem.

"I'm starting to sail. Ya with me?"

"Right into that Michellene."

"Oh, yeah."

Kaseem's insides came alive at the mere mention of her name. He squirmed to keep it from becoming too obvious to Fox.

"You a nasty-ass motherfucka," sneered the latter. "I hear you."

"But you know, brother man, that ain't all there is in this world," Kaseem started. "Coupla goddamned bitches. With their silly-assed giggling and always talking about this dress and that dress and this one's so cute and that one can take me anytime. Sheeeit. After a while, begins to get boring, y'know what I mean. Make me wanna climb through the roof and punch something. Yeah, we gotta have 'em. But we shouldn't let them become so important. 'Cause ain't a one of them worth a good goddamn no-how. You know, the bitch we took off this morning. When I had her from behind, I could feel her butt pushing into me. Made me wanna stop and cop me some. But no, business first. And it's about that, see. Me? I'm gonna get me some bank, googobs of it so's I can get me a nice crib, some threads, some wheels, and I can go where I please when I please. And pay by cash. Always have my bank on me so's I don't have to owe nobody nothing, y'hear what I'm saying? Get me a good business. Throw some bucks to some needy people to look *good* to the community and keep up my thing. And every time I feel like it, snap my finger and the finest foxes come running. Hanging on my arm. Throw some of that knee into me. Make every dude around me jealous to his toenails. And then strut on. Strut on. Now that's what it's about."

Fox gazed at him. "You crazy," he said. "Look, all I wanna do is get over. Don't have no simple turkey don't got a pot to piss in gettin' up in my face buggin' me. Nobody trying to chump me off. That's what it's about."

"Yeah, but don't you ever want more than that?" asked Kaseem as he drew an arc in the grass with a broken twig.

"Like what?" Fox put his leg up on the bench.

"Like … I dunno. Like … *more.*"

"Oh, you goin' into your deep bag now. Gone get heavy on me with that *New York Times* shit." He fanned his hand at Kaseem. "End up with nothing but a headache."

Kaseem glanced at his watch. He'd planned to be in bed before his mother got home from work. He gave his last stick to Fox, popped a cube of peppermint candy into his mouth and another of Clorets, and began to chew furiously.

"I'm pushin'," he said. "Okay, now, I probly be outa circulation for a while, but we still work our early morning thing. I got some plans."

Fox watched his friend cross the street and head for the two-family house section to the north. He loitered on the bench for a short while and then started for his home in the housing project across the street from the school.

He climbed up the four flights of his building, trying to ignore the dank odor of urine mixed with grease. The elevator, another smelly place, was usually out of whack. Exhaling after holding his breath, he entered his apartment and went into the kitchen to inspect the noisy refrigerator's contents. Many cans of beer filled the bottom shelf with a sloppily wax paper-covered plate of meat loaf that he took a bite of.

He heard a stirring behind him and turned.

It was his mother, Claudine, a zoftig brown-skinned woman with reddish eyes that pierced the apartment's semi-darkness. She was in her pink housecoat, half opened. "I thought I heard somebody come in," she said, a slight slur to her voice. "Thought maybe it was one of your slutty sisters. Come to find out it's just you."

Fox took another mouthful of meat loaf and put the rest back into the refrigerator.

"You wash your hands?" she snapped, her hands on her hips.

"They clean."

"Don't look clean to me. You come in here out the street and put those

58

filthy-ass hands on the food. Boy, what's wrong with you? Lookit those hands. And you smell. You been smokin'?"

A man appeared behind her, bare-chested and in his briefs.

Fox didn't know him.

"What's this I hear? Boy been smokin' pot?" the man asked, leaning against the jamb. "I dunno what's getting' into these kids today." He boldly walked up to Fox and sniffed. "He sure been."

"Now how you gonna come out the bedroom, your no-nothings showing all over the place, and get up in's face like that?"

The man began patting Fox down until he came to the boy's right pocket and squeezed. "Uh-oh, what's this?" He reached into the pocket and extracted the extra stick of marijuana Kaseem had given to Fox.

"Who told you you could go in my pocket?" Fox protested.

The man snapped his finger in Fox's face. "Hey, don't step outa line now, youngblood. Chill." He pushed his finger against Fox's nose.

"Hold on here," said Claudine as she stepped between them. "Hello, this's my child. Don't be manhandling my child."

The man leaned close to Claudine and stretched his arms outward, wiggling the cigarette with his right hand. "It's all right, sweet pea. It's gonna be all right. See what I'm sayin'?"

Claudine's face softened. Then she snapped to Fox, now fighting tears. "Go wash yourself up! And get to bed. You got school tomorrow! And don't you start no cryin' in here. I give you something to cry for!"

The man laughed and returned to the bedroom. Claudine followed.

Fox stood frozen in the middle of the kitchen.

Later, he lay on his bed and smelled the odor of marijuana being smoked and listened to the squeaking of his mother's mattress.

Neither sister came home.

Kaseem's block was quiet. Only the flickering lights of a distant tv screen showed any signs of life. Even the parked vehicles seemed to show their disapproval of him and pity for him, considering what he was in for.

All was stillness in the house when Kaseem entered. His grandmother was still up, way past her bedtime, a bad sign. Then he saw the bills on the dining room table. Well, things couldn't possibly be worse for him now. What the hell?

"I don't know what wickedness got into you, Rodney," his grandmother said to him in quietest, almost resigned tones. "You don't do what's right. You do all this mess. I dunno where it comes from. And then you got the nerve to ask me to intercede for you. Do me a favor, huh? Don't ask me for the time of day anymore."

"Grandma," he said, his voice uncharacteristically low. "I know I ain't been right lately. And I ain't making excuses for myself. I got things on my mind, and I been sorta upset. Please understand. I love you and Mom."

"What about the other times?" she asked, softening.

"What other times?"

She stared at him for a few moments, rolled her eyes, sucked her teeth, and went upstairs to her bedroom. Tight in his stomach, he followed her to his.

His mother was lying on his bed, reading one of his comic books. When he entered, she sat up, closing the magazine and staring at its cover. Then she tossed it aside and just stared ahead into space.

The room got darker and warmer for Kaseem.

"Kung fu, huh?" she said. "That all you put into your head? Violence and muscles. Half-naked women with some man attacking them? Do you have a library card?"

"No," he mumbled.

"No what?"

"No, ma'am."

"You don't have the school people protecting you now. I'll smack you right into that wall. I might do it anyhow. Y'hear me?"

"Yes, ma'am."

Suddenly, Mrs. MacNeil was at the door. "Julia," she said pleadingly. "I know the boy is wrong, but don't do anything you'll feel sorry for later."

"Mom," Julia said, sighing. "I'm gonna have to ask you to go back to your room. I don't mean to be rude, but I'll handle this."

Mrs. MacNeil disappeared.

"Now how come you don't have a library card?"

Kaseem paused and regarded his mother. There was grave threat in the air—that he knew—so he would weigh his answers to her curt questions carefully, as well as the way he answered them and the tone of his voice. One wrong move here and he would have on his hands a roomful of trouble.

"'Cause I lost the book and—"

"What book?" Her eyes widened.

"Johnny Something. I dunno." He looked away. *Johnny Appleseed* came suddenly to his mind but he held back.

"Johnny Something, I don't know, huh? How'd you lose it?"

"I left it in my locker, and somebody took it while I was in gym," he answered, swallowing.

"Go on." She leaned forward, stiff-armed, on her knees.

"And I didn't pay for it, so they took away my card," he said.

"How come I wasn't told about this?"

Unsure, he didn't answer that. He knew any jive answer at this point would only bury him deeper.

"I love this communication between us. Very informative," she quipped.

She looked down at her feet as she moved them about on the floor. "Well, my son. Please listen very carefully to what I have to say. You are in this house until further notice, which may never come. The only time you will see out is when you go to school. When you leave school, you're back here by three thirty. No stopping at a candy store, schoolyard, ballpark, or ice cream truck. I am going to the library with my checkbook to settle whatever account needs to be settled, and you're gonna have a *book* to read before this week is out. By the way, you stop at the library, you're still expected home before three thirty. Your grandmother sends you to the store, you're back here within thirty minutes."

"But mom, how do you expect me—"

"Shut up! Now you make one more of your bonehead moves, clown, or say something out of line, and I'm having you put away. Closing the book on you. Boarding you out to some military school or whatever—and I'll find one that I can afford so help me, God—if I have to work twenty-four hours a day to pay for it. I'll send you so far outa this city, you'll have to come south to the North Pole. Am I communicating to you?"

"Yes ma'am."

"I hope so. Now get yourself to bed."

She marched out of the bedroom. She then came back and said, "Did you eat?"

"Yes, ma'am," he lied.

"What'd you have?"

"Cheeseburger'n fries," he said.

"Cheeseburger'n fries? Grease. Sugar. Sodium. Tell you you'd better get with it. And you can chew a ton of Clorets, you still stink! Celebrating your last out, huh? You forgot you're dealing with a nurse's nose."

With that, she regarded him for the longest time before she left.

Chapter 8

The stairs went up three long flights in one direction, broken only by three landings. The first landing went to a modeling school and agency of sorts. The second landing went to a mystic, roots reader, and fortune-teller. The third, where they were headed, was the meeting hall of The Black Resurrection. On one side, through the narrow walls, could be heard the seductive throbbing of disco music from the bar next door. On the other, fragrant lavender incense was burning from long sticks scotch-taped in zigzag formation to the walls. Under each stick was a small sign: WELCOME, BROTHERS AND SISTERS! THE CLIMB IS GOOD FOR YOUR HEART. THE BLACK RESURRECTION IS GOOD FOR YOUR SOUL.

The top third floor landing turned into the rear of a large rectangular hall containing some twenty rows of folding chairs, ten each row, facing a makeshift platform-like stage. The hall was three-quarters full of restless people, mostly black, a few whites and Latinos, and one sleeping baby.

Somehow, to Earl, they seemed to lack the fire that even the phonies had during the peak Civil Rights years. They sat and listened, attentive but skeptical and tired. The sleeping baby, comfortable in a portly woman's arms, seemed not to have any less enthusiasm than many of the more adult, less distant members of the gathering.

Still, they were there, which said something to Earl about the current times and what they were doing to so many lives around him. The Civil Rights Movement may have succeeded in stirring the hearts of hopeful men and women throughout the nation and world, a point reiterated often in the speeches of earnest VIPs, but the presence at this gathering of these ordinary folk, many wearing masks of desperation, gave a contradictory testimony.

One young man with a Vandyke beard and strange Afro hairstyle, which had what looked like avant-garde cornrows where his sideburns should have been, sat quietly but distantly and stared. A very dark young woman wore a wig that almost convinced one that it was part of her and clutched a copy of *The Mountain People* on her lap. Another light-skinned woman with a freckled nose rested her hands on a paperback copy of *Tracy and Hepburn*. A brown-skinned man had shaved all the hair from his head and wore an earring, evincing a Saracen pirate masculinity. A few people were nodding or, like the baby, asleep. A couple looked at their watches and then each other before they quietly slipped out.

On the walls were large photos of Malcolm X, Patrice Lumumba, H. Rap Brown, Angela Davis, Joanne Chesimard, Barbara Jordan, Martin Luther King, Jr., Eldridge Cleaver, and Jesse Jackson.

Shehab was a small, thin, dark man with burning eyes, with a trace of a scar on the bridge of his nose, thin lips, and a scraggly beard. Obviously, he was a man who kept himself in shape, but his bleary red eyes hinted at the presence of not a little drink in his life.

He stood on the platform-stage in his gray Lincoln University sweater and jeans, glanced around at his various bodyguards flanking the audience, standing at the rear, a few also on the platform with him; and he then turned to the audience. He allowed a faint smile on his face and, with his knuckles, rapped the clipboard in his hand and then fingered a few newspaper clippings attached to it.

Dionne leaned closer to Earl and whispered, "He's such a hambone."

"Brothers and sisters," he said. "We're in a trick. More and more people're losing their jobs. That means our community goes down faster. They getting ready to ship our youth to Africa to fight our brothers over there or to Latin America to become worm meat on the battlefields there. They closing our neighborhood hospitals, and don't expect our schools to get any better. The occupation forces called the police department seem bent on protecting the special economic interests here rather than the good people of our community. Here, the junkies, pushers, and thugs reign supreme. And nobody's lifting a finger to do anything about them.

"Check it out. You notice how the transit fare keeps creeping up, up, up? Pretty soon our elderly'll have to jump the turnstiles to visit their grandchildren. The rope is closing tight around us, folks. Watch they don't turn our community into a 1980s slow-motion Warsaw ghetto."

Occasionally, people said from the audience and the security guards, "I hear that!" and "Tell it, brother!" which punctuated the speech. It had the feel and rhythm of a Baptist service.

"Grandma, what big teeth you have," he went on. "What's the deal here? How would you like to have your subway stations closed so that the express goes right through? Bus stops reduced in number and serving as checkpoints? You'd have to take a cab to get to transportation. And then they set up sentry posts in the park, around Columbia U., let City College go—half the niggers'n spics there hanging out on Convent Avenue anyhow or on the campus lawn smoking herb—the 157th Street Viaduct, right across 165th Street, river to river, yeah? You think I'm kidding? You paying at least seven-fifty a week just to go to work. That's almost two days' groceries for a family of *one*. If you're a Muslim, maybe two-and-a-half. It's happening all around you, and you think things're bad now. The man said, 'You don't learn your history, you sure as hell gonna repeat it.' Read what they did with the Warsaw ghetto and tell me that can't happen here. Only here they won't need no wall. Your Star of David is your big lips, wide nostrils, kinky hair, and *black skin*!"

A large part of the audience broke into applause as the speaker stopped, pranced about on the stage, taking five from two of his guards, and postured like a dusky Mussolini.

Dionne pulled away from Earl and leaned forward on her other elbow, peering skeptically at the grinning center of the hoopla. Suddenly, he thrust his hands above him, and the audience quieted down.

"Now, I don't have to point out to you that the government is no longer in the business of aiding us. Ain't coming up off the bucks no more. The private sector—same thing. Y'all're on your own now. Which means it's even more important that we pull together, pool our resources. That we take charge of our own destiny. Most people don't think we can. But we got to 'cause if we don't, I don't give two cents for our future. We got to come together with trust for each other. Exorcise this political elbowing bullshit that's plagued us from the giddyup. We got to organize, and we got to raise necessary funds. We got to do all this … like yesterday. The man already got our throats in his crosshairs."

The applause was moderate, though not lacking in some enthusiasm. Dionne did not applaud. She merely humphed and stared at Shehab. Earl, applauding, looked at her curiously.

"You heard of *Godfather II* and *Rocky II*," Shehab went on. "Well, the Black Resurrection proposes to head up The Civil Rights Movement, the Black Revolution II. In striving for our goals, we will have two programs that we will need help on. One, we will engage in fund-raising in the community, which means, ladies and gentlemen, carrying the canisters around. We got to have those funds to develop an economic base for the organization and use some of the monies to develop security patrols for as many of our minicommunities as possible, hopefully raising overall property values. We also want to pull the community closer to us through their contributory involvement.

"The second program is to get back heavy on our voter registration so that your voices can be heard. Without that political visibility, brothers and sisters, Chuck ain't gonna do diddly for ya.

"Once these programs're established, we'll go on to other things like youth programs and political activism. But right now, we've got to get these basics down first. Give yourselves to us so that we can give ourselves to the big *us*! I'll now take questions."

Applause started again, but he quickly signalled it down. He waited, looking around until a hand went up in the rear of the hall, off to the right of Dionne and two rows behind. Earl noticed a slight tension on Shehab's face.

"Yes, Brother Ignatius," he said, readying himself for an ordeal.

The questioner was a portly man, brown-skinned, with tiny, almost slitlike eyes and a Mexican bandit mustache that almost offset his prominent widow's peak. He stood up, as if it were a great production he was trying to downplay. Earl noticed a slight anticipatory stirring in the audience.

"Brother Shehab," the questioner said, glancing surreptitiously around to make sure everybody was paying attention. "You made the statement before about a creeping stranglehold forming around the good community of Harlem. And you compare it to the Warsaw ghetto, which is interesting indeed. But could you explain this to me? In certain areas of the outer edges of Harlem, there seem to be appearing increasing numbers of white couples moving in to brownstones, renovated co-ops, and the like. Now if what you say is true, does this make them suicidal or well— How do you explain that?"

There was a faint chuckle in the outer reaches of the hall. The guards looked menacingly around.

Shehab tried to conceal the glare he was shooting at the questioner.

Dionne made no effort to suppress her snicker.

"Brother Ignatius," said Shehab, a false sleepiness coming to his eyelids.

"Call me Iggy."

"Brother Ignatius, I am not going to refer to you as Iggy, all right, and we been through this already, 'cause, one, I don't particularly like the sound of the nickname or whatever you wanna call it. Sounds like some faggot steppin' barefoot in shit." Shehab smiled.

"Why you gotta be hostile?" the questioner said then.

"And, two, I don't want these good folks here to think there's any kind of connection between us other than mutual confusion. I'm confused about your insistence in coming to these meetings. You're … just confused."

"All this's uncalled for. Why don't you just answer my question?"

"I'm not gonna answer your question, all right? And I'll tell you why. 'Cause you don't ask questions to be informed. You ask questions to disrupt. Disruption's your thing, Brother Ignatius. That's how you get off."

Ignatius turned to the rest of the audience. "Ladies and gentlemen, I tried to pinpoint the man on his program, but he won't accommodate."

"You're trying to pinpoint me? Who're you to pinpoint me?"

"Then answer the man's question!" Dionne shouted out.

Earl placed his hand on her forearm and squeezed it. She patted his hand gently.

Shehab looked at her, saying, "I'll gladly answer the question, sister. But not with him present. With him here, what should be a forum becomes a circus."

Earl saw Shehab make a slight movement with his head so subtle as to seem not to have made at all. Two guards from opposite sides of the hall began slowly moving toward Ignatius. An acrid fear gripped Earl, and he moved to the edge of his seat.

"Aw, what is this?" said Dionne.

"Shush, willya?" said Earl.

"I would like the brother to leave," said Shehab.

A few people near Ignatius changed their seats or just stood up on the side. Ignatius didn't budge from his seat. The guards closed in on him like two cautious lions focused on an unwary wildebeest. Only this wildebeest was wary and undaunted.

He snorted. "Can I ask for a point of order?"

"Would you please leave?"

"Can I ask for a point of order?" Ignatius insisted.

One guard was now next to Ignatius's row. He jerked his head toward his besieger.

"What's he gonna do?" said the questioner whose eyes never left Shehab. "Pick's nose and gross me out to death?"

Shehab turned to the audience. "Do you see what he does, brothers and sisters?"

Dionne stood up, Earl trying to pull her back down and she slapping his hand away. "Then why don't you answer the gentleman's question? It would save all of us a whole lot of wasted time and trouble. And we really don't need this." There was mild applause.

"Sister, don't take his side," pleaded Shehab. "Please. Don't help'm."

"I'm not taking his side. Try clarity. I'm sure I'm not the only one either.

I mean, you urged us to come to this meeting, didn't you? Accommodate us!"

The closest guard to Ignatius had begun moving the few remaining people who separated him from the aisle into the row over. Another lady got up and moved away from the stalking guard and his intended target, joining those standing on the side. A few people left.

One lady said over her shoulder, "I got food shopping to do. I really don't need to come by here and listen to this same ol' bullshit!"

Earl, too, looked toward the exit, planning his route of departure. He wanted no part of this, and if need be, he would lift Dionne off her feet and carry her out.

"You'd better tell your boy something," said Ignatius, a hollow balefulness coming to his voice.

"For Christ's sake, Shehab," said Dionne.

Shehab stared at Dionne and gestured with his hand. The guard stopped in his motion, and the other guard on the other end of the row relaxed slightly. The speaker looked down and jammed his hands into his pockets.

"Okay," he said. "For the Black Resurrection, I am willing to bend over backward to get the word across to you, even if it turns me off, because certain people are present."

"Make that sacrifice," she said and sat down.

The people, still there, who'd gone out to the aisle also sat down, and the general tension in the hall seemed to lessen.

"Suicidal, huh?" Shehab began. "What makes you think their presence in Harlem's gonna make any difference? I mean, do I have to tell you they could easily be evacuated on the sneak? But more likely, they would buy it with you. The man don't care about you. But he don't care about his own all that much more. What did Adam Clayton Powell say? 'If Chuck had the choice between losing Miss Ann to you and losing his bread,' Miss Ann would have to go. What happened to those white communists in North Carolina? One lady got a bullet between her eyes. And not a thing happened to the KKK gunmen. Look at Goodman and Schwerner. Violet Liuzzo, Bob and John Kennedy, John Lennon, the Pope, for God's sake, Abraham Lincoln, Jesus Christ! Hey! So what makes you think a few white families moving into East 120-whatever's gonna make a difference if Chuck decides to move on your asses? The one thing we can't afford in these times, brothers and sisters, is naivete. No, it won't make one goddamned bit of difference, take it from me. So get involved. Put money in our coffers. Give us your time and energy. It's later than you think."

The sneer on Ignatius's face did not abate, but at least, now he was quiet. The guards continued to glare at him.

Earl now put his arm around the back of Dionne's chair.

"And with all that's been going on and with all that we have to do," Shehab went on, "we get into things like what went on just now. That's what bugs the shit outa me."

As Dionne and Earl were walking out the door, a particularly muscular guard stopped Earl with a firm grip on his forearm. "You gonna help us out, ain't you, bro?" he asked, a gravity in his manner. "We need you."

"Sure, I'll be around," lied Earl, smiling as he pulled away and continued his way out.

Dionne stopped in front of the guard. "I think you oughta know that he's a schoolteacher in our city school system. And you know how busy they are. I'd say he's already making his contribution to our community."

"That's all right, Dionne," said Earl, pulling her along downstairs.

In the car, he focused on his driving, because he knew there was great unexpressed anger at him. The issue was in his face. Why was he pulling her down? Why didn't he support her and Ignatius? He knew she didn't like unexpressed anger to fill the air either, and he knew he was safe because of the previous night. She would be watching her P's and Q's with him now.

"'Brothers and sisters, put money in our coffers!'" she raged. "Crissakes, how these assholes keep coming outa the woodwork. Every time you turn around, there they are with their goddamned schemes, their great plans for the salvation of the race, and their stupid paranoia. Sure, things're bad, and who better knows it than us? But 'Let me be your leader, and I will guide you to the promised goddamned land! I have all the answers and don't dare question me, or I will descend from the great mountaintop and put a curse on you! I'll make you stay black for the rest of your life!'"

Earl parked his car across the street from Dionne's building. It was easier to find a spot here than in most neighborhoods because of the sparseness of its population. And because of this, the crime problem here was not as acute. Still, because it was always acute enough, he turned on his alarm and fixed his various special locks for the radio, the glove compartment, and the ignition.

She slid her arm through his as they strolled toward her apartment. "Y'know, I miss 'em," she said, a sad thoughtfulness now coming to her voice.

"Who?"

She paused before she said, "Martin, Malcolm, Stokely, Mac, H. Rap—all those giants, voices, lights in the darkness. What do we have now? These pipsqueaks with their hysterical peeping in a hurricane. How they make me feel the absence of the others. How they sadden me."

Later, as they were undressing for bed, she said, "Why don't you consider becoming a leader?"

Annoyance crawled through him as he lay in bed naked, staring up at the ceiling. He said nothing, because he sensed a melancholic mood coming over him. This masked anger beneath it, which meant, at best, sarcasm or teasing from him or, at worst, another argument.

The day had worked out fairly well for him; he didn't want anything to spoil it now, so he focused on his horniness. When she came to him, he took her with a poignant but controlled hunger. He pulled out of himself and watched their coupling from a distance: his hands' movements around her body, the featherlike brushing against her erect nipples, she inhaling slightly, the grasping of her supple buttocks, the caress of her hips.

There was a momentary stiffening in her before she wrapped her legs around him when he pressed more seriously. At the same time, he rejoined himself. She grunted, sighed, and moaned as he poignantly strove for her very center. He increased in force as he felt her being drawn up to him like a water drop drawn by another. Then the control slipped away as the desire spread and deepened in him, and she became more animated. Her arms tightened their grip around him, and she thrust herself upward as he burst within her, she gasping as if stabbed with a sharp object.

Early morning yanked him from a deep sleep. He disentangled himself from Dionne and stealthily raced through his morning rituals. When he was three-quarters through them, Dionne awoke, jumped out of bed, and rushed to him, pressing her warm body to him and holding him tightly.

"Hey, last night," she said. "What was *that* all about?"

He knew that something in him enabled him to get to the deepest core of her being and this disturbed him. He was in no psychological position to explore any unchartered territories at this point in his life. His answer to her question was to escape to work.

Chapter 9

The lady was slightly portly, pleasant looking, dirty blonde, wearing a light, tan alpaca coat and the loveliest gold necklace. She exuded Bloomingdale's and Henri Bendel. Daydreaming, staring off across the street, she was possibly tuning herself out for the coming day's office interactions.

Two other women and one man were also at the bus stop. One woman was engrossed in a copy of *Redbook* magazine; the other, *The New York Times* crossword puzzle. The man, furiously chewing gum, a lit cigarette between two fingers sending languid ringlets of smoke into the morning air, studied *Sports Illustrated* magazine.

The gold-necklaced woman stood apart from the others, as if she were trying to be of another world from theirs. This braced Kaseem's attention to her while Fox ambled with bogus nonchalance to her other side.

The man glanced cursorily at Kaseem, who tensed his body like a leopard about to spring. The youth looked far to his left again and saw, about ten blocks away, an approaching bus buried in an army of traffic. Now!

He nodded to Fox, who, concealing his face, began coughing violently, attracting the gold-necklaced woman's attention. Kaseem sprang at her, grabbed the necklace with his right hand, and, with his left, pushed her away from him toward the street, she falling backward.

The two youths didn't see the car, its horn complaining forlornly, swerve around the screaming woman, scrambling to her feet. They were too busy sprinting toward a small opening in a clump of bushes thirty yards away, whose path would cut right to an alleyway between two houses on the other side.

70

Nor, until Kaseem turned at the path's mouth and glimpsed him, had they seen the man behind them in full chase, the cigarette no longer between his fingers, his magazine in one hand rolled up like a makeshift baton in a make-believe relay race.

"Oh, shit," he said breathlessly. "Sucker's on our case. Bookin' time."

They squeezed extra speed from their legs as they disappeared into the thicket, a short half-block run to its other side. They lunged across a dirt path to the alleyway, where they quickly picked up their books from behind a knotted wood fence divider. They jogged to the other end of the alley to a street where there was another bus stop. Kaseem glanced back through the alley to make sure they weren't being pursued. *Humph, man had better sense than to go into that thicket after two crazy niggers.*

Shortly, a bus arrived, and the two youths, feeling more secure, boarded it, flashing their stolen bus passes. They sat down near the back. Kaseem shoved the necklace down into his socks as Fox studied the passengers in front of him.

As the bus pulled away, Kaseem looked back again toward the alley.

And tensed.

Their pursuer, accompanied by a policeman, jumped out of the alley's mouth, and the two men quickly began looking around. A patrol car cruised up to in front of the patrolman, who leaned down to the passenger window and conversed with the two men inside.

Now, though the bus was a good distance away, Kaseem, ducking back into the nonwindowed corner and cautiously tapping Fox's knee, became aware that his heart was pounding.

An invisible hand seized him by his throat as he observed the patrol car moving away from the alley and toward the bus. Kaseem quickly checked the rear windows and the door for a possible escape route. They were trapped.

The car, however, caught up to and passed the bus to a distant corner where it made a right turn to somewhere out of Kaseem's life.

After a short while, he chuckled inside, noting with some curiosity that part of him was almost ready to embrace what would have happened to him had the police stopped the bus and boarded.

Spriggs was standing at the school entrance so that the two youths decided to split up and bury themselves in the entering crowd. This didn't prevent the policeman from eyeing Kaseem closely as the youth passed him. A commotion in the rear of the line diverted his attention from the outlaw, who slipped past him with a quickening movement. Kaseem looked toward the rear of the line and noted that Fox was in the center of that commotion.

Kaseem rushed to his new classroom, greeted his teacher now deep in thought at his desk, and immediately began looking about the room for something to do. He straightened out the desks, swept paper out of them into the wastepaper basket and washed the board. (Most of this work had been done by the custodial helper the evening before.)

"Sit down, why don'tcha?" said Earl. "Save some of that energy for your schoolwork."

"That's okay," Kaseem answered. "I got energy to spare."

Soon, the students were forming into their various cliques around the classroom prior to the morning exercises. Kaseem had not yet meshed with the class, so his movements were unrestricted and minimally noticed except occasionally by Vinny.

He ambled over to the window and looked down on the street. Spriggs was standing on the center now directing traffic.

He studied the policeman, though the mere sight of him always tightened his stomach. Still, it was better to keep his eye on this man he considered his mortal enemy, because keeping him in sight was in itself a kind of security.

The security was short-lived.

His back to Kaseem, Spriggs suddenly turned and looked up toward Kaseem's floor.

The youth backed away from the window. He glanced nervously around the classroom. His classmates were too involved in their separate worlds to notice his discomfort. Mr. Chaney was standing in the hall, supervising the arriving pupils.

He peeped back out the window and saw that Spriggs was no longer in the street. Panicked, he turned to make a move; but "The Pledge of Allegiance" came over the loudspeaker, and everybody had to freeze, stand, and salute the flag, which hung over the chalkboard near the window.

His right hand on his chest, he looked around quickly at his hiding spot on the rear bulletin board and then at the rest of the class focused in various degrees of intensity on the flag. Mr. Chaney was standing at the doorway so that he could keep part of his eye on the hallway.

Moving subtly, Kaseem did a half-knee bend to retrieve the gold necklace from under his sock. He then inched as quickly as he could to the bulletin board. That Spriggs might be approaching the classroom made him increasingly uneasy. He had to rid himself of the necklace now while everyone was facing front. Plus, their sitting after would isolate and reveal him.

He backed into the bulletin board, and as he faced the front of the classroom—they were now singing the national anthem—he pulled the staples out behind him. Then, quickly, he turned, placed the necklace under the loosened spot, and replaced the staples. He glanced around the class again to make sure he was still unnoticed. Because he felt a little less uneasy now, he turned back around and pressed the staples as hard as he could to make sure everything was secure there. Then he moved away from the bulletin board to his seat.

As soon as he could, he would replace those staples.

The morning exercises ended, and Mr. Hanley began his announcements.

Spriggs thrust half his torso into the room, Kaseem's heart jumping, and crooked his finger at the youngster.

"Oooooooooooooh!" went his classmates as he got up and moved his pounding heart toward the officer.

Bemused, Earl joined them in the hall.

"No big thing," said Spriggs. "Just wanna ask the young brother here if he knows anything about a gang forming in the neighborhood."

The teacher regarded them for a few moments before he nodded and returned to the classroom.

Spriggs took Kaseem to the teacher's room, now empty.

"Okay, my man, whaddya say?" the officer said to the youth, who feigned puzzlement before a baleful finger pointing to the wall urged him to do what he was told. Annoyed, Kaseem spread his hands on the wall and took a wide stance while Spriggs proceeded to pat him all over his body—his torso, sleeves, trousers area, and socks.

Then, satisfied, he stood up. "Okay."

As he straightened up, Kaseem looked at Spriggs curiously. "I guess somebody else got robbed," he said.

"Know anything about a gold chain snatching east of here?"

"Which way's east?"

"Cut the bu'shit, turkey. This woman had her gold chain snatched by two young dudes over near Mickle Avenue. One of them pushed her out in the street that almost got her killed by a passing car and almost caused a traffic accident." Spriggs studied Kaseem for reaction. "Fact, you fit the description of him."

"All us bloods fit the description of somebody."

"You trying to say the people was white who gave the description?"

"You putting words in my mouth," Kaseem said. "I didn't say nothing except all us bloods fit the description of somebody. And I'm sayin' it 'cause it's true."

"And you got the inside line on what truth is," pressed the officer.

"Y'know, this's police harassment. I could have you up on charges."

"Here's my badge number."

"Can I go back to my class now?"

"When I'm ready to let you go," the officer said. "Don't run this outraged, blinking your wide eyes innocence shit on me, see, 'cause this's Spriggs here. I been where you are. And I'm still there. I had you tuned in from the giddyup. All right, you kids got your little capers. I can dig that. But you, Kaseem, got something else in the middle of you. Something mean … even vicious. And when something's going down, I'm gonna look your way. You'n that other schlurb you hang with. Now go to your class."

Kaseem turned to go and then turned back to the officer. "I don't think it's fair you should keep singling me out."

"Ain't fair that that woman'll have to spend a wage-earning week in the hospital. Hey, life's not fair. But you keep your nose clean, ain't a thing I can do to you. Look, if it's any comfort to you, not that I ever wanna make you comfortable, you ain't being singled out. You happen to be an outstanding member of a very big club. Damn, speaking of noses, don't you bathe, brother?"

Kaseem stiffened. "I was running around outside. Then I had to come right in."

Spriggs smiled and nodded at him. "Playing basketball?"

"No, just general running around."

"Gettin' that good exercise, huh? Well, you need to give a party and introduce your body to a stick of deodorant."

Chapter 10

An uneasy frown masked Earl's face as he filled out the daily section sheet on which the class, at the end of a lesson, would receive its behavioral ratings—excellent, good, fair, poor and, occasionally, "a nightmare"--from their subject teachers. Departmental (in which classes travelled from classroom to classroom for their various subjects) necessitated this because this way a homeroom teacher could monitor and control how well his official class conducted itself while elsewhere in the building. Control was important for Earl.

This is why the furtive conference in the hall with Kaseem and Spriggs had so disturbed him. It took everything out of his hands, undercut him, emasculated him, heightened the satrap feeling he always had about himself, reaffirmed his essential ineffectualness in everything in his life, and he loathed the feeling he got from these qualifications of his manhood. There certainly was, after all, enough in his life not in his control, and here, in the case of his guardianship of Kaseem, he would need more than ever to have control.

Furthermore, he was displeased with himself for running away from them so fast and returning to the classroom. He'd told himself that he was needed always with his students to keep the authority, that the special psychological needs of the eighth grader dictated this. In fact, he'd accepted what was, to him, a not quite transparent dismissal of him by Spriggs and escaped.

As Kaseem reentered the classroom, the teacher studied him. There didn't seem to be any undo concern on the youth's face, but he was slightly measured in his movements as he took his seat.

As he glanced almost subliminally at Spriggs walking by the room and waving to him, he handed the section sheet to the class president, Maria Rose Baez, a tiny, wide-eyed brunette, just as the bell rang for the first period class.

He went out into the hall to see his class off and supervise the interclass passage of the pupils. Another day had begun. He'd promised himself he'd do even better in his work. The positive "good mornings" from the passing students told him he already was doing all right, but in his heart of hearts, they weren't enough.

"Excuse me," said Kaseem, snapping him from his thoughts. He realized the youth had been standing next to him for some time and became aware of his body odor, pungent, now subtle. "You looked a little worried. I just wanted to tell you that that little talk between Officer Spriggs and me wasn't nuthin', no big thing. He wanted to know about some new gang forming around here. I told'm I didn't know anything about it, which I didn't—square business. So thanks for being concerned about me."

As he told himself the boy was being candid with him, Earl watched him proceed down the hall to his class.

Mrs. Stanton was an attractive woman, brunette, with large eyes and pinkish cheeks. When she looked at one, she always gave the impression she was seeing though a lie being told to her. Her occasional smile was dimpled, seeming to sparkle, but the half scowl dominated her face.

"What?" she bellowed at her husband one morning, "You bought a what?"

"Take it easy, sweetie," he said to her. He was a handsome man, thin with longish black hair. "Let's just back up, get off the hyper."

"Don't tell me to back up," she returned. "I'm not some drunkard you have to calm down on the street!"

"I'm not going to say anything further until your voice comes down a few thousand decibels."

He leaned back in the chair and folded his arms, glancing occasionally out their terrace door. *Defensive position*, she thought, and this enraged her more. She checked herself though. She had to be careful with his delicate male sensibility. He was, after all, an artist, a composer whose work seldom saw the light of day. When he hit, it was fairly lucrative for him, but it was necessary for him at other times to take short-term teaching jobs and tutoring assignments to tide him over between the "hits." This kept them in a fairly safe, "nice" Fort Lee neighborhood but one she had to live with as well as in. Mrs. Joyce Stanton was not one to accept "living with" anything.

She strained to control her voice. "My voice is down. Well?"

He leaned forward and placed his hand on hers, which she removed.

"Look, sweetie. I'm a composer of serious music. It's an art I must continue learning every waking hour of my life. I must learn its poetry."

"Please don't lecture me on what I already know," she said.

"Its lyricism, its harmony, its disharmony. I must sensitize myself to its diverse complex subtleties."

She spoke over him. "What does that have to do with the price of carrots? Hey, am I in this conversation here?"

"A two-speed monaural's fine for Joe Schmoe who just wants noise or to listen to pop or punk rock, but I need a little more. I need … engulfment. And I don't think three hundred dollars—on sale, mind you—is too much to pay for an excellent Magnavox."

Now it was her turn to fold arms, this time to defend herself against her surging fury. "Last month, it was the top-brass card holder for five ridiculous dollars. All right, I lived with it."

"You want to get over, you have to make that impression," he pleaded.

"What about the house?"

"We'll get the house."

"When?" she asked. "How? With two attendants wheeling me up the front walk?"

"Your voice is going up again."

She stood up. "You don't see what you're doing, do you? You never do. You and your dreams—all right, I'll do what I can to support you, to help out. But for goodness sakes alive, don't sentence me to life imprisonment with those animals I have to deal with six hours a day. Or at least allow me to have something to show for it. What about *my* dreams? The house! Kids. A garden. Something that'll tell people we're class, we're somebody! Civilized, boring neighbors. Space! So that my blouses don't smell of shaving cream mixed with scent! I mean, I'm trying to work for this, but you keep pushing it back farther and farther with your outrageous stupidity with the money I'm working my buns off for! It's not fair! There's just got to be a time when this garbage comes to an end!"

And now they had transferred Kaseem into one of her classes. Social studies was hard enough to teach eighth graders. Now she would have to deal with the Demon Pazuzu himself. Why didn't they ever ask teachers who had to teach these kids how they felt about the transfers?

That first day, she had stared at the young man as he took the seat she had assigned him. This pattern continued until one day she decided to confront him.

"Mr. Wilson," she said. "Is there a problem?"

"No, ma'am. Why?"

"You seem to be having difficulty getting to your seat."

"I didn't take anymore time than anybody else. Why you singling me out?" He sat down as he commented.

"Singling you out? Am I doing that? My apologies."

"No big thing," he said.

"Of course, I realize that social studies is not the most *relevant* subject to you people, long on *dry* and short on interest. And I have to overcome that, you see, through your prejudices, disinterest, and resistance. Plus, take the attendance, check your homework—those of you who bother to do it—monitor your various marks, and make sure no one is marking up a desk and do it inside of forty-five minutes. So if I'm a little testy, please forgive me."

"Could we start the lesson now?" Kaseem said.

"Mr. Wilson wants me to start the lesson. Well, will wonders never cease?"

Kaseem became silent now as his classmates allowed faint snickers to fill the air.

"With that kind of eager dedication to knowledge and understanding before me, I suppose I'm duty-bound to proceed with the lesson."

The end of the period came with a doleful bell, and the class filed out like water pouring through an open drain. It had been a mediocre, dull lesson, and she knew it. Dry pieces of information with no rhyme, reason, order, or relevance to their lives were hurled desultorily at them like thrown, stale popcorn and the pupils responded with continuous low-key chatter.

Her sense of fairness made her mark down a "good" on their section sheet. It wasn't, after all, their fault. Even Kaseem had sat in his seat, staring expressionlessly at her without doing or saying anything to disrupt the classroom proceedings. That, in itself, was enough to warrant the "good."

She didn't go out into the hall to supervise the student interclass passage, because she simply didn't feel up to it, reproaching herself for her bad lesson added to all those unpleasant urchins surrounding her in their disorderly corridor movement.

So she lingered at her desk, staring down at her lesson plan.

Suddenly, she looked up.

Kaseem was standing by her desk, looking at her.

"Yes, what is it?" she said, her unfriendly mask on.

"Sorry to bother you," he said to her in his lowest, most subdued tones. "I'll only take a moment of your time. Can I say something?"

"What?" She readied herself for an attack.

"Well, I feel there's a problem between us that's getting in the way of your teaching."

"What do you mean?" she asked, now curious.

"No, really, Mrs. Stanton, I don't mean no harm."

She studied him for a few moments. "Go ahead," she said, swallowing, bracing herself.

"I got a bad rep in this school, and I'm sorry about that" he started. "And now I'm in your class, and you're uptight. I know that. Well, I just wanna say that I'm in your class to learn, that's all. I'm not gonna break on you or cause any kind of disturbance to your lessons. You're a good teacher, and the only thing you have to worry about with me is whether I understand what you're teaching. You teach which is your job, and I'll learn, which is mine. That's all I wanted to say."

Dumbfounded, she gaped at him.

"Thank you for listening," he said and started to go. Then he stopped and returned to her. "Sorry again," he said. "Could you give me a late pass? I'm trying to avoid any charges."

"How many charges have you gotten since you've been in Mr. Chaney's class?"

"None."

"None?"

"I'll write the pass, Mrs. Stanton. All you have to do is sign it."

She went into her desk drawer and produced a blank piece of paper that she proceeded to write on, saying, "Now you know that if they see your late pass with your handwriting on it, it'll be suspect."

She handed him the pass, and he gratefully started out. Then he stopped at the doorway again and turned to her. "I'll even be your monitor for you if you'd like," he continued. "I know you have your own monitors, and I do a lotta work for Mr. Chaney; but I'll be more than glad to help you out anytime you want."

"Well, that's very nice, Kaseem," she said. "I'll certainly take you up on that very soon."

Later that week, she went to Earl's classroom when he was alone during an unassigned period. She immediately began searching the top of his clothing closet, his pupil desks, behind the door, and inside the rear cabinets.

"What's going on?" he asked.

"All right, I give up," she said, turning to him. "Where is it?"

"What?"

"The magic wand. Where'd you go for it? The Middle East? Far East? Darkest Africa? Oh, is it all right if I say that?"

Earl chuckled. Now he'd caught up to her.

She approached his desk, gesticulating. "What did you do to that kid? You turn the worst monster in the history of humankind into the best kid in the school in just a week's time. I'm sure somewhere around here I should drop to my knees and shout hosannas!"

"Come on, Joyce," he said. "Cut it out."

"All week, he sat there, watching me. I figured he's waiting for his opening to spring. I'm in for it."

Ingram appeared at Earl's doorway, gave her back a "has she gone nuts?" look and then disappeared.

"Please excuse my effusiveness but thank you," she continued. "My hat is off to you. You have got to be the teacher of the century."

"Of the hour maybe," he quipped.

"You're too modest," she said, laughing, as she walked to the door. She turned to him again, a faint seductiveness having come to her manner. "Hey, do you think you could come home with me some evening and tap my husband on his head with your magic wand?"

She left, feeling part of Earl's triumph. Maybe she would make love to her husband that night

.

The man chewed his gum furiously as he studied the children exiting from the school. A plump man, he was sitting in the backseat of a patrol car parked across the street. Spriggs, in the front seat, watched him and then watched the students. The driver took photos of certain students.

"I wanna thank you for doing this for us," Spriggs said to the man. "I know it's an inconvenience."

The man shrugged. "Ah, things're dead at the shop right now."

Fox emerged from the building, his class engaged in an unruly dismissal. The man's eyes fixed on the young man, and Sprigs' eyes fixed on his face, searching for any signs of recognition. Something inside the officer had tensed.

Another boy pushed Fox, and the two engaged in fake rough play. They were quickly joined by others. The teacher tried to get order but, fanning his hand at them, went back into the building.

The gum-chewing man frowned and then smiled at Spriggs. "Tell you. I was so busy ducking branches smacking me in my face, and those two kids were burning rubber. I don't wanna take a chance and get some innocent kid in trouble, ya know?"

"You saw somebody?" asked Spriggs anxiously.

"No, sorry, I can't be sure." He looked down, somewhat uncomfortable now.

They waited around for a few more minutes. Spriggs saw Kaseem's class come out in their orderly dismissal, but there was no Kaseem. Then the patrol car drove away.

As he came downstairs, Kaseem had spotted the car through the stairwell window and seen the silhouetted figure sitting in the backseat. Because he didn't want to take any chances, he decided to go back upstairs with Mr. Chaney and clean out all the desks. He would have to race home after taking the long route.

Mr. Chaney would call his grandmother.

CHAPTER 11

Earl called Dionne. Eagerness filled him.

"Well," said Dionne on the phone. "Don't we sound bubbly."

"Just want to see you, that's all," Earl said.

"To what do I owe this? Hunger? Or yearning for my dynamic company?"

"You mean they're not both the same thing?"

"You can come up with a better answer than that," she said.

"To be clumsy is to be sincere."

They laughed.

"C'mon, give. Tell mother," she persisted.

He didn't care for her occasional ventures into making him feel like a little boy, but he was feeling too good about himself not to push any displeasure aside.

"Well, it comes from those rare times when you're positive about things. When you do feel like going in to work, dealing with all the problems, struggling to some accomplished end. That it's not all empty waste and mere finger exercises. And that energizes you. Sends those lightning bolts right up the spine."

"You're talking about the boy, Kaseem."

"The school has turned upside down," he admitted. "They're staggered at this boy's turnaround. A teacher came to me today almost crying from admiration."

"Okay. Come down. Don't get too full of yourself."

"Hey, I know I'm not Professor Higgins. And I know the job's far from

82

complete. But can you imagine? I've finally risen above the ho-hums of the world."

"Do you have a need to be above the ho-hums?" she asked.

"I need to be something more than what I've been."

"Hush. Please. I don't like to hear that. To me, you're a beautiful man with a lot going for'm. You're a pain in the ass sometimes, but I thank the good gods above every day that you're in my life."

"Sorry. Didn't mean to pop my own balloon."

"Look, baby. I'm going to be a little tied up this evening." She sounded slightly annoyed and concerned.

"Oh?" he said. "What's up?"

"Black Resurrection business."

"Oh, well, why don't I—"

"I'd rather you didn't," she exhaled. "Not this meeting. Might be a little drawn out. Can I come to your place … if you're not otherwise engaged yourself?"

"No, I'll hang out in a diner and come by see you later tonight."

She seemed to hesitate. "Oh. Okay."

The phone conversation left him somewhat uneasy. His first impulse was to take in a movie and forget the whole thing, but he had to stop running from things. Yet, he didn't want her to think he was following her or checking up on her. He didn't want to crowd her. He would try to find some middle road here.

He drove to the Black Resurrection meeting place and saw a sign in the front that said the following: Meeting tonight—7:30 PM. Because he knew she wouldn't arrive for another twenty or so minutes, he started to go but then changed his mind and decided to wait near the subway exit she usually came out of. He took a position about forty yards from the exit and settled himself down in his double-parked car for a wait.

She emerged from the exit, and he rose from his car. He began to walk toward her to catch up with her but then stopped. Another man, somewhat familiar to Earl, came up to her, and both went into a nearby restaurant.

As he felt annoyance and a stomach-turning rage in this darkening evening, he started toward the restaurant, Tommy Lee's Victuals. The good feeling of earlier that day had begun to fade.

He went up to the front window and looked in.

He stiffened.

The man with Dionne was Ignatius, the argumentative questioner of the first Black Resurrection meeting Earl had attended. His recognition of the man, however, was not what made his stomach catch.

The man's lips were swollen, and there were the remains of contusions on both sides of his face. One eye was puffed up a little, and one hand was bandaged. Plus, he seemed to move with difficulty.

She was listening intently to something he was telling her. On her face was outrage mixed with shock and pity.

Neither touched what appeared to be two cheeseburgers and coffees.

Before long, she stood up, glancing at her watch. It was now seven-twenty. Obviously, he was going to pay the check.

She threw a dollar on the table, probably for the tip, and started out of the restaurant. He walked her to the door.

Earl ducked back into the darkness of an adjacent alley.

"Watch'm," he heard Ignatius say. "He's treacherous. He smiles up in your face, all calm and sadiddy, and does this to you. He claims he's all for order, but the man belongs in a cave deep back in the jungle somewhere. That ain't no brother. That's a sneaky scumbag. He don't even have the heart to do this himself. He uses his goon boys. Then comes on all horrified. So I can't prove a goddamn thing."

"Why don't you come to the meeting and confront'm with this?" she said.

"No way. I had enough confronting to last me a lifetime. You just watch yourself, you hear? I heard your mouth too that night. The man is crazy."

"I have to run," she said, glancing at her watch.

"Okay. Remember, he don't know how to deal with anybody contradicting'm."

Dionne rushed away, and Ignatius returned to his table. He was devouring, with some difficulty, his cheeseburger when Earl reached the window again. Ignatius took two bites out of Dionne's cheeseburger as well, paid the bill, and walked out of the restaurant, going in the other direction.

Earl decided to catch up to him to find out exactly what had happened, but the man was moving much too swiftly through the streets despite his injuries. It took some effort on the teacher's part merely to maintain the distance between the two. But slowly, Earl began to close that distance.

Finally, he had to call him. "Ignatius! Iggy!"

The other, without turning around, ducked into a large crowd going around a distant corner. By the time Earl got there, he was nowhere to be seen.

Kaseem's model behavior bubbled over into his home as well. He spoke only when spoken to, worked industriously on his homework, and did all his chores without argument or grumbling. He'd done an especially good job on the stairway rug and washed all the dishes as well.

The deep-seated resentments, rages, and hatreds, still there in him, were well concealed. His periodic "expeditions" with Fox afforded him his few opportunities, if intense, to spew his inner venom in outward physical form. He was thus able to wear his "good" mask on other occasions.

Julia was spending one of her rare afternoons and evenings off, cleaning the Venetian blinds and dusting the furniture. The couple downstairs had paid their rent on time, so there was no real pressure anywhere. Beethoven's "Moonlight Sonata" was playing on her stereo. It would be followed by a few of Chopin's etudes and collections of Billie Holiday, Dinah Washington, and Sarah Vaughn's works. She liked working to this music. In fact, it often inspired her to put a little extra elbow grease into her efforts.

After he had passed their morning's booty to Fox to sell, Kaseem had arrived home feeling somewhat "up." Mrs. MacNeil kissed him and studied her beloved grandson before she returned to the kitchen.

He looked at his mother on her knees, working on the mahogany coffee tabletop and frowned, concealing well the inexplicably deep rage and fear he felt toward this woman, who had brought him into this life. "Aw, Mom," he said, grabbing the rag from her hand and kissing her head. "Lemme do that."

Momentarily, his love for his mother grabbed him. It was nice feeling. Perhaps, someday it would be all right between them and he would make her glad she gave birth to him. Perhaps he would find his father and his father would tell him to love his mother which he would gladly do.

He lifted her up and began to spin her around in a pseudo-waltz while, at the same time, he negotiated a few swipes here and there on the various items of furniture.

"You cut this out, you crazy nut," protested his mother, laughing. "Besides, that's not gonna get it."

As she dried her hands, Mrs. MacNeil came back out of the kitchen and watched them. She shook her head in bogus disapproval.

Kaseem's mother snatched the rag back out of his hand, tweaked his nose, lovingly ruffled his close cut 'fro, and resumed her work. "What kind of homework we have tonight?" she asked, laboring on the coffee table.

"Have to read this short story, "The Most Dangerous Game," by Richard Connell," Kaseem admitted.

"Mmm. You shouldn't have any trouble identifying with that."

"Huh? Oh, okay." He put his hands into his pockets.

"What else?" she asked, wiping away like a sailor swabbing a deck.

"I have to find a book on a black or Hispanic person and read it for social studies and be—"

"Fiction or nonfiction?" she asked.

"Doesn't matter."

"*Native Son*," his mother said. "Richard Wright. I have it upstairs."

He resented it when she took things out of his hands like that. But with the skill he'd developed, he contained it. "And a buncha algebra examples to rupture my brain with."

She chuckled. "You can do it. So do it. Bye. We'll call you for dinner."

As he walked upstairs his attention was caught when he overheard Mrs. MacNeil mention his name. He slowed his ascent, but her voice suddenly went lower, probably at the signal of his mother.

He went into his bedroom and closed the door, but he could still make out, though barely, what they were saying. His mother said something about knowing he'd been good lately but that she still had to be sure. Mrs. MacNeil said something about it not being right to coop the boy up in the house like this. Wasn't healthy. His mother returned with a willingness to think about it. *Go, Grams*, thought Kaseem, seeing a distant light at the end of the tunnel.

The dinner, as usual, was eaten in relative silence. There were sporadic comments by the women on a stunning dress seen today in a dress shop window on Fordham Road, Mrs. Lothario's impressive flower bed down the block, how beautiful the day was at midday, or the nice job the doctor had done on a young patient's cut finger or abscessed tooth, all which tended to drive Kaseem quietly crazy with boredom.

"How ya doing on your homework?" she asked him, jerking him from his thoughts.

"Pretty good," he answered. "The algebra wasn't as hard as I'd thought. "The Most Dangerous Game" was a pretty good story, and *Native Son* kinda grabs you right away."

"Why?"

"Well, the main character's got an attitude on'm. You know that's gonna lead'm into trouble later on."

"Why does he have an attitude?"

"Not sure," Kaseem said. "Something to do with's father, I guess."

"I read it so long ago," she said, chewing, now deep in thought. "I remember feeling sad. Especially for his mother. And so terribly afraid."

Later that evening, there was a soft knock on his bedroom door that he knew was from his mother. He'd been flipping through a few martial arts magazines at his slightly cluttered desk.

She immediately commented that he should clean that desk off a little. Then she sat on the foot of his bed, where there would be greater cushion for her behind. He noted that she had closed the door behind her, even though, he knew, his grandmother would be lost in *Family Feud* at this moment, making her precautions unnecessary.

She looked so tired in the tensor lamp, shadowed glare of his room. He wondered briefly if she ever got laid. He tried to recollect the image of his father, but he always remained a shadowy figure, ghostlike and indistinct, for whom Kaseem yearned but at the same time was unable to get his memory's grip around.

There had always been something back then between his parents that remained vague, unfocused, and yet somehow terribly significant in the course of his life's development. She never spoke of it to anybody or even hinted by facial expression or action at any connection she'd had to that past. Even the times he attempted to ask her, she quickly hushed him up or deftly changed the subject. Moreover, there was that remembered look of fright on her face when she'd discovered he'd been watching her talk harshly to his father just before the distraught man vanished from his life. The totality of this mystery continued to foment his smoldering anger toward her.

Kaseem knew she loved him deeply, and he certainly loved her. But those resentments and hostilities in him always kept his acknowledgment of his affection in check.

"Look, son," she said after a pause. "I've been hard on you, I know, and I'm really sorry. I just have to be sure you stay on the straight and narrow. I took you away from a bad environment, and now it's caught up to us. There're so many bad influences out there now … all over, as a matter of fact. I have to be supercareful, 'cause you're all we have."

"Where's my father?" he blurted.

She inhaled slowly. "I dunno. And I'd rather not talk about him."

"But—"

"I said I'd rather not talk about him. Next topic."

Her fired eyes and the edge coming to her voice told him to drop the subject.

"I'm alone," she went on, only a faint suggestion of complaint now in her voice. "There's mostly been nobody in my life except you and Mom. Let's leave it at that."

Mostly?

"Your grandmother won't be with us forever. So, all right, maybe it's unfair of me to put it all on you, but I'm doing it in the hope that maybe someday soon that man inside you will start coming out. If you go, I might as well pack it in and crawl off to the happy hunting ground, because that's it. Last stop for the MacNeil line. So please, Rodney, I'm asking you to see it from my point of view, huh? Don't make me join that army of mothers out there chewing on their hearts all day. I don't think I'm as strong as they are."

For a few moments, she was silent, regarding him closely. Then she looked down at her folded hands. "I have to tell you you've been a good boy these last couple of weeks. You've been industrious, responsible. You've done all the things I've wanted you to. There hasn't been the attitude. Well, maybe a little now and then. But you've been pretty decent. I don't feel the dread anymore about you. Now, if I can get you to get up early Sunday morning and go to church with us, that'll be just about perfect. But I can't have everything, right?"

Kaseem felt a strange welling up in him so he fought any moistness that might burst into his eyes.

She got up, went to his door, and then stopped.

"Anyhow," she continued, "I'm lifting the punishment at the end of this week."

He managed a wan smile.

She regarded him momentarily and then said, "You're welcome."

CHAPTER 12

Earl was sitting in his car, which was still double-parked a block away, when Dionne emerged from the building. She stood at its entrance for a moment, looking up and down the street as if searching for someone. Seeing no one, she then stepped to the curb to hail a gypsy cab.

Because there were three cars parked in front of Earl's, she didn't see him, and he didn't want her to see him there. He was still deeply uneasy about Ignatius.

Suddenly, his heart jumped.

Two of Shehab's guards stepped out into the street from the doorway through which many people were now leaving. The two men watched Dionne as a cab slowed down in front of her. One of them said something to the other—probably uncomplimentary and vulgar—and then the two proceeded down the street in another direction, chuckling to each other.

Earl, now starting his car, smoldered as the objects of his ire disappeared around the corner. He had wanted badly to see her, but now, suddenly, he didn't, so he decided to call her instead. He found a candy store with a working phone a block away from her house.

"Look, can I beg off tonight?" he said. "I'm not feeling up to par."

There was disappointment in her voice. "Is there something wrong?"

"The way my stomach feels, I probably have horrendous breath."

"I have a toothbrush, Lysterine, and I'll take bad breath over an empty bed any day."

"Some meeting?"

She snorted. "You wanna go to bed restful? They're getting ready to hold so-called open nominations for president. Coupla Shehab's citizens worked Iggy over."

"No, don't tell me that."

"Well, Iggy had expressed his desire to run, and they did a job on'm. Naturally, he declined."

"Anybody else running?" he asked indifferently.

"Not as far as I know. Anyhow, I tried to bring up what had happened to Iggy and was shouted down."

"Hey, honey, you wanna be careful." He suddenly wanted to get off the phone. Also crowding his mind was the frightening picture of two goons crashing into her apartment to get her.

"Don't worry about me," she said. "I'm too much woman for those pipsqueaks."

"But still, watch it. For me, please."

"I did so much want to see you tonight."

"Me, too."

"Where're you now?"

"Across town," he lied.

"Go home to bed. You'll call tomorrow?"

On Friday of that week, Earl asked Kaseem to stay after school and act as a monitor for him, because he'd been doing such a splendid job for Mrs. Stanton, saying this last comment in a kidding, pseudo-jealous, and complimentary manner as he patted the boy on his back.

Happy about his forthcoming release from punishment, Kaseem eagerly volunteered but said his mother would have to know about it.

While Earl went down the hall to Mr. Rako's office to call Mrs. Wilson, Fox dropped by the classroom to pick up the gold necklace from Kaseem. Kaseem was beginning to amass a sizable sum of money now, having had no opportunity to spend it. Fox showed his fortune with a radical improvement in wardrobe, a fact not unnoticed by Officer Spriggs.

Kaseem told Fox of his imminent release and that brought the response: "Alllllll riiiight! I'll set it up for Saturday night. Friend of mine's crib. Try to hook it up with, you know, Michellene." They slapped each other five, and Fox went downstairs.

Earl stopped by Mr. Devonshire's classroom. A few after school students were busily writing an extra credit essay on the responsibilities of The President. Their teacher stepped out into the hall.

"My god, man," Earl whispered. "When somebody makes a mistake, you can hear his breathing stop."

"Your magic is catching," responded Mr. Devonshire as he glanced back at his class. He turned to Earl. "You'd never guess who apologized to me yesterday."

"Kaseem."

"Came right up to me in the hall. Begged my forgiveness. Took responsibility for everything. Was that your idea?"

"Not even a hint," said Earl.

Mr. Rako walked by. "My office is open," he said to Earl.

"Look, I'll tell you," said Mr. Devonshire, puzzlement in his manner. "I felt good after…but…I don't know…something bothered me. His turnaround seemed almost …unnatural. Ah. Maybe it's just me."

"I have to make this phone call," said Earl, pulling away.

"Yeah, go ahead," said Mr. Devonshire. "Forget what I said." He returned to his students as Earl continued to Mr Rako's office.

He was not going to let those last words disturb him.

"Mrs. Wilson," he said on the phone. "This's Mr. Chaney. How are you?"

She seemed to hesitate. "Oh, I'm just fine, thank you."

"Look, I know you're busy now. I just called to ask you if it's all right if I keep Kaseem after school today. I need'm to do some monitorial work for me. He's really been doing a fine job for the teachers here."

As Earl listened to a faint sigh on the other end, Mr. Rako, returned, shuffled papers on a large conference table and nodded to himself in slight astonishment.

"While I have your ear, I must tell you that he's been a fine student," Earl said as much for Mr. Rako as for Mrs. Wilson. "Marks're up. Always does his homework. Right now, he's working on an A in conduct."

"How can I repay you?"

On the way back to his room, Earl passed Mr. Devonshire on his way out.

Earl watched him going for a few moments, wondering why he'd never developed a closer relationship with the man. Both "brothers" had the same hopes for their students, particularly the black ones. Yet, there was something very foreign about the man to him.

Inside his classroom, Kaseem was putting the finishing touches on the bottom panels of his windows. The board had been completely washed, and the desks were all in order, chairs up for the custodial helper and free of every crumbled piece of paper.

"Well, that's not quite what I had in mind," he said, entering. "But I'm not going to turn up my nose at it. Excellent job."

He then asked Kaseem to alphabetize his official class students' names and to make up a few class lists for him in preparation for some upcoming attendance and racial-ethnic quota reports he would have to do.

Kaseem whipped through his duties. Then he sat at his desk and proceeded to do his homework. He worked concentratedly until Earl looked up from his work. "Oh, you don't have to stay! You're finished. Why don't you take off?"

"That's all right, Mr. Chaney. Just thought maybe I'd knock off some homework."

Earl returned to his work for a few moments but found his concentration waning. He looked up at the young man and regarded him for a few seconds, tapping his thumb with the ballpoint pen. The boy looked up from his homework and met Earl's eyes with his. The teacher looked back down at his work, snorted, and looked back up at Kaseem.

"Peeping at each other like two owls," Earl joked. "What's that you're doing?"

"The composition you asked us to write."

"Good. Rewrite it at home, bring it in on Monday. Maybe we can send it down to the principal's office. He's looking for samples of pupil writing."

"You sure you wanna do that?"

"I know it'll be good." Earl noted a tendency in the boy to low rate himself.

"Can I ask you a question?" Kaseem said.

"Ask."

"When I asked to be put in your class, you knew my rep, and you coulda said no. How come you didn't?"

"Somebody told me the more people I had in my class, the more money I'd make."

"Square business?"

Earl chuckled. "No, only ribbing you."

"Which you wish was true."

"Hey, the times. Inflation. I'm never one to turn my nose up at extra coins."

"But how come?" Kaseem was determined to hear reasons for things that happened to and around him.

"I saw that you were a kid getting the business," Earl said. "I knew a lot of it you deserved, but still, what I saw didn't hit me right. So I figured why not give the kid one more chance. If he blows it, he blows it. What can you lose?"

"And you didn't bother me or nothing," Kaseem said. "Didn't get on my case or start in on me. Gimme a buncha warnings and rules. How come?"

Earl gestured with his hand to the young man and stared wide-eyed at him.

"I guess with what's happened, it's a dumb question," said Kaseem, looking down.

"No such thing as a dumb question now," the teacher pointed out. "Never hesitate to ask a question. Question askers don't end up sorry about things." He immediately thought of Iggy.

"See, that's what I mean about you. In a way, you're kinda like ... not like the teachers I'm used to. You're patient. You lay cool and listen. You don't come outa your face alla time. Yet and still, none of the kids give you a hard time. It's like they know their role with you without you having to sell woof tickets."

"Well, don't put me above the other teachers. I'm no better. No worse."

"There's a lotta kids'd disagree with you. Everybody looks up to you as, like, the top. The white, black, Spanish kids—don 't matter. They all think you're the man."

The teacher squirmed a little under this "assault."

"I'm sorry," the boy went on. He was not pretending. "I don't mean to make you uncomfortable."

The teacher smiled and regarded the boy. "May I ask you a question?"

"My turn, huh?"

"No, no game," Mr.Chaney said. "This's something I've been curious about since you've been in my class. I look at your mother, a fine, beautiful lady. Knocking herself out for you. Now I'm not trying to lay any guilt on you. But, well, look at what you're doing now and what you were doing before. Frankly, I don't think I really did anything to change your behavior. Why were you doing all that nonsense before that put you in such bad stead with everybody and gave your mother so much grief?"

Kaseem leaned back against his chair, clamped his hands behind his head, and looked up at the ceiling.

"Okay," he said after a pause. "I know I can trust you."

He stood up and leaned back against the desk, his eyes fixed on the floor space between his jogging shoes.

"I been looking at things very immature, I guess," Kaseem started. "Stupid. I dunno when I started having a attitude. But long as I know, I had one. For days. Stayed evil. Go to movies or watch a TV show, and there's a happy ending. I fan my hand at the screen and suck my teeth. And I can't stand it when they show somebody—all teary-eyed—running in slow motion to something happy. Corny music up all loud and like that. I mean, sometimes I applaud like the other people in the movie when the bad guy gets his, but I'm always sorry the bad guy wasn't smarter, faster, or stronger. And I'd walk out the movie unsatisfied. Like, take *Jaws*. When they make it like you're the shark going through the water and that baaaad music's in the background—boomp-boomp! boomp-boomp!—and you know you the baddest thing in the sea. Or on TV when those Japanese monsters're destroying cities and ain't nothing anybody can do about it. Godzilla blows on a steel beam and turns it into a wet noodle. Boy, that just knocks me out."

He checked himself, pushed off the desk, and walked over to the window, where he stared at a blue jay-standing post on a high tree limb before it flew off. Then he turned to his teacher, who had closed his pen and put it down on his survey form. He picked up a chair, placed it close to the teacher, and sat, leaning forward, his elbows on his knees. He stared into his folded, veiny hands, their thumbs playing with each other.

"The things you said about my moms," he said, his voice low, a faint quaver in it. "You're right. What I been doing ain't been right. But, well, see … I love her and my grandmother both. They done a lot for me—I know it—and sometimes I think they missed a lot in their own life doing it. This tells me something. And I appreciate that. But sometimes I look at her and get so mad I can't see straight. She bugs me about something, bosses me around, which I know she's supposed to do, snaps on me when I'm wrong. She don't hit me anymore, but boy, she used to go to town on my butt. I don't have to tell you when those black mothers get to you, the dust flies. And part of me appreciates what *that* was for, too.

"But, Mr. Chaney, deep inside me, I couldn't stand the woman. I used to look at myself in the mirror and say, 'Wow! What kinda guy're you? Can't stand your own moms. That's heavy.' Then I got to feeling real crummy and wishing I could step outside myself and kick my butt all up and down the house.

"And it was the same with the women I had to deal with—teachers, women on the bus, looking down their nose on me like they my mothers, saying, 'Well, aren't you gonna gimme your seat?' Or, 'Why're you in school? Why don't you stay home and torment your family instead of us?'

"And the girls. Now, I dig the girls. They got those sweet, cute faces and dimples, big-eyed smiles, and nice figures. Then they get to giggling and opening their mouths, talking all kinds of stupidness, and I wanna put my fist right through the wall."

"Is your father around at all?" the teacher asked.

"No, he was killed in Nam." Kaseem cleared his throat.

"Look, Kaseem," Mr.Chaney said, leaning forward on his desk and toying with his pen. "In life, we're given choices. We can say, 'The world's not perfect. Let me outa here!' Or add to its imperfection with negative behavior. Or say, 'I'm going to get involved in it and make my contribution.' The final test of your choice is what it does to you inside."

"My feelings? I mean, you can know all this but still—"

"They'll change along with everything else," Mr. Chaney added. "You can't stay angry at the world for not being what you want it to be. You'll only end up old before your time. Besides, this world has tried. And sometimes it's come pretty close."

"Like where?" Kaseem asked innocently.

"A work of art for instance. Rembrandt. Reggie Jackson's swing. Palchabel's *Canon in D*. A day in the country with your girl. Mother Theresa and a smiling child Your mother's happiness when you've done something that pleases her."

The teacher then paused and stared at the youth now deep in thought.

"Suppose I don't want 'good'?" Kaseem said . "See, where I used to live, you had to be 'bad' to get over, that sorta settled in and got to be my way. When bad things happened, you laughed, or you were considered a goody-goody. I'm just askin', y'understand, because I seen the error of that now and I'm gettin' it together."

"All right," said his teacher, regarding him closely.

Kaseem nodded thoughtfully, gathered his books, and started out. When he got to the door, he stopped and thanked Mr. Chaney.

"Say, listen," said the latter. "Are you free Sunday? About one o'clock?"

Kaseem looked at him blankly for a second. "Yeah, I think so."

"My son and I're going to a basketball game at the Garden, the Knicks and 76ers. Like to come? On me, of course. And we can hit MacDonald's or someplace after and argue over the game."

Now Kaseem was dumbfounded. A teacher was asking for his company on the weekend, taking him into his other world.

"Come on, come on. Say yes so I can get back to my work."

"Yes."

CHAPTER 13

Early Saturday morning, Kaseem was dusting furniture, washing Venetian blinds, straightening up his room, watering the garden in the back, mowing the front lawn. He went through the house and its immediate environs like a magic cleanser in a TV commercial and finally sat down at his desk to read *Native Son*.

He was having some difficulty concentrating on the book now. He found the smoldering anger of Bigger Thomas too disturbing, too similar to his own. Mirrors were not for him, his soul's reflection even less so.

His mother slipped into the room. Her hand shot up to her forehead, and she staggered back against the doorjamb. "Oh! I can't stand this. This boy's trying to turn me to stone."

She was dressed in a light blue oversized shirt and loose-fitting jeans. He liked her like this. She sent out calm vibes that quenched his uneasiness.

"Go on, get outa here," she said, reaching into her pocket and producing a twenty that she pushed into his shirt pocket. "Have yourself a good day. You deserve it. But be back here at a decent hour, hear? Big day tomorrow."

When she was gone, he added the twenty to the sixty in his trousers pocket, and while she was out back in the garden and Mrs. MacNeil was downstairs in the cellar, he called Michellene.

"Well, well, well, well," she said. "As I live and breathe. What have we here?"

"Just thought I'd give you a ring, find out what's happening."

"How'd you get my number?"

"I confess. I got it from the attendance folder when I was still in your class."

"Go-get'm dude, ain't ya?" Her voice became early teen sexy.

"When I see something I like," he said.

"Oh, yeah? Well, Mr. Go-Get'm, I would appreciate it if you'da asked me straight out instead of sneaking it like that. You coulda got me in a lotta trouble. My mother don't like our telephone number getting around all over the place. It's embarrassing, ya know?"

"Hey, I'm sorry. I didn't get you in any trouble."

"No, she's at the coin launderette now," she said.

"So how'd you like to hang out with me tonight?"

"On such short notice?"

"Hey, this's my first night out and—"

"Oh, that's right. Your mother had you in solitary confinement all this time. And your first night out you wanted to share with me? That's nice. Well, you're on. Don't take that literally now."

"Bet." They made plans for meeting and then hung up. Kaseem went to the cleaners to get himself ready. He had a hard-on the whole time.

Michellene had already known the date was coming even before the phone call. Elva had scooped her of the upcoming double date earlier that morning, and now plans were finalized.

She thoughtfully hung up, entered her bedroom and glanced out the window at the launderette a block and a half away. She saw no one coming out, and turned to Vinny lying on her bed and gesturing to her. She sucked her teeth and fanned her hand at him as she walked to her dresser mirror, smugly primping. Her blue silk blouse was open at the top and she wore tight jeans.

"Why didn't you come in here with the phone?" he asked, turning over and leaning on his left elbow. "Your extension wire's long enough. Make me suspicious."

"Was private," she answered, studying the launderette. Her fourth-floor window overlooked the wide front walk to the main entrance of her Latimer Houses building . The laundry in the basement was on the blink, so her mother had to use the one in the mini-mall where the supermarket, pizzeria, candy store, dry cleaners, and check-cashing place were. It would take her mother considerable time to wheel her load home, after which Michellene's job would be to sort it and put the items into their appropriate dresser drawers, clothing and linen closets, and onto the towel racks.

"So you're going out with the guy?" Vinny asked, pulling idly on a loose thread on the bedspread.

"None of your business," she snapped. "And stop messin' with that."

"It is my business," he said, a bogus pout on his face. "I'm jealous. Like that guy Macbeth."

"Othello," she snapped. "you're so ignorant."

"Othello. Yeah, right. And you know what he did with his woman when he thought she was two-timin'm."

"That a threat?" she looked at him challengingly. "You know better than to threaten me."

"Hey, I'm upset. Dude's in my official class, and you gon' go out with'm. Dis'n me. A hurtful thing you doing."

"So?" She chuckled provocatively.

"Ooooh," he said. "Hard-backed bitch, ain't you?"

"Like you care."

"You don't think I care?"

"Why don't you just stop it?"

"Okay, baby. I'm cool. But while you out with the Big K, I want you to find out those little things for me like I asked you."

"You gonna go over this again?" she asked, sighing.

"Find out where Fox is getting all that bread for his threads. And if he's got that kinda bread, you'd better believe the Big K's got it, too. Find out what they into."

"Why should I?" she asked, teasing him.

"'Cause you wanna know, too. And you my woman, ain't ya?" he purred.

"Am I?"

"C'mere."

"Whatcha got in mind?"

"Just c'mere."

"She's gonna come outa that launderette any minute now." Desire was stirring inside her.

"With the load she had? She'll be in there another hour at least. And you know that. C'mon, sweet thing, don't run this game on me."

She crossed to the bed and let him seize her wrist.

"You like me?" she asked, her voice lower.

He pulled her down to him. "If I didn't like you, you think I'd put up with all the shit you put me through?"

"Respect me?"

"I can't like somebody unless I respect her." He began kissing her under her ear, her eyes closing with pleasure.

"Quickie draws. That's all you think about."

"Now you know that ain't true," he said.

Her efforts to push him away began to weaken.

"Just don't make me pregnant," she said, half a whisper, half a sigh.

After, she pushed him out the front door, careful that no one was in the hall or looking through a peephole, cautioning him once more to go down the staircase and exit when her mother entered the elevator with the laundry load. Vinny found the instructions unnecessary.

The four teens went to see a chop-socky film in one of the theaters on Time Square, where they sat in the center section and laughed and oooohed and aaaaahhhhed at the spectacular events on the screen before them. Occasionally, the girls would push their foreheads into the smalls of the young men's shoulders when the going got too rough between two rabid, would-be gladiators or when a Samurai sword found its mark. Meanwhile, the boys just guffawed, slapped their knees and each other five, and pointed.

Periodically, Kaseem's fingers would play with the underside of Michellene's breast before her fingers gingerly pulled them away. When events on the screen became dull, they passed a stick of grass among them. The odor soon permeated their whole area.

A portly woman behind them stood up in anger. "You can't go to a damn movie anymore," she growled, storming to another section.

A small wiry man in front of them turned around. "Could you put out the pot please? I paid my money for this ticket, and I would like to see the movie without having to put up with that awful smell."

"Aw, you just jealous 'cause you don't have any," said Kaseem. "Want some?"

"Would you put it out please?"

"Here. Take a nice drag'n everything'll be real cool."

The man got up and started toward the rear of the theater.

The four laughed and moved to the erstwhile smoking section on the far right side, where a similar odor awaited them. They saw the man return with the usher, a tall black youth who looked like he was doing this between basketball seasons. He whipped his flashlight beam around the area they had been sitting in before, and then the two men appeared to be talking to other people in the audience to no avail. The man thanked the usher and sat back down as the usher now walked down toward the screen and crossed the front toward the aisle lining the smoking side of the theater.

By now, what was left of the roach was under Kaseem's heel as the usher, whipping his flashlight beam about, ambled up the aisle. Then his beam hit Kaseem's and Fox's faces. He held it there for a few seconds.

"Hey, what is this?" said Fox. "Get that light out my eyes, man."

"Smoking pot is prohibited in this theater," the usher said to them. He now seemed much taller than at first.

"Hey, you right," said Kaseem. "I think it's a disgrace what goes on in these theaters. I'm glad to see you on the case."

The usher stood there for a few more moments, staring at them. "I'm glad we understand each other," he said finally and continued up the aisle.

After the film, they went to Popeye's Chicken, where they sat at a table and talked about the movie, laughing and chomping on a chicken leg or thigh. They told jokes and made comments, often derogatory, about their school, fellow students, and many of the teachers.

Shortly, however, Kaseem began to notice something that shot a sour jolt through him. Each time Michellene reared back to laugh she would bend forward and drop her hand on Fox's wrist or grab his arm. Elva also noticed, though she said nothing.

Fox seemed to be too busy clowning to notice anything. Also, quite frequently, his Elva-side hand would disappear from the table, and Elva would look like she was straining to maintain a cool facade.

In the bathroom, while they were drying their hands, Fox leaned close to his friend and said, "Man, I don't like to step outa my place, but you shouldn't let her pull that shit she pulled before. You spend all this bread on her—I mean, we risking our butts for this—and she's pulling that shit. Don't let her vic you like that. Chill the bitch out. She's outrageous. Y'understand what I'm saying? And I'm telling ya again. Watch Vinny. He's after her butt, if he don't already have it."

"Don't sweat it," said Kaseem. "I got it covered."

Fox placed a key in his hand. "The guy's out of town for a week, so don't worry about being interrupted. 'Sides, he likes activity in his crib. Keeps the burglars away. Just don't forget to put the sheet in the hamper when you finished."

"And you?"

"Elva's moms is working the night shift at the hospital. Ain't nobody else home. And I got her sewed up. Gonna get me some serious trim tonight."

The couples split up on East Gun Hill Road. Kaseem and Michellene took a gypsy cab to Fox's friend's place on a quiet street on Bronx River Parkway. Michellene was prattling on about one thing or another that Kaseem was scarcely paying attention to. His mind was on the last time he'd made love to a girl. It'd been two months ago with a seventh grader he'd taken to a party. She'd been given a little too much to drink, so he'd whisked her to an empty bedroom on the pretext of helping to sober her up. With hungry ease, he'd mounted her atop a few coats and jackets lying on the spread. She'd wept, after which had angered him, so he'd slapped her. After that, her family moved from the neighborhood.

When Kaseem and Michellene entered the apartment, a tension immediately seized him. This took the moment briefly out of his hands and unsettled him. He watched her walk about the apartment, examining the furniture, as if she'd planned to move in permanently. A sudden urge for her gripped him.

He strode over to behind her to wrap his arms around her, but just as he reached her, she moved away from him.

"You think maybe we could lead into, well, you know, let's be civilized," she said. "We're not two dogs in the street."

"I took you out."

"Yeah, you did."

"We been talking all afternoon," Kaseem said.

"You're missing my point."

He sat down on a chair, feeling frustration pushing its way into him. How dare these girls hold so much power over his appetites! "Well," he said. "What is the point?"

"There's no point. God, you're making a whole discombobulation outa all this."

"Then I'll shut up. You talk. You tell me, for instance, what all that crap was before in Popeye's with Fox. With the dropping your hand on his arm and shit."

"Say what?" she said and then started for the bedroom. "Forget it. Come on."

"Just like that."

She whirled on him. "Didn't you understand what I was doing? I was getting next to *you* to make *you* more interested in me, to turn *you* on."

"Then what was this 'let's lead into it' business all about? You stringing me along? You some kind of cock teaser?"

"Say, listen, where you get off talking like that to me?"

"Then what was it all about?" he asked.

"What's your problem?"

"I don't have a problem. You have a problem?"

"Why don't you take me home?" she said.

"I don't wanna take you home, all right? I have the hots for you, all right, and I wanna get down with you. I thought you were a down babe. So what's up with you?"

"Because—" She regarded him momentarily. "Nothing," she sighed. "Never mind."

They undressed silently in the bedroom. He watched her, noting how truly beautiful she was naked and regretting that there was something wrong in the air between them, something that was spoiling the flow of the evening. He noted also that she didn't seem a bit shy in front of him.

He hesitantly approached her, and this time, she didn't move away. They embraced and kissed tenderly. Her smooth brown skin felt like a warm nylon veil touching his, and she smelled of lilac. "I like you," she whispered.

"I like you, too," he said, slowly laying her down on the bed.

Suddenly, her hands shot to his chest. "Look," she said, turning her head to the side. "I'm really sorry about all this stuff before. I didn't mean to upset you."

"It's okay."

"One more thing," she said, turning her stare to him. "I'm not exactly a virgin."

"So?" he said. Something inside him swallowed.

"I been brazen with boys. My way of getting along, I guess. My mom don't know. I have the feeling she'd really care if she did. And it might do something to her. One boy once bought me a skirt, which I hid in my closet for over a year before I put it on. Mom never noticed. Yet and still— Oh, I dunno."

For the next few silent moments, he lay on her, absently fondling her breasts.

"Hey, I like us getting close like this," she crooned and looked at him. "Ever since we were in the seventh grade, I thought about this."

"I always liked you, too. From the time I first moved up here."

"Can I ask you something?"

His need was growing stronger. "What?"

"How do you two guys come to have so much money?"

"So much what money? Me'n Fox? We're thrifty. We save our coins."

She peered at him. "Okay. Your turn to ask me something."

"Yeah, can we get it on now?"

"Not yet. Not ready yet."

"When?" he asked impatiently.

"In due time. You don't mind if I put you in when I'm ready."

"Hey." He shrugged and regarded her. "What's the story on Vinny?"

He felt her muscles tighten, and she averted her eyes. "Oh, him. Jerk. Always bugging me. Thinks he's God's gift to women. He's had his nose open for me since even before you were transferred out of our class. I ain't thinking about'm myself. He needs to get his act together, that's what."

He tried to enter her, but she gripped his member.

"I said I'd let you know when I'm ready."

Suddenly, rage flooded through him. He whipped his hand across her face and hit her again with his other hand.

"Hey, what the—"

He pummeled her arms, shoulders, and the top of her head, she covering her face with her arms. Then, after he again tried to enter her and failed, he jumped off her. "Think you slick, huh? Think you slick, bitch?" He banged her again on her shoulder with his fist.

She was now whimpering. "Please don't hit me no more!"

"Aw, get dressed. I don't want your damn draws. You think you can hand me this bullshit, and then I'm supposed to open up like a damn elevator door and scoop you to all the happenings in my life? Well, you can suck this, ho! Always trying it!"

In a flash, the door was closed and the sniffling, crying girl was running up the street. "You'll pay for this!"

He fumed for about fifteen minutes before it occurred to him that he'd have to be home soon. But he couldn't leave just like that. There were tracks to cover.

For a day that had begun so beautifully to end like this and for him to have lost so much control. Tears of rage welled up in him, and he punched the pillow.

He stared at the large crater his fist had made and suddenly thought of the apartment's owner and his connection to Fox and the world, it seemed.

He pushed himself up to a kneeling position, thought of what might have been, and masturbated over the sheet.

CHAPTER 14

Dionne walked out of the Black Resurrection building, stepped to the curb, and waited. She was a little discouraged about the way things were going in the organization. The election was fast approaching, and no opposing candidate to Shehab had come forward.

Since the Iggy incident, Earl Chaney had shown diminishing interest in the organization, not attending the last couple of meetings. Dionne had even offered herself as a possible candidate, but the inbred male chauvinism stifled that idea. She briefly entertained the idea of going the way of Iggy and leaving this "lost cause." Her time was too valuable to waste.

She folded her arms. Shehab's security guards came out, flashed dirty looks at her, and proceeded to some destination up the block.

Then, suddenly, Shehab was standing next to her.

She instantly knew what he was after. She had been down these alleys so many times that she could almost orchestrate the dynamics in her head.

"I haven't seen your teacher friend lately," he said.

"He's been very busy, dealing with school problems."

"I hear ya. Teaching's a bitch of a profession. My hat's off to'm. I was hoping we'd have more access to'm as a resource."

She didn't respond. She only looked toward the corner, hoping Earl's car would be coming.

"Do you think sometime we could sit down have a cup of coffee together?"

She turned to him. "Why would you want that?"

"Get to know each other better. I think, maybe, you got me all wrong."

"What do you mean?"

"We could be good friends. I could do a lot for somebody like you."

"That so?" she said.

"I could take you to new levels."

"Levels?"

"Put you into a high position in the organization. Intelligent person like you. Put some dollars in your purse. Things're about to break with us. You can be part of that. Things can happen with you and me as well. Situations that could be good for both of us."

She stared at him for the longest time and then crooked her finger at him. He leaned toward her, and, after she smiled and waved at some of the people who were leaving, she cupped her hand over her mouth, which she moved toward his ear.

"We can't be friends," she whispered. "We're from different planets, you'n I. Worse, I don't like you, never have. So there is no way in my time on this earth or yours that you're going to get into my pants. Now don't take that as a provocation or tease. Take it as what it is, an irrevocable fact."

"You're locked up with somebody else, and you're not open to any new experiences."

"You might say that. But if there was absolutely nobody else, our situation, you'n I, would not be any different. Do you comprehend what I'm saying to you? And why're we having this conversation?"

At this point, Earl drove up. Shehab's eyes flashed as he looked at the teacher and then smiled. "There he is. The man of the hour. What you know good, good brother?"

Earl nodded to him as Dionne got into the car.

"Hear you been busy. When you have time, Mr. Professor Sir, don't forget us."

"You're never out of my mind," responded Earl dryly as he drove off.

Dionne looked back at the receding figure and sucked her teeth. "Would you believe that sonovabitch just tried to hit on me? I guess he's got it in his beady brain that if he gets to screw the teacher's woman, that validates him somehow."

"Can't say I blame'm," said Earl as he turned right at the far corner.

A moue crossed Dionne's face. "I'm going to make you pay for that when we get home." She dropped her head on his shoulder and then kissed him.

———

His mother and grandmother's stirring on Sunday morning awoke him. He'd been having dreams of being in a cloudy chamber and hearing derisive, mostly male laughter somewhere nearby. Fox's, Vinny's, Mr. Devonshire's,

Officer Spriggs's, and Elva's faces—all smiling, laughing—flashed through the fog. He tried to splash them out of his memory with a few handfuls of cold water in his face, but it didn't completely work.

"Do I hear Rodney up?" he heard from downstairs.

His mother came to the foot of the stairs. "Rodney, what're you doing up?"

He spit out his mouthwash and, wiping his face, came to the bathroom door. "I'm going to church with you, Mom. Wait up."

He went into his bedroom and quickly started to put on his Sunday best, a navy blue, three-piece polyester suit that he'd gotten from the cleaners the previous day.

"You wanna run that by me again," his mother said.

As he put his tie on, he went to his bedroom door. "I said I'm going to church with you."

He was buttoning his vest when he saw, through his open door and the hall balustrade, his mother's face, rising above the landing. Her eyes were as wide open, it seemed, as her mouth.

The Baychester Presbyterian Church was now a modern building, almost futuristic in its angled, sharp-edged architecture. It was as if it had skipped ahead in time past its congregation, who had moved there from an older building two years ago. This one was now larger, resting on wider grounds, and it had a well-equipped community center, a beehive of continuous activity, mainly youth, from basketball to basket weaving to senior citizens' disco or bingo, which Kaseem's mother occasionally attended when time allowed her.

Reverend Boston, a large, black, ex-pro halfback, bespectacled, whom many people called "The Jolly Black Giant," stood at the entrance to the church, greeting his assemblage. A man from the streets, he knew what life was all about and was willing to "throw down" if necessary. He was known to roll up his sleeves and pitch in with his deacons, scrubbing graffiti off the buildings' faces. If the perpetrator was caught, he was made to join in after a few well-aimed whacks on his head.

His eyes flashed, and his head went back in a slight movement of incredulity when he saw Kaseem with his mother and grandmother. He grabbed the boy's hand and shook it. "It's good to see you, young man," he said, smiling. "God bless you, Mrs. Wilson. Mrs. MacNeil. The Lord has truly blessed you on this fine morning."

Kaseem sat through the services without moving a muscle. He'd contained his strong claustrophobic feeling and his boredom and hadn't allowed his mind to dwell too long on the events of the previous night.

He looked around at the congregation of mostly women, their earnestness and focus on the pulpit like his mother's and grandmother's. The aroma of heady lavender filled the air, and the ornately designed fans in white or dark gray sheer net-gloved hands oscillated like butterfly wings gathered in a flower bed.

The presence of the men puzzled him. He had the feeling they'd been dragged there or simply were there, fighting drowsiness, to keep peace in their respective homes. Yet, there were men in the pews who seemed to be perfectly at home with their assenting, fanning wives.

Suddenly, all singing stopped, and there was Reverend Boston at the podium, his eyes scanning the assemblage of faces in the electric silence except for a few clearings of throats and the ruffling sound of a busy fan. His "flock" was ready.

"I want to thank you all for coming on this beautiful Sunday morning to spend some time with our Lord in His house," he began. "And how pleased I am to see some young faces among us. Bless you. I know how hard it is to pull yourself out of bed after an arduous evening at the local disco."

Laughter.

"But the Pepsi generation ain't all at the Pepsi machine."

"No, they're not, Lord," chorused various people from their pews.

"Most of them right here, side by side, with us."

"Thank you, Jesus," the people sang again.

"But we don't hear about them. They don't make interesting copy in our newspapers and magazines."

"Tell it."

"They won't make lines form at the box office to see movies about them," the reverend continued.

"You know it, too."

"Stories about them on TV won't help the bigwigs sell you their shampoo and mouthwash."

There came more laughter and general clamor.

"I could say the ones here don't really need to be here."

"Tell it like it is 'cause it's right anyhow," the audience chimed.

"Don't get me wrong. We all of us need to be here."

"Word!"

"I'm talking now about the ones who really need it, the others."

"Mmmmmm-hmmmmm."

"The lost ones."

"Who you tellin'?"

"The ones who make you clutch your pocketbooks, lock your doors, look over your shoulders, and stay in your homes at night," he said. "The ones who prevent your child from learning in school, because they dominate the teacher's time and attention. The ones who seek salvation in the funny cigarette, the pill, or the needle. The ones who will come to your house and try to sell dope to your child. The ones who put terror in our hearts even on a lovely Sunday morning like this. They're the ones who need to be here."

Intense clamor.

"But it's not as simple as that. If we were to root out all those lost children and lock them inside Yankee Stadium, will the problem be solved? No. Because the problem really isn't them. Those children are not the disease. Yhey're the symptom."

"Thank you, Jesus."

"They're crying out to us. They're saying, 'World! Society! Community! Yes, family! Painful though it may be to admit. There's something wrong going on. Somehow you've gotten off the track. You bypassed the path of righteousness and love a coupla miles back.'"

"Word up!"

"'Our inner moral compass is out of whack. The needle's jerking back and forth. So therefore, we're having a bumpy ride of confusion, darkness, and evil.' And is it any wonder that they're saying this to us? After all, what're we presenting to them? We play cutesy number games on our income taxes and tell the children, 'Don't cheat on your tests.' We talk about each other like dogs behind our backs. And when we're face-to-face, we show all the ivories in our mouths. We make secret visits to our neighbor's wife or husband and then tell our children, 'It's not nice to steal.' We see a Vietnamese child on fire, running in fright along a dirt road, gasp, and say, 'How awful war is and how terrible the violence.' Then we say, 'If that Mrs. Jones cuts in front of me one more time at the checkout counter, I'm gonna bash her head in with the Clorox bleach bottle.' And the children are looking at all this and saying, 'We don't understand your mixed messages. And our confusion fills us with dismay and anger. So acting out's the only way we know of sounding the alarm. We have not been given any other way.' Somewhere along the line, brothers and sisters, we didn't make the grade for them. We, through our actions, inactions, through losing our values and our strength, have turned them off the path of righteousness."

"I wanna tell ya," the audience sounded.

"'*Yea, though I walk through the valley of the shadow of death, I will fear no evil: for thou art with me; thy rod and thy staff they comfort me.*'"

"Praise the Lord!"

"We've got to get everybody in our community back inside those words," the reverend said. "Only then can the lost ones be found again. '*Surely goodness and mercy shall follow me all the days of my life, and I will dwell in the house of the Lord forever.*' Let us bow our heads and pray."

Kaseem only half heard the prayer and the benediction after. His mind's ear, instead, was straining to focus on his soul. What was it? Where was it? Where was it going? What was to become of him? He searched for some sign of an answer, some indication. What answered him, however, was only frigid silence.

Furthermore, he saw, with a furtive sidelong glance, moisture forming in his mother's eyes. He chose not to deal with the self-reproachful implications of that.

After the service, he stood on the top of the church steps, looking out over the mingling of people on the sidewalk involved in various pockets of conversation. Everyone looked beatified, even with their occasional sidelong glances his way. He somehow knew that sermon had to be for his sake. How much did Reverend Boston know about his life? The congregation? He felt uncomfortable.

He looked at his mother and grandmother deep in conversation with the reverend, and he thought he heard someone say, "Thank God for Mr. Chaney." At this, his stomach caught, and he felt the ground shift sideways under him.

Despite one or two strands of gray hair, Ida still looked like a woman in her twenties, hardly one who had a sixteen-year-old son. The figure was still there, the dark brown skin absent of wrinkles, the face, wide-eyed, pug-nosed and dimpled, and the high cheekbones still provocative.

She was not happy, exposing her son to this Kaseem person. Who was he? Why was the school having so much trouble with him? What did he do with himself after school?

Earl could always tell when she felt qualms about something. She would suddenly become overly involved in the finest details. Anthony would patiently bear her fussing, look mock helplessly at his father, and smile. "Mom," he would say. "Believe me when I tell you the day won't be totally destroyed if I leave my Afro pick home." Finally, he would be released and sent to wait in the car for his father.

"It'll work out fine," said Earl.

"I suppose so," Ida returned, sighing with pretended resignation. "He's a big boy now. Might as well meet the Kaseems of the world now as later."

He looked at her and frowned accusatorily. "You make it sound like I'm taking him out with Attila the Hun." *How dare you of all people question my judgment.*

"For my son, everybody's Attila the Hun until proven otherwise," she said.

"My son? I like that. What'd you have? An immaculate conception?"

"Don't challenge me, Earl. I'm not particularly thrilled with this, putting *our* son—okay?—on exhibition for the great unwashed."

"Don't insult my intelligence by stating the obvious," he said.

"And I won't be put on the defensive about my feelings."

"Then don't announce them."

"Stop giving me a hard time, will you?" she said, backing off.

"Stop giving *me* a hard time."

She regarded him for a few moments and then chuckled. "Listen to us," she said. "Like a coupla kids. Maybe the wrong people in this family are the parents."

"Are you complaining? Or bragging?"

"The story of our communication these days," she said. "I say something. You respond. You say something. Ditto. Always on the defensive with each other."

"That word again. Defensive," Earl said, sighing. "Watching a lot of talk shows lately, are we?"

"The dance goes on," she responded, waving her arms as if conducting an invisible orchestra. "Nothing like that ol' sexual tension."

He gave her a quizzical look.

"Come on,".she persisted. "You know you still have your nose open for me. And I do for you. It's a fact of nature, that's all. Playing all these games."

"How'm I supposed to respond? Ask for a quickie in the bedroom for ol' times sake?" He hoped he was concealing his arousal better.

"Aha!" she said, putting her hands on her hips. " He's threatened by that, so he has to belittle it."

"All this because Anthony's meeting Kaseem?" he parried.

"Okay," she sighed. "I mean, how come you didn't ask one of the good kids?"

That stung. Earl squirmed under his discomfiture from that but brought it under some control. He sighed inside. "Who died and made you my guru in early adolescent education?"

"You never trusted my judgment in things."

"I tried."

They locked eyes for a few moments. Then his eyes dropped down to her legs.

"Legs still good, huh?" she said.

"Yeah."

"How's Dionne?" She regarded him closely.

"She's okay," Earl admitted.

"More power to her."

"Still putting me down."

"You haven't been putting me down since you walked through that door?" she asked.

"Habits die hard."

"Another defensive response. And look at him. He's starting to get mad." She placed her hand on his back and pushed him toward the door. "Go on, get outa here. I got five on the 76ers."

"You would," he said as he left.

It could not have been a more perfect afternoon. Not at first, though. When Kaseem in a tan blazer climbed into the front seat next to Anthony, he was obviously uncomfortable.

When Earl introduced Kaseem to his son, Kaseem nodded stiffly and clammed up. Anthony, however, the outgoing and warm young man, was not going to let his new acquaintance off that easily.

"What?" he said to the uneasy young man. "You're a 76ers man? Well, you have just let yourself in for a terrible afternoon. I'm gonna hafta send you home mumbling to yourself."

With that, Anthony lifted his hand, palm down in a semi-cup, and, when Kaseem placed his under it, brought it down with a resounding smack. Later, during his raillery, he did the liberation handshake with Kaseem, something Earl always considered "metaphysical nonsense," and then the well opened up.

Never had Earl seen so many fives being slapped, so much raucous laughter that grew louder as the afternoon progressed. The two boys jumped and marveled at every move Dr. J. or Michael Richardson made. They ooooed and aaaaaaaahed over each spectacular ballistic image that crashed to their senses. Kaseem perhaps laughed a little too hard at times, especially when someone fell, and he would slap his forehead with perhaps a little too much drama when Bobby Jones would put in some unexpected or unheard of shot or would grab an impossible-to-get but crucial rebound.

Earl watched Kaseem jumping out of his skin with enjoyment and marveled pridefully at his son and felt that he had done the right thing for both boys. That the Knicks finally lost seemed secondary to the total joy he felt at how everything was working out so smoothly.

At the restaurant after, they gobbled down their Big Macs and talked animatedly about how great a game it was—Anthony did not have to eat crow—and Earl, with some certainty, began to entertain the notion that he was pulling this boy, Kaseem, inside out and that, thanks to him, the world would never again see the hostile young wretch who had first come to his class.

"I'm glad you enjoyed yourself," he said to him as he pulled up to in front of his house.

"It was a trip," said Kaseem as he did the liberation handshake with Anthony while he pushed himself out of the car. "Fantastic."

"Say, listen, keep this under your hat for future reference," said Earl. "I'm thinking of renting a cabin in the woods upstate one of these weekends, take Anthony up. How'd you like to join us?"

Once again, Kaseem could only gape at his teacher and nod dumbly as he staggered backward up the walk to his house.

Fifteen minutes later, Earl was pulling up to in front of Ida's house. "Let's sit here and talk for a while," he said to his son after he gave him ten dollars to give to his mother.

"We haven't had much chance to talk to each other, have we?" said Anthony.

"No, we haven't." Earl looked at his son.

"Today was a good day," Anthony said, nodding. "Even though, at first, you were a little uptight."

Earl stared at his son. "And I thought you were concentrated only on Kaseem."

"I was. And I wasn't." Anthony looked briefly away.

"What'd you think of'm?"

"Nice guy. But a little too on edge. Sometimes he's a bit much, and there's something eating'm inside."

Earl nodded. The frightening notion occurred to him that this young man was a walking antenna, picking up every signal within his range. How the debacle of Ida and him must have devastated him.

"May I ask you a question, Anthony?"

"You mean, I'm old enough to be asked if I can be asked a question?"

"Don't be cute now." Earl gave Anthony a light right hook to the jaw. "When your mother and I split, one of the things that greatly concerned us was—"

"Me?"

"I—"

"I already— I—" Anthony shrugged.

"You seem to've turned out so—"

"Straight."

"Together is the word I'm looking for. You're calm. You appear to have everything under control. You ace your schoolwork. You're informed. Aware. There don't seem to be any stickers in you. My parents're still together, and I wasn't one-quarter as together as you. How'd you do it? Mirrors?"

Anthony smiled to himself and then looked off, the faint suggestion of a spiritual shadow crossing his face. "They're there—the stickers, as you call'm. I just try not to let'm take over. Like when you guys split up, I was very angry at you, at mom, at me—yeah, me. Then it was, 'Why me?'—you know. 'What'd I do?' Stuff like that. Lotta confusion. Fear. Marks started seesawing. Forgetting things. Walked outa the house with mismatched socks one morning. You shoulda seen me that day, my hands deep in my pockets trying to push my pants down so that the bottoms would stay over my shoes. Hard to do when you're carrying books. I figure, if I ever go off later in my life, that's the form it'll take—mismatched socks.

"But I dealt with it. Came to see your reasons. Mom can be a trip sometimes. Dug myself. Realized it didn't affect your love for me at all. And now I can live with it, although it still hurts when I see you two having words. Things are as they have to be, I guess. Fantasy games in the head got the heave-ho."

Anthony looked at him. "Can I make a suggestion, Dad? If you do this cabin thing, maybe you should have another coupla your students along so that your class won't think you're playing favorites."

"So?" said Dionne later as she caressed Earl's chest. "The two of you blundered into a class kid. Happens."

A drowsiness was creeping into Earl. It was not just from good lovemaking but also from the euphoric release he felt after he had had a nearly perfect day. He was certain, also, if he read the signs correctly, that the same was true for his son and Kaseem.

So teacher and pupil slept soundly that night, heartened by the knowledge that such days do exist in one's lifetime.

CHAPTER 15

Fox was starting to roll a joint. They were standing in a small alleyway behind the handball courts in a schoolyard far across town, far from the piercing, early morning eyes of Spriggs.

Also, the rush hour crowd hadn't really started yet, so those people waiting at bus stops or walking toward the nearby elevated subway were still relatively isolated.

"Do me a favor, man," said Kaseem. "Don't light up. Smells up your clothes'n shit. And I don't wanna be walking in on Mr. Chaney with that all over me."

"Yeah, you right," said Fox, putting his works away. "My teacher's so dumb she wouldn't know the difference."

Kaseem stared at his buddy for a few seconds and then looked down, and shook his head slightly. The gap between them had widened.

"So come on, brother, before somebody comes along," said Fox, doing his slight jerking, knee-bending movements that always signalled a champing at the bit to Kaseem. "You cop or what?"

"I tore the bitch up. Wasn't for me pulling up on her, I'd had me a woman doing the streets for me."

"Yeah. Saw her yesterday. Didn't say nothing. Looked kinda glum. Well, all right!" Fox's palm smashed down on Kaseem's. "Me'n Elva worked a mean taste. Moms almost caught us, too. I hurried up'n got my behind outa there. We definitely got to do that again." Fox guffawed, but Kaseem only managed a wan smile. After the former stopped, he looked down the block impatiently. "Come on, somebody."

"How much time we got before school?"

Fox gave Kaseem a look. "'Bout a hour. Why you ask a question like that?"

"Nothing." Kaseem stretched himself and then, looking off, leaned against the wall.

Fox's eyes returned to the still-empty streets. He scanned them like an eagle studying a field for rabbit movements.

"Look, man," said Kaseem. "I think I'm gonna be chilling on this."

Fox slowly turned to him.

"I'm not down for this anymore. Time to stop. Get into something that counts for something. Start making something of myself. Y'know what I mean? Start looking ahead."

"What kinda shit is this? You letting that goody-goody crap you doing at the school go to your head."

"No, Fox," Kaseem started. "Don't run that on me. Now I set this up—all right?—got you some bread. I can't help it if you piss it away. Now it's time for me to move on. Mr. Chaney's been okay with me. My moms. Other people been off my back, and lemme tell you something, it feels pretty damn good. See, you sneaky. Nobody gives you a hard time 'cause they don't see you. It's me catches it. So don't jump all hinky with me!"

"Who's jumpin' hinky? You jumpin' hinky. You lay this on me, how you expect me to react? Pat you on your nappy head and say, 'Go forth, my son?' Sheeeeit."

"Look, brother man. Don't make me no never mind whether you pat me on my head or not. A new day's coming."

"Aw, who you kiddin'?" Fox said. "You tryin' to make me split my ribs open laughin'?"

"I'm disappointed in your reaction, Fox. I woulda thought you'da been understanding. I thought you was my ace boon coon. 'Stead, you coming up all shaky."

"I'm comin' up shaky! You got balls on you."

"You start raising your voice on me and I walk away from you," Kaseem said. "You can do this all by your lonesome!"

"Now you gettin' your nose bent all outa shape. We was discussin'. Can't we discuss?"

"Not when people three blocks away can hear you."

Suddenly, they were silent. Fox, obviously thrown off balance, stared down the street. A kind of perverse affection for him touched Kaseem.

"Look, man, lemme explain somethin' to you," said Fox, looking away. "I'm not into much. I mean, what I got? Teachers callin' me stupid every day, even when they smilin' at me, which is hardly ever. My moms spreads her legs for every scroungy sucker crawls in, and a old man only comes home to work her over. And cop. You know it's true. I wouldn't lie to you on that. See, it's goin' pretty good for me now. Elva's comin' across. I can buy some threads and herb. And, yeah, I'm saltin' a little bread away. Now lemme clue you in on something case it ain't got across to you yet. Without this, I'm nothin', hear? I ain't no better'n the bent beer cans in my hallway. Now you ain't gonna jack me up with some goddamn moral majority bullshit. You ain't punkin' out on me, homes. I'll scream all over your butt all up and down the street."

Though Kaseem knew it was an idle threat, he acknowledged Fox's feelings. He was, after all, his buddy. He would have to compromise at least.

"All right," he said. "We'll do one more big one after this. Then I'm out. I don't care what you say or think."

"Okay. How about a couple, 'cause I gotta lay the bread on Elva if I'm gonna cop and you probly do, too, on Michellene. Well, maybe not, but come on, at least lemme put some long bread away."

For the first time, the idea of more than one job ahead of him made Kaseem uneasy. Still, he reluctantly agreed.

"All right," exclaimed Fox, slapping Kaseem an enthusiastic five. "And, hey, I promise you I'll—"

Kaseem gestured to Fox, who turned to see an elderly black woman approaching them carrying heavy grocery packages. The youths' eyes swept the area for blocks around. There couldn't have been more than five people out in the street within a three-block radius.

Though she was almost a perfect target, Kaseem was tempted to let her pass. She reminded him too much of his grandmother, which now filled him with strong qualms.

One thing, however, reaffirmed his initial intention.

She was wearing the most expensive-looking gold necklace he'd ever laid eyes on. This made no sense to him at all.

Cautiously checking around them, the two youths decided to follow her to her apartment house. She was obviously out shopping this early in the morning because she deemed it safest. After all, most young people—her most feared enemies—would be on their way to school or just getting up. And there was bound to be some store open somewhere.

She didn't notice them as she climbed the front stairs to the vestibule of the five-story apartment house she lived in.

A block and a half away, three sanitation men were putting the night's garbage into a truck. Two blocks in the opposite direction, a large black woman was walking a small black dog.

The two boys moved up the stairs like lightning and caught their victim in the vestibule while she was struggling with her packages and getting her apartment keys ready. They grabbed her around her frail waist from behind, covered her eyes, and wrenched the necklace from her neck. They raced away amid her screams, and in what seemed like no time at all, they were standing beneath a tree, admiring the necklace's workmanship and wondering what the hell had made the crazy woman wear the thing in the first place. Was she senile already? Didn't she read the newspapers? Who was she trying to impress at that hour in the morning? That dumb pride of elderly people. Or maybe she didn't trust leaving it in the empty apartment.

Something inside Kaseem made him kick the tree trunk several times.

Fox looked at him oddly. "Man, you need to renew your membership at the dee jay."

Halfway to school, Kaseem became aware of a faint discomfort in him, a subtle knot in his stomach. Looking out the bus window, he saw a stern elderly lady glaring at him as the bus passed her. His grandmother? No, she didn't travel this way and she didn't work near here. *Get your head on straight.*

He managed, however, to live with this discomfort the remainder of that day. It helped that Spriggs wasn't around.

During the following evening's rush hour, they went to an underpass at the IND subway line, Forty-Second Street station and loitered, keeping their eyes sharp for any policemen. In their minds, they'd already mapped out what exits to use.

No patrolman showed up, but a young woman, foolishly trying to save time, did. They grabbed her and took her chain from her neck, as well as a few bracelets from her arms. They were through the exit and into a Forty-Second Street movie house before anyone could react.

The next evening, they went to a semi-suburban shopping mall in the East Bronx. Behind the mall was a housing development for the fairly well-to-do, and though it was getting dark, there seemed to be close to a hundred cars in the parking area. Of this, the two boys gave quick and thorough surveillance. There were no police officers around, and only a few men sitting impatiently or sleeping in their cars, scattered throughout, kept the parking lot from being completely empty of people.

So the stately lady they spotted coming out of the jewelry store was practically alone. Why was she advertising that expensive gold necklace? Were these women so arrogant in their wealth that they thought none of the dreadful things they'd read of in the newspapers could ever happen to them?

The two followed her to her car, parked in an isolated area of the parking lot, pounced on her, grabbed the necklace, and raced away, she screaming.

As they dashed through the exit at the far end of the lot, Kaseem glanced back to make sure there were no pursuers.

There were.

A small crowd had formed in what had to be seconds and were close on their tails.

"Oh, shit!" he exclaimed, hitting Fox on his shoulder, and the two increased their speed twofold, cutting into a nearby alleyway, racing its length. When they emerged on the far end, they hailed a gypsy cab after two medallions passed them by and rode back to their neighborhood.

"That was too close for comfort," said Kaseem breathlessly. "That sews it up—that's it."

Fox caught his breath and said, "Brother, you don't have to convince me. Those dudes were so close I coulda reached back and combed one guy's hair."

They went to one of their jeweler-customers to get rid of their booty, which, they were sure, would get them quite a bit of money. It would carry Kaseem a long time, and maybe, if he ran out of money in the future, they might do one or two more jobs, or he might take a job, if there was one available.

Whatever, they were, as of now, retiring from the gold necklace-snatching business. He was not one to press his luck, and he was having an increasingly bad feeling about their activities. He would take the money and run.

They turned the corner and stopped.

In front of the jewelry store, there was a man reading a magazine and glancing around as he leaned against a parked car.

Kaseem cursed to himself. News of the chain snatchings was now widespread. That necessitated more caution. Undoubtedly, this man was a detective casing the jewelry store. There'd been arrests in this area of both snatchers and buyers. They would not be able to get rid of their booty this night.

For a few minutes, they stood at the corner, watching the man. Kaseem hoped that something would happen to pull him away from the car, away from the store, but knew they would do best to return home.

Then the jeweler came out, locked the door, set the burglar alarm, and pulled an iron gate down its front. He locked the gate to its foundation, and the waiting man slapped him on his arm with the magazine before the two men climbed in. Then the car was gone.

"Well, I can't take this shit to my crib," said Fox, somewhat disheartened. "Can't trust nobody there, not even the statue on my mom's dresser."

"Then I'll have to take it home," Kaseem told him, uneasy about this, frowning worriedly, "bring it to school tomorrow'n keep it in my special hiding place. First thing after school, we jump on it."

"Sure nobody'll nose around at home?" asked Fox, staring at Kaseem.

"Fox, this's Kaseem you're talking to."

So Kaseem took the stash home, where he hid it among his folded jockey shorts in the bottom of the dresser drawer. He organized the clothing on top so that there would be no need for anybody in the house to go into his things. His grandmother had recently done the laundry and therefore would not have to go into the drawers for some time. He just needed the night.

Of course, Spriggs would be around.

Earl stayed in his classroom, did his clerical work, read school bulletins, and thought about his inner reality. That debacle in that southern town seemed so far away now, not as hurtful in its recall. Deep down, he felt an inner satisfaction, at one with his sense of purpose and accomplishment. His father would often say to him, "Whatever you choose to do in your life, make sure you do a creditable job of it so that inner voice won't tsk-tsk you to death." And there were times when he'd done just that. When he walked the halls, Earl was egregiously unassuming. He was at rare peace with himself.

Kaseem was determined to show his appreciation to his teacher for the previous Sunday and make up for the evil of his "extracurricular activities." He had upgraded his class work still more from the eighties in his marks to the nineties. He dominated most of his subject classes with correct or near-correct answers, pointed questions, and quality class work. He handed in volumes of extra-credit work in addition. His reading assignments were now completed with amazing comprehension, interest, energy, and thought. He read beyond his assignments as well.

He'd finished *Native Son*, understanding all, except that he'd somehow managed to deny any connection between Bigger Thomas and himself. He looked upon Bigger as a fool who really didn't know what he was doing, for which he deserved to go to the gallows.

He was now reading *Black Boy* and trying his hand at *Julius Caesar*; though most of the latter was incomprehensible to him, he stuck with it and was somehow touched by the character Mark Antony, having lost his "father," Julius Caesar, in the third act.

His classroom behavior was nearly perfect, and other teachers beside Mrs.

Stanton and Mr. Chaney began using him as a monitor. Even the main office occasionally used him to carry various special messages to teachers.

Needless to say, an underlying resentment in Earl's official class students had been growing since he'd taken Kaseem to the basketball game, and the teacher immediately picked it up. Again, the coward inside him prevented him from addressing this problem, but it wouldn't be long before his hand would be forced.

One morning, Earl asked for a monitor who would take his monthly attendance report down to the office. A few hands went up. He chose Maria Saez, the class president, whose preadolescent, movie-star beauty had moved ahead of its elementary school physicality, only now showing early signs of trying to catch up. She took the attendance report and a pass from her teacher and started for the door.

Vinny snickered into his hands at his desk, and the young lady flipped the bird at him before she exited.

"Oooooooh!" responded the class, and Earl looked up from his lesson plan book. He quickly stepped to the door, called Maria back to the room, and then turned to the class.

"Be ready to give a brief oral report on the book you are reading for your book report," he ordered as his eyes scanned the classroom. "You may make notes if you want. In fact, it's strongly suggested. Please don't be unprepared."

He stepped into the hall to the waiting Maria.

"What just happened?" he asked her.

"Nothing," she answered as she averted her eyes.

"Maria."

Meanwhile, Kaseem, quietly studying *Black Boy,* became suddenly aware that he was being watched. He looked up to see Vinny staring at him, a slight smirk on his face. Vinny quickly looked away. Kaseem continued to regard Vinny, who looked back up at him. "Who you looking at?" he said to Kaseem, who continued to stare at him before he resumed with *Black Boy.*

"You think you being funny?" continued Vinny, who turned his whole body toward Kaseem now.

"No problem, man," said Kaseem, looking down at his book. "Peace. Read your book."

"Oooh," went somebody in the class.

Vinny started to stand up. "You come in, take over the class, and now you think you gonna chump me off?"

"Come on, Vinny, lighten up," said Kaseem, furiously groping for a way out of this. "I ain't paying you no mind."

"He dissing you," mumbled another student from the far end of the room.

"Vinny, sit down," said a girl near Vinny, "before you get us all in trouble. He ain't botherin' you. Why you wanna dog'm like that?"

Vinny sat.

Too late.

Earl had returned to the classroom, Maria lingering by the door.

"What's going on?" he asked, which got silence from the class.

"Mr. Chaney, can I say something?" said Maria from the doorway. She stepped inside and closed the door.

Earl gestured for her to speak. He was a little annoyed that this would put his planned lesson off schedule. Something inside him, however, told him that resolving this matter was important if his otherwise good relationship with his class was not to turn into the negative chemistry he'd seen between other teachers and their official classes.

"The class is mad at you," she went on, a faint trace of a Latino accent still in her speech. "We're hurt that you took Kaseem to the basketball game and not any of us who've been with you longer. I mean, haven't we been a good class for you? It seems like Kaseem gets all the monitor jobs and the approval of everybody, and it ain't right."

Earl felt the floor moving under him. Still, he did not let himself look down at his desk, though the impulse to do so was strong. Instead, he fixed his eyes on those of his students.

"I'm sorry, Mr. Chaney," Maria went on. "We understand what you're trying to do, and we support you. Kaseem chose our class, and we're a good class, so he made the right choice. It's just that ... we're hurt, that's all."

"Shoot, I'm not hurt," injected Vinny.

"You need to be quiet, Vinny," Maria said to him. "You the one ran your mouth the most about this."

Earl regarded the young man, now chidden.

Kaseem raised his hand. Earl nodded toward him, and he stood up. "I like this class," he said, gambling with a trump card. "And I would like to stay. But if it means it'll cause trouble for Mr. Chaney, I'll go to another class."

Vinny turned in his seat and gave him a you-gotta-be-kidding-me look.

Maria stepped to the center of the room front. "That's not the point, Kaseem. You've been good for the class. Making us look good. No, we don't want you to leave. We just want more fairness from Mr. Chaney, that's all."

She turned toward her teacher and searched his pensive frown for anger. "Thank you, Maria," he said finally. "Your points're well taken. I made a big mistake in judgment, and I'll now make it my business to make up for it. I plan a weekend at a cabin upstate in the woods. I've already invited Kaseem, and I'll add two more of you to that group. I'm also planning a trip to the Stratford Shakespeare Festival in Connecticut to see *Julius Caesar*. Then, later on, when the summer nears and things really start to get hairy in this school, I'll take you to a Yankees day game. And I promise to distribute the monitorial duties more evenly. How's that?"

The class in general nodded. Vinny just stared at his teacher.

"Problem with that, Vinny?" he asked his student.

Vinny looked around at the rest of the class and just shook his head.

"Is whatever was going on between you and Kaseem before finished?"

"Yes."

Earl turned to his class president. "Thank you, Maria. I know this wasn't easy."

Maria continued with her appointed mission to the general office.

Just after lunch one day, Fox was standing in the corridor talking to a couple of ninth graders when he heard a familiar voice behind him.

"Fox with the 'boks." He didn't have to look to know who it was. It was Spriggs, approaching the small group.

The young man became slightly uptight but maintained enough surface nonchalance to convince himself that his repose was convincing.

"Where *did* you get the mean kicks?" the patrolman asked him. "Florsheims?"

"Aw, man," said Fox. "You raggin' me again, ain't ya?"

"No, I'm just complimenting your sneakers. Don't you know how to take a compliment? How much they run ya?"

"Hundred'n change," Fox answered, looking uneasily around at the others.

"Ooooooweee!" responded Spriggs, who gave Fox a vigorous five. "Some long coins. Where you get that kinda bank? You must work for Rockefeller."

"Appreciate the compliment, Officer Spriggs. Look, I gotta make this social studies class."

"Yeah, you do that little thing, hear?"

Fox turned and, with the other boys, walked away. He didn't want to see Spriggs's eyes following him down the hall."

Earl had entered the school earlier than usual. He wanted to mark some compositions and catch up a little on his pupil attendance figures. Only a custodial helper and a secretary were in the main office.

"Your boy's waiting for you upstairs," said the former to Earl as he clocked in. "I got to give you credit. I leave'm up there by himself and don't even feel nervous about it."

Earl smiled as he proceeded upstairs.

Kaseem immediately went to work on the room as his teacher went down the hall to the bathroom.

The boy quickly checked the corridor and then rushed to the bulletin board corner. He would have to pull out more staples than usual, because the load he had was larger than usual.

He worked quickly, pulling the staples out along the side but leaving them in on the bottom so that the jewelry would not fall through as he shoved it behind the paper. Putting the staples back in took a little more effort, though, because the larger bulges under the construction paper made their purchase more difficult.

He pressed harder on the staples and then, hearing his teacher's returning footsteps, stepped back to look at the spot. Yes, the bulge was there, but unless one were looking specifically for something at that spot or scrutinizing the area, one would not notice it.

No, won't work, he thought with panic as he quickly grabbed the jewelry and jammed it into his pocket, covering it over with tissues.

Then, fearing Officer Spriggs coming by, he took the jewelry out of his pocket again and looked around. He spotted a large photo of Langston Hughes near the rear window!

He darted to it and carefully pulled the staples out of the right side of the frame, the window side. Jamming the jewelry into the slim space, he kept his back to the front of the room and pushed the staples back in. It worked! There was no tell-tale lump and nobody messed with the honored poet.

He glimpsed Spriggs pointing a warning finger at some student he had pushed against the front gate.

Mr. Chaney entered the classroom and went straight to his desk. He glanced at his industrious monitor, smiled, and plunged into the stack of compositions. He worked as diligently as he could on the largely error-ridden, poorly thought-through essays—some of the penmanship almost indecipherable—but his enemy time brought him under.

Even his determination to get at least half of them done was frustrated.

Ingram walked into the classroom then.

The latter looked at Earl and the stack of compositions with a look of exaggerated amazement on his face and then turned toward the busy monitor, still working near the rear bulletin board. Bogus disbelief jumped onto his face that then went blank.

"Mr. Chaney," he said earnestly. "May I borrow your monitor a sec?"

Earl gestured toward Kaseem. "You don't mind, do you?"

The boy looked at Mr. Ingram, hesitated an imperceptible second, and then, nodding his head, walked toward him. The two disappeared from the room.

Earl had gotten halfway through one more composition before Ingram returned and sat in one of the pupil's desks near his.

"I let'm take over the room, fix things up. You don't need'm anymore. Your room's standing tall," he said, looking around the classroom before his eyes settled on Earl in a long scrutiny.

"The miracle worker," Ingram announced. "But to what end? Will it increase your lousy salary? Will the public appreciate you more? And who's to say he'll keep up this level of behavior with the next teacher? Then again, maybe you don't mind your efforts flowing into the wastebasket. Because that's where they're going come June, Pilgrim. Right into the wastebasket along with last year's compositions. Look, you know Rako wants to get rid of'm, and he's eventually going to have his way first time the kid slips up. Hanley just wants you to keep'm out of his hair while he slithers upward to the higher ranks. And next year there you'll be, playing with little numbers in little boxes in still another roll book. Now tell me what I say isn't true."

Rankled, Earl stared at him.

"My god," Ingram continued. "I've popped your balloon. We will now hear from the chastened miracle worker."

Earl was about to open his mouth when the morning bell rang.

"Ah," said Ingram. "Posts. To our cages to await the arrival of our lions."

It was then that the idea hit Earl.

After the morning ceremonies, Kaseem, who had found Mr. Ingram's "little chores" much more than described and took more than 'a sec', accepted the teacher's thanks expressionlessly and started back to his classroom. He spotted Michellene down the hall and stopped for a moment to watch her. Because she didn't see him, she went into her classroom. When, his heart now pounding, he then turned to enter his own classroom, he noticed Vinny wandering around the room, talking to a few pupil clusters and glancing at him with the most peculiar kind of mockery in his eyes. How much did he know about that Saturday night?

He ambled over to the rear of his classroom to check the photo of Langston Hughes.

He stiffened.

Two shafts of ice stabbed his eyes and nuked his insides.

The staples had been pulled off the frame so that the whole side frame was ajar. Something squeezed his neck.

Then the first period bell rang.

His ears hot, he began to breathe with some difficulty as he inched closer to the photo. The class was now lining up, and Mr. Chaney headed for the hall.

The space behind the photo was empty. Thumb-tacked there was an unsigned note, obviously hastily written, saying, "Sucker!" Panicked, he turned and furtively eyed the remainder of the class as they filed out. He saw no one he could suspect.

Mr. Chaney looked in. "Don't you think you'd better get going?" he said to the staggered youth. "You don't want to be late for your first class."

"Right," said Kaseem, clumsily gathering his books together.

"Something wrong?" asked the teacher as Kaseem passed him.

The young man turned awkwardly to him. He was now almost choking as he squirmed slightly under his teacher's gaze.

"No," he squeezed out and proceeded to class.

CHAPTER 16

Fox saw Kaseem's blazing eyes as he approached him in the pupil's cafeteria.

"What happened?" he asked as the other pulled him to an isolated corner behind one of the cafeteria's six columns.

"The stash is gone! Some scurvy sonovabitch racked it on us! Left this!"

He handed the note to the dumbfounded Fox, who read it and then glanced confusedly at his buddy.

"Wait, wait a sec," Fox stammered breathlessly. "Hold up here. What the fuck is going on?"

"I just told you, man. Somebody discovered my hiding place. The jewelry's been stolen!"

Fox stared at Kaseem. He began to tremble slightly as he pointed a threatening finger. "Don't play with me."

"I look like I'm playing with you?"

Fox grabbed him by his shirt.

"You'd better get your hands offa me. You crazy or something? Get'm off me, hear?"

A teacher came over and said, "Problem here?"

Fox released Kaseem, who turned to the teacher and smiled toothily. "Everything's cool. Real chilly. No problem."

"Doesn't look like it," commented the teacher, eyeing both of them.

"No, really," Kaseem said. "Fox here was scooping me on something. Something he saw outside. Officer Spriggs and somebody."

The man placed a gentle hand on Kaseem's elbow and suggested that they return to their seats.

The two boys complied.

Kaseem turned to say something to Fox, but the latter had stalked off. He sighed and walked to his class's table, glancing briefly at Vinny, whose eyes appeared to have just moved away from him.

At lunch dismissal, he bumped into Michellene in the basement corridor. The two eyed each other momentarily.

"Look, Michellene. I'm sorry about that night," he said, clearing his throat.

"You wanna get outa my face," she said, averting her eyes and walking off.

Kaseem watched her and then turned around. Fox was behind him, still grim-faced. "You'n me got more work to do," he said.

———

As he tried to slough off Kaseem's strange mood—perhaps it would improve before his class came to him later that day—Earl went first to Mr. Rako and then to Mr. Hanley, who said he'd think about the nomination.

Ingram said it was a good idea, though he seemed to be sucking on a mouthful of mud at the time.

To think, "The Most Improved Student" Award to Kaseem Wilson.

———

Kaseem glowered as he sat in Mrs. Stanton's classroom. He seemed far away. This did not go unnoticed by Mrs. Stanton, though she tried to proceed with the lesson, as if nothing were different on this day. Things had been going fairly well for her at home. She had not been so angry with her husband, and her hostile attitudes toward the students had mellowed considerably. Her life had become more livable, and for this, she partially credited Kaseem's turnaround. So, with this consideration, she decided to try to pull the sulking youth into the lesson.

"Kaseem?" she asked nervously. "What is your opinion of the Carter presidency so far?"

The young man didn't respond.

She decided to leave him alone and go on to another student, who gave an evaluation considerably inferior, she knew, to the one Kaseem would've given.

Later in the lesson, she tried again with the same result.

"Kaseem, would you stop a moment after class?" she said. "I'd like to speak with you."

"Oooooh," went the class before her baleful look stopped them.

Surly, he ambled up to her desk after class. His class had gone on to their official teacher for English. The corridor was emptying.

"Is there anything the matter, Kaseem?" she asked.

He fixed his eyes on a chalkboard spot and said nothing.

"Well, all right, I guess you'd rather not talk about it. Do you think you could be a monitor for me this afternoon after school?"

"No."

Abashed, she gazed at him.

"Later this week?"

"No," he said again.

"Well, I guess that's it then," she said embarrassed.

"Can I go to my class now? I'm missing work."

"No, we don't want to miss that, do we?"

He walked to the door.

"Wait," she said, taking out a piece of paper and writing on it. "You'll need a pass, won't you?"

He stood facing the door.

"Obviously, something terrible has happened," she said. "If there's anything I can do to help—"

He left but returned a second later, stepping to the side of the doorway and looking down. "Look, I'm sorry about last period," he mumbled. "Something did happen. Don't worry about it, though. I'll deal with it."

"Good luck," she said as he walked out of the classroom again and started toward Mr. Chaney's room.

He stopped and ducked behind the narrow strip of wall between the corridor dividing swinging doors.

Michellene was far down the hall ahead of him, near Mr. Chaney's room. She stopped in front of his rear door and tapped lightly on the window. Then she gestured for someone inside to come out before she ducked into the stairwell.

Kaseem waited a moment and then saw Vinny come out of the classroom with a pass. Jolted slightly, he watched him also enter the stairwell. He knew where they were going.

There was a basement landing on this stairway, whose exit doors were chained shut to keep intruders out. Because there was thus no need for a patrol in this area, it was a perfect spot for "making out" during classes, a kind of lover's landing.

He rushed by Mr. Chaney's room, hunkering down so that he couldn't be seen through the door windows, and stealthily slipped into the stairwell. Fortunately, there was no movement at all in the halls and stairwells; any patrolling teachers would be near the trouble spots in other parts of the building.

Immediately, he heard the *sotto voce* giggling, punctuated by long silences, as he crept down the stairs. When he got almost to the first floor, he leaned slightly over the banister and saw them locked in a tight embrace, their lips melting torridly into each other. A bitter flame burst in his stomach, but he strained to maintain his control.

He moved closer. Though they whispered to each other, he was able to make out words hinting at some great time they would soon be having.

When he returned to class, Mr. Chaney was approaching the middle of the lesson. As he proceeded to his seat, he could feel his teacher's eyes on him.

"We were just talking about the difference between the simile and the metaphor in both prose and poetry," the teacher said to him. "I'm sure you'll catch up with us." He glanced at the pass in his hand and tossed it into the wastepaper basket.

As Kaseem trailed his class out of the room at the end of the period, Mr. Chaney said to him, "Whatever it is, worse'll happen in your life ... and better."

The boy managed a smile and proceeded to his next class.

Earl went to Mr. Rako to check on the progress of his "most improved student" idea. He knew some morale fortification for the youth was in order.

"Look, I wouldn't count on it," said the administrator. "We have some full programs coming up in assembly. Other problems to deal with."

"This'll take five minutes of assembly time at most," Earl insisted. "And it'll serve as an example for others."

Clenching his jaws, at a loss for an answer, Rako looked off.

"I'll do all the work," Earl continued. "All you have to do is sign it and present it if Mr. Hansen can't. Look, you got me into this. Now help me do the job."

"I didn't get you into this," said Rako resentfully. " Don't pressure me."

The teacher looked at the administrator, whose laziness, inaction, and belligerence he despised, tolerating these as long as they were kept away from the students. Then he reproached himself for being so self-righteous.

"You'll handle it?" said Rako, staring down at a paper on his desk.

"Yes." Earl pressed his lips together and gazed at the administrator.

The latter crumbled up a piece of paper and threw it into the wastepaper basket. "I don't want to know from nothing," he said, turning and returning Earl's gaze. "They have me whirling like a dervish with these assembly programs and special visits from educator hotshots Getting some of these teachers to turn in stuff on time—you get yours in but some of these bozos…."

"You won't miss a step," answered Earl, one of the "bozos."

He met less resistance from Mr. Hanley.

That evening, Kaseem and Fox had mugged three women and a sixth grader and sold the booty.

"No more," he said to Fox. "I've had it."

"Don't have the stomach for it no more, right?"

As he jabbed his pressed together fingers toward Fox's face, Kaseem whirled on him. "You keep it up, hear! Keep it up!"

"Get your fingers out my face, Homes. What's up with you? All hyper'n shit."

"Just get off my case! I ain't Silver, and you ain't the mothafuckin' Lone Ranger! Now let's divvy this fuckin' bread up so I can get home. Some of us got things to do."

"If I'da knowed you'd act like this. Forget you."

Earl was slightly manic as he returned to the coffee shop booth and Dionne. He rubbed his hands together eagerly as he sat and eyed her voraciously. "All set up," he said. "There'll be four city rats in the upstate woods less than a month from now." Though she smiled back empathically, there was reserve in her.

He caught the reserve and turned to his menu. He wasn't going to get dashed with any of her quibbling this evening. That Sunday had been a great success. No, it was not likely that would be duplicated—it never was—but it could possibly be even better. Who knew? The point was that he was doing something, and in doing it, he was going beyond what most of his colleagues would do. And Kaseem was showing the results of that. Who would or could argue with that?

Moreover, he was back on track with his class.

A weekend in the woods in Monroe, New York, with his son and two students. This would give them the healthy air they all needed. It would afford them the male camaraderie, bivouacking while they did male, woodsy things. There would have to be the parent-consent slips and long telephone conversations.

Dionne would have been a lovely addition to this, but it was an addition that brought with it complications he was not yet ready to deal with. He would think about that. Whatever, surely, it would finish the job of turning Kaseem around.

The waitress, a pretty redhead of middle years, took their orders. Earl put on some music, played low, a disco version of "The Chorale" from Beethoven's *Ninth Symphony* that, in that modest diner, considerably above a greasy spoon, did not seem out of place.

They toasted with the glasses of water the waitress had left and sipped as they locked eyes. Then Dionne put her half-emptied glass down and placed her hand on his.

"Darling," she said, the soft magenta coffeehouse lights seeming to highlight the brownish glow of her skin. "I understand where you're coming from, and I love you deeply for it. I think it's beautiful what you're doing for that boy. But sometimes things go whack."

"Hey," he said with slight testiness. "I have a life full of things going whack on me. Don't you think I would've developed a set of reflexes by now? Please. Don't cloud my head with negativisms."

"I'm not poking pins in your balloon. I'm just saying you've got a lot to offer us. Don't throw all your irons in one basket and not make provisions for anything else, because if the basket falls apart on you, the rest of us're put in a trick."

"I hear you," he said, squeezing her hand. "I didn't mean to get touchy on you."

"I'm uptight, too. I'd rather we went to a movie tonight or just to bed."

"Great idea," he said.

"Which? The movie? Or bed?"

"Both."

"Good answer. You know what I'd like? I'd like to get married. Give Anthony a sibling." She bit her lip for having let that out.

He gaped at her. "Where'd that come from?"

"I don't know. Scratch it. We have to go to this meeting, right? I guess fulfilling moral obligation's not too bad as long as it doesn't intrude on our misbehaving *all* the time."

Shehab's face dropped when his eyes fell on Dionne entering the hall; then he smiled. He looked through Earl, though he nodded.

The hall was less full than usual—attendance was dropping—but the same number of baleful guards formed a perimeter around the hall. They folded their arms, making their forearms seem thicker, more rippled, and scowled at everybody.

"All right," Shehab said after a few flat introductory witticisms. "We're at the same point as last week. I need candidates to run against me. At least one. If we're to get any legitimacy, we must have an election so we can begin with a viable program. Are there any nominations?"

Dionne leaned not too closely to Earl and whispered not too softly, "He's praying there'll be no candidates, because he really doesn't want the trouble of an election."

Shehab gave her a sidelong glance.

Earl put his finger over his lips to shush her.

"Why don't you let me nominate you?" she said to him.

"No way."

"Excuse me, Dionne," said Shehab. "Did you say something?"

"I was talking to my friend," she snapped boldly. "Or is that prohibited now?"

"I must ask you please not to carry on little secret conspiratory conversations."

"You trying to say I'm afraid of you and your thugs?" she said.

"You got something to say, let us all hear it," he said, a strained calm in his voice.

"Don't try to make me look like I'm ducking from you with your phony laid-back grandstanding."

"See, folks, that's why we have to have an election," he said. "There're too many malcontents waiting on the sidelines to—"

"Excuse me?" Dionne stood up. "Are you trying to say I'm a malcontent? And talk to *me*. Don't talk about me to this audience, as if I'm somewhere else."

Earl anxiously pulled on her sleeve. One of the guards had started moving in their direction, but Shehab waved him off. The others remained still.

"Why're we going through this?" Shehab half-pleaded.

"Because I'm sick to my stomach of you paper leaders with your schemes and your mouth and your carelessness with people's time and hard-earned money."

"You keep coming back," Shehab pleaded.

"I never learn. I keep hoping." She leaned on the seat in front of her.

Shehab stared at her. "Peace, sister. We got too much to do to be wasting our time and energy wrangling with each other. There're other issues and matters that should concern us. Wouldn't you agree?"

"No, you're not gonna put me in a box with your equivocating oily charm."

"Then what is your beef?" He tensed, knowing the answer coming to him.

"You know what my beef is," she returned, her voice a wolf's warning growl. "It's an issue standing between us plain as the nose on your face."

"What the sister's referring to is Brother Ignatius and his foolish attempt to co-opt the integrity of this organization."

"You're doing it again," she said. "I don't need you to interpret me to the meeting here. Anything to hold onto control, right, Shehab?"

"Tell it, sister," came from the far end of the hall. The security guards looked around, spotting no one.

"Dionne! Try contributing, huh? Don't destroy. We have enough forces out there *destroying.* All I'm asking you to do is show you're on the right side by taking a step forward."

Dionne took a deep breath. "All right, I'll take that right step forward. I nominate Earl Chaney to run for president."

One part of Earl knew it was coming, but most of him was still caught off guard.

"I decline," he said, disappointed at what he finally heard himself say yet knowing that no other response would come from him. He cleared his throat.

Shehab's eyes moved to him with a mixture of faint surprise and condescension. Already, all the guards' eyes were on him.

"Our in-house educator. Brother, er ... Earl Chaney. Your lady friend obviously thinks a great deal of you. She thinks you could be of great help to our organization. Now why do you want to disappoint that trust by turning us down?"

"I'm sorry," she whispered to Earl. "He cornered me on that one."

"I have limited time, energy, and resources, that's all," he said to the meeting. "Nothing personal. This would require a lot of me that I don't have to give."

A guard whispered something to Shehab.

"Please," said Dionne, her eyes blazing, as she placed her hand on his. "For me."

"I just learned," said Shehab, half-announcing to the audience, "that you were a participant in the Civil Rights marches down South. You would be of tremendous help to us. Your experience, knowledge. Come on, man."

"You're doing just what he wants by refusing," Dionne said.

"I have to," he said, now racked with self-loathing.

The couple was silent all the way to her house. He knew a big blowout was coming but not what the consequences of it would be. Still, he both hoped for one and dreaded it.

She went right into the bathroom and definitively closed the door. Momentarily, he stood in the foyer, not sure what to do with himself. *No movie, no nooky tonight.* At length, he acknowledged that she'd been in there an inordinately long time. Leaving seemed his best recourse.

He walked to the bathroom door. "Look, I'm going. Lock the door."

When he reached the front door, he heard the bathroom door open behind him. He briefly closed his eyes with dread and turned to see, thrust through the opening, her mask of outrage, glaring at him.

"You're unreal," she said and repeated it. "You're going to go just like that."

As he felt his annoyance swelling, he stepped toward her. "You know, I would've appreciated a little warning tonight. A little consideration. Fairness. Maybe ask my permission to throw my name into that cauldron the way you did. Give me a chance to get my bearings."

She continued to gape at him as she came out of the bathroom. Her eyeliner had run, but he wasn't sure if it was the result of crying or cleaning her face. "All right, I apologize. *Mea culpa.*"

"Don't do me any favors," he responded, exasperated.

"There's no issue between us that needs dealing with?" she pressed. "Maybe it's not really that important, right?"

"Now you're trying the tactics you accuse Shehab of using."

"Hey! Don't try it, hear? Don't even try it. You know what the score is. And, knowing that, you're willing to let this greatly needed organization fall into the hands of that sociopolitical pimp."

"I don't owe anybody anything," he said.

"You're right. You don't. So good-bye."

He walked to the door, paused a moment, and then turned. "All this because I wouldn't jump into that mess."

"You could clear up that mess."

"How can I with the little time I have?"

"Uh-uh, sweetie. Don't try that either. You make time. Like you're making time for that boy. You sure made your time to work your way into my pants. You made time for those marches. And you're no more busy now than you were then."

"You know, you're very selfish. *You!*" he said, taking a step toward her. " That's who you're concerned with! The question is ... what bug is up your ass about this Black Resurrection thing? That you're willing to toss me into it. You get something on with Brother Iggy? And this's payback time?"

"For an educated man, you can sometimes be a total asshole, you know that?"

"What's my education got to do with it? I'm an asshole with or without it. When I was playing musical chairs in kindergarten, I was already an asshole. It may come as a surprise to you that my education has had very little to do with the way my life has turned out."

"Listen," she started. "I'm thinking of that woman with the wart on her neck and run over shoes and wig that's not on right who drags her butt up there to that meeting after a horrendous day, looking for something to work herself up about besides that reward in the future. I'm thinking of an organization that has the potential to give her that, to do something substantial in these bleak times, and that we'll more than likely blow the opportunity. I'm thinking of you ... with your deep unhappiness that I can't seem to do anything about, your crying need to do something like this to save yourself."

"I don't need to save myself, thank you." He straightened up, indignant.

"Darling, you sleep with somebody enough times, after a while you get to know the hell's going on inside him."

"That so?" he said.

"Yes, and rehabilitating Kaseem is not enough."

That last had found its mark and stung profoundly. Reeling inside, he marched to the door.

"What happened to you down South?"

A tremor rolled through the floor under him. "What do you mean?"

"Something happened to you down there, and it's been sitting on your guts ever since."

He stared at her for a few seconds. "You know what your trouble is," he said. "You're still looking for your husband Georgie Boy to return to your bed. Well, I'm sorry. I can't fit the bill."

"There's not even any oomph when you try to be vicious," she said. "All you do is come off looking off-the-wall and stupid. It's such a pity that such a beautiful man has to be trapped inside such a great big baby."

"One more reason why I should decline, isn't it? After all, do we want that wart-necked lady's dreams tied up in the bunglings of such a great big baby?"

With that, he left.

———

The phone was ringing as he was walking through his front door. He hesitated before he answered it. It was Dionne, curt, business-like. "If you have a woman with you, get rid of her. I'm coming over."

After lovemaking, she laid her head on his chest, her hair redolent with lavender hair spray and perspiration. For a long time, they were silent.

"Every now and then," she said finally, "this noggin of mine gets a notion, and I get carried away. One of these centuries, I'll grow up, but in the meantime, please be patient with me."

"If you promise to be patient with me," he said, peace now inside him.

"If you promise to listen to my Oscar-winning life story."

"You don't have to do that."

"Hush," she purred. "You must listen while the listening's good. You must not say a word. I'm asking you to do what I don't do very well—listen. Then, hopefully, you'll emerge with a deeper understanding of me, which, by the way, I myself don't have."

She paused, and he could feel her heartbeat quicken.

"Once upon a time in the land of skyscrapers, there lived a little girl named Dionne," she started. "Now this little girl had a husband—you know who—she was very much in love with. Are you with me so far? Well, you know who, Georgie Boy as you called'm, was an up-and-coming lawyer in a large, very prestigious, very lily white law firm. That he might've been the token nigger never entered his mind. Never dared. We lived … nice. High-rise co-op like *The Jeffersons*. Orchestra seats. Monk's Inn for after-show onion soup. And no children to hamper us. Then things happened. He woke up one morning and made the terrible discovery that he hadn't made any progress at all at the firm. And I lost the baby my fifth month."

"So suddenly he's not a man anymore," Earl commented.

"You got it. Boy, you know the territory well, don't you? The arguments about this'n that. The touchiness about everything."

"The waiter forgets to bring the breadsticks, it's part of a grand conspiracy," Earl quipped.

"And it got to be much. I was starting to get headaches for days. Then one day, to avoid paying a fine and messing with our very tight budget, I returned a library book he hadn't finished. Well, what'd I do that for? He went off. We ceased being a couple and became two vicious mouths. And when the smoke cleared, I was by my lonesome.

"Now it was my turn to go off—liquor, pills, sleeping around. Then King was killed, and I was suddenly awake. You know, how the worst part of your nightmare wakes you up. Got straight. Went back to school. Took courses in self-organization, editing, and administration at The New School. Met Rex, the great ambitious black leader of the future. He opened my nose. I inhaled deeply. He wanted to take over and lead the masses in a new movement. I taught'm all I knew about leadership, organization, proper planning, use of personnel, resources, and the designing of needed programs. I helped'm set up his agenda and kept his fingers on the rank and file pulse.

"So when he's made chairman of the National Conference of Equality, what does he do? He appoints some hussy as his running mate, a Ruby Wall, because of the intraorganizational political power she could bring with her. A sorry number with big tits who chewed gum with all her teeth showing. And saliva, to boot."

"Now, now," Earl said.

"There's more," she continued. "Rumor had it they'd had a closer than political relationship behind my back. When I confronted'm with it, he tried to hand me some bullshit about the existential imperative, faith, and political expedience. Cliches, the refuge of the sleazebag. Well, one thing was proven. I didn't have to fall to pieces again. I was stronger."

She paused thoughtfully.

"It bugs me that integrity and class have slipped off somewhere hiding out. We've got all these accumulating perils around us, gathering forces, and steam, and all we've got to reach out for are tiny flickering candles inside dingy lanterns instead of beacons for when the ride gets bumpy. What hurts so much is that they're there, those beacons, but they're not coming forth."

Then they were silent.

"I heard what you said," he said finally, "but I still decline."

She didn't move off him.

CHAPTER 17

Days later, inside a brightly lit apartment, Officer Spriggs took out a small class photo and handed it to the elderly black lady sitting across from him at her living room table. It was a photo of Mrs. Reinking's official class and had a picture of Kaseem in it, standing in the back row.

Two detectives stood by the hallway leading to the kitchen, from which a short, thin, brown-skinned young man emerged with two cups of tea, handing the men one each. They sipped concentratedly as they watched her study the photo. Spriggs had turned down a cup. He only studied the woman's face, as if he were looking through a microscope.

She frowned, twitched slightly, and then handed the photo back to Spriggs. "Sorry for taking up your time," she said. "I hear so much about these young boys getting railroaded into jail because they look like somebody. All our boys seem to look like somebody, y'know. I just don't know."

"Shouldn'ta worn it, Gran," said the man.

"What you mean I shouldn'ta worn it?" she snapped. "Was given me by your father, wasn't it? Before he went off to that awful war in Korea and got killed? He wanted me to wear it in dignity. And that's what I did. Wicked children. I'm telling you. All right, it's gone now. But if Wesley come up outa the grave today and give me another one, I'd wear it in the street tomorrow."

Spriggs put the photo away and gave her one more glance before he thanked her and left with his partners. Her face had answered a lot of questions for him when she looked at that photo.

Thank God for Mr. Chaney

Earlier that day, Kaseem had been studying Vinny all morning. Though his fury lingered, he was thinking more clearly now, and he was more observant. Little things took on greater significance for him—the suppressed smile, the discreet distance Vinny now kept between them, the eyes that once stared boldly and now averted whenever they met Kaseem's, and, most significantly, the nonchalant stroll by the bulletin board spot during homeroom, after which he glanced around uneasily to see if Kaseem was watching. This last, of course, Kaseem observed with his peripheral vision, which he had developed playing basketball. The surveillance continued into math class. At one point, tired of studying the back of Vinny's head, Kaseem inadvertently let his eyes drop to his shoes—brand new, expensive, obviously imported nylon and polyurethane running shoes—and he went into a quiet rage.

At length, his glare turned into scheming watchfulness. He noted, during the afternoon homeroom period, that Vinny hid his textbooks in one of the rear cabinets, where they would stay until the next day. As he watched his foe, his mind was already formulating a plan.

The boys' gym locker room inadequately served its purpose. A single teacher had to patrol it to make sure as many of the rules as possible were followed. Despite gym being a double period, there were simply no facilities or time for the boys to shower, so a quick and thorough wipe-off followed by heavy applications of cologne or deodorant (those who had them) were in order. Naturally, the classrooms to which these boys went after gym had somewhat game atmospheres.

Moreover, many locker doors were either almost off their hinges or bent from karate chops, so they didn't open or close properly. Combination locks and much prayer were used. Yet, the number of thefts was surprisingly low.

The energies were used in other ways. The din was murderously high, the hijinks never-ending (constant running back and forth, with towels snapping in the air and on many behinds like miniature whips), and there were the many cliques forming for this or that matter. The teacher who drew this patrol assignment (usually low man on the tenure totem pole) earned his salary there alone. Still, few major disasters occurred.

Kaseem, having dressed very quickly, strolled down the aisle, surveying the empty or very busy rows of T-shirts, bare, skinny torsos, and textbooks stacked carelessly on the benches in front of the lockers. He always trusted his improvisatory sense, that his reflexes would make the right moves should the correct opportunity arise.

It arose.

He spotted a locker of one of his ex-classmates, Mario, carelessly left open and unattended, the books stacked on the bench next to his sneakers. The row was empty, and everyone else seemed to be involved in some aspect of the surrounding chaos.

He slipped into the row ,and there on the locker door hook was the gold chain he'd often seen on Mario. In a flash, the chain was off the hook and in his pocket, after which he continued up the aisle, upstairs, and out to the corridor for his next class.

He'd had math earlier that morning, and just before gym, he had seen Vinny shove his rather large math textbook into one of their official room's rear cabinets, closing the door. It was one of the many cabinets in the school whose lock was either broken or nonexistent. The custodial helper would "get to it someday."

Kaseem's mission was to get up to the room before Mr. Chaney's subject class got there.

Sure enough, the room was empty, and Mr. Ingram was bending Mr. Chaney's ears. Though he was still glancing around to make sure he wasn't being observed by anyone, Kaseem quickly slipped into the room to his destination. He pulled the cabinet door open and saw the large math book with a few of Vinny's other textbooks. Stooping, he produced Mario's necklace and placed it between the pages somewhere in the algebra section, which the class had been working on at that point in the semester. It was scarcely noticeable. He closed the door and slipped back out of the class just as Mr. Chaney's subject class was arriving on the floor.

During the next class, social studies, he wrote a note with his nonwriting hand: "I saw Vinny put a gold chain in one of his textbooks." He placed the note into his shirt pocket and joyfully focused his attention on Mrs. Stanton.

Just at that moment, Spriggs looked in, and Mario's face appeared at the rear door window. Mario was a mixture of Italian and Cuban with a pale, ashen face and shining black hair. When Mrs. Stanton asked what the problem was, the officer informed her that Mario had lost a fairly expensive gold chain. She clucked and shook her head. "Why do they wear them to school?" she asked rhetorically.

He merely shrugged his shoulders.

She walked to the door and conversed with Spriggs, her back to the class. Kaseem could see Spriggs explaining something to her as a low murmur started up in the class. Suddenly, Mario appeared in the front of the room and joined the conference. The young man was obviously shaken.

Then Spriggs's eyes fell on Kaseem. He whispered something to Mrs. Stanton, who looked at the young man, turned to the policeman, and shook her head. She said something to him, which obviously dissuaded him from what appeared to be suspicion. She turned to look at Kaseem again and said something else to the policeman, who nodded and left with Mario.

Mrs. Stanton turned to the class and told them what had happened to Mario and that they were touring all the classes that had been in the gym with his earlier that day.

After, Kaseem stopped by her in the hall. "What'd Officer Spriggs say about me before?" he asked her.

"He asked how you've been in my class. I told'm how horrific you are. How you're driving me into an institution."

Kaseem smiled and looked down. "He did suspect me though, didn't he?" the youth asked.

"He did," she said, now more serious. "But after I spoke to'm, he thought differently."

In language arts, Kaseem volunteered to go downstairs to the general office to pick up Mr. Chaney's mail.

"That's a very good suggestion," said the teacher as he wrote out a special pass.

Vinny raised his hand. "Mr. Chaney, you're doing it again. You're letting Kaseem do everything for you and don't give nobody else a chance."

Kaseem tensed.

Maria Saez turned to Vinny. "No, Vinny, you're wrong this time. It's better, and you know it. You're wrong."

The teacher regarded Vinny for a few seconds. Then he smiled and shrugged his shoulders. "If you still feel that, I'm sorry. Of course, someone else could have volunteered. You have but to say the word, and the job is yours. But I can't read minds. Thank you for bringing that to my attention though. I'll take it under advisement and correct it ... if you're correct."

Kaseem was still frozen at the door, staring at Vinny. "Don't make me no difference, hey," he said. "You wanna go on the next ten errands, be my guest. Won't find me whimpering like no baby. You wanna go on this one?"

"Naw, bro," responded Vinny offhandedly. "Your gig, y'understand what I'm sayin'?"

Kaseem went quickly to the general office, showed his pass to one of the secretaries, and then went to the staff mailboxes. After he pulled Mr. Chaney's mail from his box, he looked around to see if anyone was watching him. The office staff was too busy with its own pressing duties to pay any attention to him, so he pulled the hand-written note from his shirt pocket and, holding it with a tissue, slipped it into the mailbox provided for Officer Spriggs.

He blew his nose and returned to his class.

Dismissal time was usually pandemonium. The all-day-pent-up energy exploded in all areas, the din almost unbearable, and the hijinks often got out of hand. The school managed to empty out, however, with a reasonable amount of order.

Mr. Chaney's official class maintained its customary orderliness. They had to if they were to get out in a reasonable time.

They had just gotten on line—the other classes on the floor headed for the staircases—when Spriggs and Mario appeared at the classroom door.

It was Spriggs's second visit to Mr. Chaney's classroom that day, so immediately, the teacher became concerned. Kaseem maintained an icy nonchalance.

"I'm sorry, Mr. Chaney," the officer said to the teacher, "but I'm gonna have to hold your class for a short while."

The students exploded in a symphony of protests, but Mr. Chaney immediately quieted them.

"Can I see everybody's notebooks?" said Spriggs.

A low murmur and a few subdued moans emanated from the pupils.

"All right, everybody," said Mr. Chaney, a slight edge to his voice. "Just do as he says."

The officer was quick but thorough as he went down the boys' line first. When he got to Vinny, he noted that the youth had only his notebook and one small science textbook.

"How do you do your homework?" Mr. Chaney asked, looking over Spriggs's shoulder.

Spriggs turned to him and said, "You don't know? You get a drop of water, sprinkle on some baking powder, stir, stick it in the oven. You wake up in the morning and—presto!--all the homework's there, ready to take to school."

"I see," said Mr. Chaney, nodding as if enlightened.

"Where're the rest of your books?" Spriggs asked Vinny.

"In one of those rear cabinets, I suspect," said Mr. Chaney. "Fewer books to lug home, you know."

"Language arts book? Math book? Social studies?" Spriggs commented.

Mr. Chaney was now embarrassed. "Well, Vinny?" he said.

"I left'em home by mistake," answered Vinny, looking down

"Then how'd you do your class work?" asked the officer.

Now the whole class was silent as a scowl crept into the teacher's eyes.

"I think you know what I want you to do," said Mr. Chaney with ominous calm.

Vinny nodded and walked to the rear of the classroom, where he opened a cabinet door and retrieved his textbooks.

"Bring'm up here'n put'm on this desk," said Spriggs, gesturing toward a front desk as he removed the chair from its top.

Vinny looked puzzled at the desktop and then the policeman. "Hey, wait a minute. Hold up," he protested. "You're not putting his missing gold chain on me."

Spriggs turned to Mario. "You see'm anywhere near your locker today?"

Mario, now frightened, his eyes widened, shrugged his shoulders. "I seen a lotta guys near my locker. I dunno."

His face a blank, Kaseem inched back away from them. He held his breath.

"Well, let's see," said the officer as he began slowly going through the books while Mr. Chaney warned that there had better not be another book in that rear cabinet or any other rear cabinet, making one other student race to a cabinet to retrieve his science book. Suddenly, Spriggs held Vinny's math book up in a strange way, saying, "Hey, what's this?" as a gold chain dropped from its pages into his free hand.

The class exclaimed. Mr. Chaney stared at the chain. Vinny was flabbergasted.

Spriggs turned to Mario. "This it?"

Mario nodded and looked down.

"You gotta be kidding!" shouted Vinny, tears now in his eyes. "This's some kind of damn frame-up!"

"Better cool your role, youngblood," warned the policeman. "Right now, you standing on banana peels."

"But I didn't. Jesus Christ! Can I call my folks?" He looked at the expressionless Kaseem. Spriggs glanced at him as well.

"You'd better," he said finally to Vinny.

A stunned Mr. Chaney took his now-subdued class downstairs for dismissal.

He immediately rushed to Mr. Hanley's office, where Spriggs, Mr. Rako, and the principal were hovering over the now-frightened young man.

"And we're supposed to believe," Spriggs said, "with all this gold chain snatching going on in this city, that the chain walked off Mario's locker hook and squeezed its way in between two pages in the algebra section of your book." The officer turned to Earl. "They taking algebra now?"

"Yeah, I think they are," Earl said, noticing Mario sitting quietly in a corner. He also noticed his students on the sidewalk outside the school bunched together as they tried to look into the office at what was happening to their classmate.

Spriggs leaned close to Vinny. "Now tell me, young brother. Where *did* you get those smoking running shoes, and how much they run ya?"

"Store downtown," Vinny answered, his voice trembling. "Got'm on sale."

"How much?" Spriggs began writing something on a pad.

"Dunno. About forty-five dollars." Vinny was now trembling.

"Those're bad. I'm gonna get me a pair like that. By the way, you work part-time?" the officer asked.

"No, my folks want me to concentrate on my studies. But I do little chores around the neighborhood—you know—clear off a front yard, go to the store, things like that."

"That get you enough pennies for shoes like that?" Spriggs pressed.

"Well, I save up from other things." asserted Vinny, a vice tightening around him.

"What things, Vinny?"

Vinny hesitated.

"Excuse me," said Earl. "I know it sounds far-fetched, but isn't it possible that somebody else slipped the necklace into his textbook? I mean, he saw you and Mario going around the rooms before. Would it make sense for him to keep the chain in his textbook and leave it here overnight?"

Spriggs pointed at Earl as Mr. Hanley nodded. "Good point. But I gotta look at all possibilities. Either this kid's dumb, or he's arrogant. And right now, he looks to be both."

"I was framed," said Vinny. "And I know Kaseem did it."

Spriggs and Earl fixed their eyes on Vinny. "Why would Kaseem want to frame you?" the teacher asked him. "Why're you bringing him into this? I know you two have your differences."

Vinny boldly returned Mr. Chaney's stare. "Mr. Goody-goody. You think Kaseem's this great big angel who turned over a new leaf. Your pet. Well, I happen to know he ain't all you think he is."

A patrol car slid up, followed by an unmarked vehicle. The street had been emptied by the long-departed teachers. Just Kaseem's and Vinny's co-students loitered.

"Let's get back to the things you save up from," pressed Spriggs.

"Well, sometimes, my mom gives me money for doing extra work around the house."

"Lotta extra work."

Detective Wenders, a husky man with reddish-chestnut hair, a few subtle freckles on his nose, and a slightly protruding stomach, entered. There were two patrolmen who stayed in the patrol car for a moment before they drove off.

Wenders gestured toward Vinny. "He the kid?"

Spriggs nodded as he handed Wenders a small Ziploc sandwich bag containing the chain. Wenders glanced at the contents and then reached his hand out to the boy. "Let's go, son," he said.

"What about my folks?" asked Vinny, his voice quavering.

"They're at the station house," answered Wenders.

"I'd like to speak to the boy for a second," Earl said, suddenly feeling diminished.

"We're short on time," said Wenders. "I know you're his teacher—I assume you are—and you feel an obligation to'm, but believe me, anyone takes a gold chain or anything off somebody else doesn't deserve that obligation."

"You can't interfere with police business," chimed in Mr. Rako. "This's now police business."

"I would still like to speak with'm."

Spriggs whispered something to Wenders, who sighed. "Okay. A few minutes."

The officers, administrators, and Mario went to a far side of the general office.

Earl regarded Vinny. "Look me in the eye, son. Did you take Mario's chain?"

Vinny swallowed and then wept. "I didn't. I swear to God."

"Then you have nothing to worry about. Sometimes, things go out of whack in life. And you get caught in the middle of it. But in the end, they straighten themselves out, and the real truth emerges. What you've got to do now is reach inside yourself for that little bit of extra and tighten down so that you can get through this. C'mon now. Let's see that strength."

Vinny pulled himself together, and then Earl turned him over to Wenders, who took him to the unmarked car and placed him in the backseat before he joined another detective in the driver's seat who immediately drove off.

Now deeply thoughtful, Spriggs got into his own car and followed them.

Mr. Rako walked next to Earl as they watched them.

"Something, huh?" said the administrator.

"The boy needs our support," Earl answered.

"There's nothing anybody can do. It's out of our hands how."

"Know what?" said Kaseem. "I think Vinny's been framed by somebody. I think somebody did a real slimy number on'm."

"He was wrong and got busted, that's it," said one of the small group of students he was walking along the street with. They hadn't made much progress away from the school.

"Hey, look," said another student, his cap on backward.

They turned and saw Vinny being taken out of the school by Detective Wenders and Officer Spriggs.

"Boy, he's jacked up now," said another of the boys. He had opened up his shirt and pulled his necktie knot down

Guilt struck Kaseem, his stomach catching, and for the first time in his life, he thought seriously of what it would be like if he were ever caught chain-snatching, if he were in Vinny's place. Was this in his future? If he continued with the chain-snatching, it very likely would be. What about his mother and grandmother? Reverend Boston? Mrs. Stanton? Mr. Chaney? Hey, why was he concerned about them? He quickly pushed these fearful thoughts from his mind and focused on his companions.

"You know, we oughta get that Mario," said a blond-haired boy, sharpening that focus. "I mean, Vinny's our classmate—right or wrong—and, like, it ain't right."

"No," said Kaseem. "Don't take it out on Mario. Wasn't his fault. He didn't know the chain would be found in Vinny's book. He was just doing what Spriggs said."

A few of his companions assented, a mostly black group with a few Latinos and one chestnut-haired white who "hung out."

"Count me out," said Kaseem.

"Aw, man, you lame," said one black youth, fanning his hand at Kaseem. "You becoming too goody-goody. You don't have heart no more. Betcha a month or so ago, you wouldn'ta backed out."

"Yeah," said another. "What's wrong with you?"

"Skeets here," said another gesturing toward the white youth with them, "more nigger than you."

"All right, y'all," said Kaseem, a balefulness seeping into his manner. "Get off my case. Y'all stupid, you wanna know. Like you gonna be doing something. You gonna get Vinny outa trouble? Hell no. You gonna get nuthin' but your butts _in_ trouble. And maybe even make things worse for Vinny. You ever think of that? Huh? Naw. Better to do some dumbass macho shit and make things worse all around."

"He trying to talk around our heads," said a dark-skinned youth with acne. "I hate it when dudes talk all reasonable to you. I don't wanna hear it."

Skeets got up in Kaseem's face. "You know what, man?" he said. "You startin' to sound like _Sesame Street_."

The others laughed and slapped him five, and he slapped them five back.

"Won't even do this for your classmate, man," said another as they walked away. "That's cold."

"Mario was my classmate, too," said Kaseem, fanning his hand at them. "Go 'head on y'all!" He turned to walk in another direction. Then he stopped. Something told him he had better follow them. He turned around in time to see Fox running toward him.

"Hey, man, what's up?" the youth said as he did the liberation handshake with Kaseem and gave him a pound. "What happened with Vinny?"

"Aw, that stupid chump tried to take Mario's gold chain and got himself busted," Kaseem answered, not wanting to go into what he had done, fearing that his explanation might involve his debacle with Michellene.

"Hey, don't nobody like to see a dude get busted, even if he wrong," Fox commented, shaking his head.

"Look, I'm gonna check you out later," said Kaseem, strutting away from Fox, almost running from him.

"You buggin'?" asked Fox.

But Kaseem had walked far enough away to pretend he hadn't heard his buddy.

He decided to find Mario and warn him. He searched the neighborhood—the woods near the school, the parks, the housing project playgrounds, the alleyways. Then it occurred to him that maybe Mario had been told already and was sitting it out in his house. He decided maybe he should go home himself and forget the whole thing.

He turned a corner and saw Michellene, weeping, standing in front of her house, Elva attempting to comfort her. He backed out of sight and felt the rage swelling in him again. *She's crying for Vinny, that bitch*, he thought as he continued home.

CHAPTER 18

Sickened by what had happened to Vinny and disconcerted by not being in control of the situation, Earl decided to go to Kaseem's house to give good news to the household. Mrs. Wilson was still at work, but Mrs. MacNeil was home, preparing dinner. He told her of Kaseem's continual improvement and his upcoming award.

Needless to say, Mrs. MacNeil was quite pleased to hear this about her grandson and promised to inform her daughter when she got home. He then told her that he was finalizing plans for taking Kaseem, his son, and a couple of other students up to the country for the weekend. "Oh, my goodness, that's so nice," she said. "Can I get you something? Coffee? Cupcakes?"

"No, thanks. I only dropped by for a second."

"Why don't you call Julia on her job? I'm sure she'll be most happy to hear these things."

As she showed him to the phone, he glanced around for signs Kaseem was home. Finding none, he suddenly thought to himself, *What am I doing? This couldn't wait?*

"Yes, Mr. Chaney, how are you?" said Julia when he picked up.

"Good. You?"

"Oh, good as to be expected, thank you."

Because she was on the job, he would not take up much of her time. He got immediately to what he'd told Mrs. MacNeil, now back in the kitchen, and emphasized the upcoming award.

There was silence on the other end that puzzled him momentarily. Then he thought he heard quiet weeping. When she was able, she responded in a voice now hoarse and quavery. "I'll be indebted to you for the rest of my life for what you did for my son. Bless you. My goodness, here I am at work, talking to my son's teacher and getting all sloppy. Well, why not? And I can say Rodney certainly deserves that weekend in the country."

Earl was now beaming. "I think I will have that cup of coffee," he said to Mrs. MacNeil.

When Kaseem came around the corner, he saw Mr. Chaney's car parked in front of his house. He ducked back out of sight, cursing to himself.

Fox ran up to him from behind. "Hey, man, check yourself."

"Look, it's nothing," snapped Kaseem. "Nothing. All right?"

"Cool your role, brother man. You know, I'm about getting tired of you coming out your face on me." Fox began to stalk away.

Kaseem watched him for a few seconds and then caught up to him. "Look, I'm sorry. Put up with me. All right?"

"What's on your mind? You been outrageous lately."

Kaseem looked at him and then started laughing.

"You buggin' out?"

"Just thinking of the look on Vinny's face when they found the chain in his book. I dunno. I'm going off, I guess."

"You sure are. But at least you not boring. Anyhow, I just came to tell you, buncha guys gonna roll on Mario. We get into it, maybe you roll up some more brownie points with Michellene."

"Sorry. Got things on my mind." Kaseem was uncomfortable.

"Okay, that's cool. Look, word is he's laying cool up in his crib. Now, you a dude can get over. You got the rap."

"Don't play me, okay?"

"I ain't playin' you," Fox said. "I'm scoopin' you to the happenins. Are we tight or what? Come on now. Look, you got this new John-Boy, goody-goody rep. But you don't wanna be totally out with the folks who count. Do you? Why don't you be a brother and go up and bring the sucker down so's we can get to'm. Be a whole buncha people there."

"That'll involve me. Why should I involve myself in that mess?"

"As a favor to me, ol' buddy. After all, you did desert me. And I ain't come up with no partner to take your place yet. I'm hurtin'. Square business. I'm down to eatin' hot dogs and potato chips. 'Sides, Michellene pushin' it."

Kaseem stared at his friend.

Earl called Dionne on her job to make arrangements for meeting that evening. He'd managed to push the Vinny affair down in his consciousness and was even able to discuss it briefly with Dionne. He would go into greater detail when he picked her up.

She hesitated on the other end. "Here I go again," she said.

"Now what?"

"All right, here goes. Seems to me, this Vinny rates more of your time and energy right now than Kaseem."

"Funny, Ida said the same thing about Anthony." He fought the irritation inside him.

"Well. Great minds run on the same plane and all that. Hey, look, what you're doing is fantastic. If I'd had a teacher like you, I'd've been much further along than I am. Same with you. Same with most of us. All I'm saying is don't allow yourself to blow up like a balloon, or you might burst in a regrettable way."

"You prefer me all deflated."

"That's not what I'm saying, and you know it," she said. "Jesus Christ, can't I talk to you anymore?"

"You can talk to me. Don't make me out to be some paranoid adolescent. Every time I breathe, you have a criticism. Yet I still listen. I still bring what few triumphs there are in my life to you. For every Kaseem I score with, there's a thousand other Kaseems I try to reach and bomb on. Nobody knows the impact of that better than I do. Okay, goes with the territory. Look, I may not be Malcolm X or Frederick Douglass, but at least I'm doing something, not just talking. Why don't you try giving me some credit once in a while instead of always stabbing?"

"Am I hearing a little child's voice in the wind?"

"Yes, you are, dammit," he said. "I'm being as immature as an Easter egg on New Year's Day. I'm tired of being nice and mature, swallowing every goddamn stab in my guts with a shit-eating grin on my face while those guts drop to my toes. Why not a little healthy, wholesome, self-pitying immaturity? About time I started showing my behind a little."

"That a warning?"

"It's a declaration."

"Your time is up," interrupted an Ivy League voice. "Please deposit a nickel for the next three minutes, or your call will be interrupted."

"Why not?" said Earl as he plunked in another nickel. "You pays your money, and you makes your choice."

"You should listen to yourself. Why do I even bother? I'm sorry I started this."

"But start this you did, baby. Wielding your sword again. And I'm not

151

getting myself involved in any way in that Mickey Mouse organization. I don't care if time *is* running out and Idi Amin Fetchit has to take it over all by his lonesome. Because that's what this's really about, isn't it?"

"Around about here—sarcastic applause," she said. "Who was that masked man who's just properly put us in our place? Now what do we do? Go to my place or sit in an all-night movie and pout?"

"Maybe we start asking some pertinent overdue questions about us."

"Ah, sobriety has descended upon us. And to think I didn't think it had a role in our little drama. Tsk tsk tsk."

"You going to keep this up?" Earl asked.

"Because I wanna keep your feet on the ground instead of flying around? Baby, I love you. Sorry about that. Makes our relationship a little more serious than maybe you intend. And so because I love you, I'm gonna keep poking needles in you to make sure you're alive and well in Earl Chaney's head."

"Which means I'm not," he said.

"I'm not saying that. God, you and your touchiness. You really take the cake."

"I wish you'd stop equating me with these black power con men you keep getting involved in through your lack of judgment."

"Your time is up," came that voice again. "Please."

"You get that nickel in," she said. "You're not gonna end this conversation on that point."

Earl was tempted to let the conversation end, but a nickel found its way to his fingertips and into the slot.

"All right," she continued. "You're right. I do have poor judgment when it comes to leaders and organizations and husbands. *Mea culpa.* I have to work on that. But I do have good judgment in other areas. I'm a demon at picking cantaloupe and blouses. I chose you to fall in love with. And though you often set my teeth on edge, I think here I made a pretty dynamite choice."

"The same for me. That's why it's important that I feel you behind me."

"Honey, when I'm critical, that's when I'm most behind you. Believe me when I tell you, the other way is much less wear and tear on the blood pressure. But anyone who smiles sweetly at you and pats you on your back when your head is up your behind is your deadliest enemy."

"I hear you," he said.

"Now let's go sulk in the movies."

"And that's another thing. I spend my day following orders. I don't relish doing it on a date, too."

Silence was the response on the other end.

He cleared his throat. "So what's playing?"

The block where Mario lived consisted of a combination of two- and three-story tenements, a few prefabricated two-family houses, and two private houses, one shanty, one frame. The sidewalk was always swept clean and pooper-scooped, and the garbage cans were placed neatly near the curbs.

Mario's apartment building had three stories and was situated near one end of the block. Across the street and around the corner, out of sight of the apartment building, mainly Mario's window, a small gang had gathered, many of them Kaseem's classmates. There were a few girls among them, egging the gang on, and a few boys were engaging in ritualistic pantomimes of fighting, punching each other or some invisible figure and ganging up on one person. A peripheral crowd was forming.

Many of them ran up to Kaseem and Fox when they arrived. Some pranced around them in hysteric anticipation of some imminent event. Others wiggled, danced, and twirled like manic street festival clowns.

"You gon' do it, man?" said one. "I mean, you the one he'll listen to."

"Just convince'm to come down here," Fox said, "and we'll take care of the rest. You don't even have to be involved. Remember, Vinny's your classmate."

"Yeah," answered Kaseem, "but Mario used to be my classmate, too."

"But, hey, he's not no more. Vinny is, y'know what I mean? And it's right that we get Mario for what happened. Am I right or wrong?"

Kaseem looked around at their assenting faces, studying their eyes. "Suppose you hurt'm. And I'm not hurt? Wouldn't that put my name in it?"

"Okay, tell you what," said another. "Like suppose we chase'm back upstairs, and it looks like you saved'm from a really bad butt whipping. That'd make you a hero. Get you more brownie points at the school. Check it out."

"Hey," said Fox, giving Kaseem a pound.

When he glanced once more at the swelling crowd, Kaseem turned and marched across the street and upstairs to Mario's second-floor apartment. When the latter opened the door, its door chain on, and saw Kaseem, he immediately started to close the door, but a shoe stopped it.

"Wait a minute, man. Lemme talk to you."

"I don't wanna talk to you."

"You don't wanna talk to me?" Kaseem said. "Your old classmate?"

"You wanna move your shoe?"

"Aw, come on, Mario. At least hear me out. What can happen to you inside your own house?"

"Hey, it is my own house, isn't it?" He tried to close the door again.

"Who is it, Mario?" came a mature feminine voice from one of the rooms inside. Suddenly, an attractive middle-aged woman with a full head of black hair was standing behind Mario, eyeing Kaseem. "What is this, Mario? Invite your friend in. You'll make'm think we don't teach you any manners. I dunno what's the matter with you today."

Mario gave Kaseem an eye signal not to say anything as he let him in and introduced him to his mother, who then returned to the kitchen. She returned seconds later with a glass of ginger ale, which she graciously handed to the guest and then excused herself.

"See, if I was gonna do something to you, would your moms have let me in?" Kaseem said. "She a fool?"

"Okay. So?"

"Look, you'n me both know there's a problem. Buncha people out there wanna get to you. You up here hiding. And the whole thing's not right. That's why I'm here. I feel that you should not have to stay cooped up in your apartment. Suppose your moms wants you to go to the store. What're you gonna do then? You have every right to the streets just like everybody else. And you should use that right."

"Yeah, the right to get my head beat in?" Mario said. "Nothing doing."

"C'mon, Mario. You gotta show your face downstairs. What happened to Vinny was not your fault. You stay up here, you're saying it is."

"You finished?"

"Is it your fault?"

"No!" Mario exclaimed.

"See how excited you said it? You know it yourself."

"Look, I'm not going out there, and that's that."

"How you gonna go to school tomorrow?"

"I'll cross that bridge when I come to it."

Kaseem was stymied, his mind working furiously. "You gonna let them dudes put a rope around your life," he said. "Make a slave outa you."

Mario answered with silence.

"Okay," said Kaseem. "I guess that's the way you want it." He got up and started for the door. "Tell your mother good-bye for me and thanks for the—" He stopped and turned to Mario. "Why don't your moms know about this?"

Mario stared at Kaseem with eyes beginning to tear.

This will surely make me feel less guilty about punking out on Fox, thought Kaseem as he led Mario downstairs. *I'll just walk away, put my back to it.* That thought sent qualms through him, but he pressed on.

His heart beat as he walked toward the corner, talking with pretended nonchalance to Mario, his eyes carefully scanning the block.

When they were out of sight of his window, Mario suddenly grew very tense and uneasy. This spurred Kaseem on even more. He wanted to get it over with, and perhaps there would be a slight thrill in it for him as well.

Suddenly, Mario stopped. He was ashen. "Hey, look, I don't think this's such a hot idea."

"Aw, man, you came this far."

"Hey, know what? I don't care what you tell my moms." He turned to rush back but froze.

So did Kaseem.

Before they knew it, they were surrounded by a rabid looking group of boys. A larger group was forming around them, and there were more people running toward them from up the block.

Then Kaseem saw Michellene, leaning against a car, and a deep rage engulfed him. He turned to Mario, and both backed against a nearby, vine-entangled, mesh-wire fence. Fox was signaling for Kaseem to move to the side out of the way.

The inside group was being egged on by the fringe group and the still accumulating onlooking crowd. Kaseem looked from side to side at their besiegers and readied himself.

"Vinny's my ace," said one wiry youth with a Boston Celtics sweat jacket on and a cigarette tucked in his ear. "You messed up my ace."

"Caused the guy to get busted," added a dark-skinned seventh grader. "Now you know that's wrong."

"We need to light his ass up," shouted a heavy-set brown-skinned beanpole.

One boy smacked Mario on the back of his head.

"Ouch!" shouted Mario, now trembling, his eyes teary. "Whaddya call this, huh? You didn't have to do that."

"Aw, the poor fuckin' booby," contributed a white youth, rubbing his eyes in fake sorrow.

Suddenly, Kaseem was in front of Mario, facing the mob. "All right now, y'all chill," he said.

"What're you doing?" said Fox.

"What's the real deal with you man?" said another boy, stepping threateningly toward Kaseem. "You crazy or something?" The attitude thinned when he discovered that no one else had stepped forward with him.

Noting the same, Kaseem fixed his eyes on his lone challenger for a moment. When the other didn't move, Kaseem suddenly took off his belt of thick leather with a brass buckle and, after wrapping part of it around his fist, swung it, nunchaku-style, making crazed-bird figure eights in the air with the buckle.

"Okay, only me'n him," he growled through clenched teeth. "You think I'm trying to play it off, come ahead."

The boys looked at each other and seemed to lose their fervor just as Kaseem grew more livid. A few started walking away, sucking their teeth and fanning their hands at Kaseem and his partner. Another nodded his head thoughtfully and said, "Brother's right, people. Wasn't Mario's fault. What we gonna mess with the guy for?"

A few others stood around in idle conversation.

"Don't move," Kaseem whispered to Mario out of the corner of his mouth.

The larger part of the mob dispersed, grumbling disappointedly.

Fox looked at Kaseem, a knowing smile fading into his face.

"Shit, I'm going back upstairs," said Mario, his voice trembling. "Ain't nothing out here for me."

"Suit yourself, man, but the street's yours. Ain't nobody gonna bother you now. You can even hang out for a while." Kaseem turned back and saw Michellene glaring at him.

Chapter 19

The class was silent, contrite. Earl marched around the classroom like a furious, caged lion. Both doors were shut.

"You didn't think I'd find out?" he said. "I have news for you, boys and girls. I was already trying to get over it before you walked into this building this morning. I haven't succeeded. You ought to be ashamed of yourselves. Right now, I'm ready to haul the bunch of you right down to Mr. Hanley's office and leave you there for the duration. How dare you resort to KKK-Nazi behavior. Who do you think you are? Judge and jury? The executioners? God? And stupid, to boot? Nobody is more upset about what happened to Vinny than I am. Do I run out and form a lynch mob? Huh? Does that help Vinny? And why Mario? What'd he do that each and every one of you in the same position wouldn't've done?" Those three men who accosted him in that town long ago briefly reappeared in his mind.

He slammed a large dictionary down on his desk, the report so loud that a few students jumped, and it brought furtive faces to the rear window.

"Now you let me hear that one scratch came to Mario's body, one nick on his skin, even the suggestion of one, and I'm on your behinds like black on tar! You haven't seen trouble! Don't even bring in a distant cousin from Hoshkosh, Arizona, somewhere to give'm dirty looks or make cracks under his or her breath loud enough for him to hear."

He turned toward the door window, and faces vanished. He marched to the front door and opened it. *"Get to your classrooms!"* he bellowed in the corridor that emptied in seconds, except for Mr. Rako standing at his office door.

He returned to his desk. "You say you didn't do anything. You were merely watching? Wrong. You're just as guilty. You participated. You didn't raise a hand to'm, but you were the inspirational force behind the blow that was struck. So that 'out' you don't have."

Maria raised her hand. She cleared her throat. "I offer my resignation as president of the class," she said in a low voice.

Earl regarded her for a few moments and then glanced around the class. "Why?" he asked. "Were you there?"

"No," she said.

"I didn't think you would be. No, I do not accept your resignation. You're a good class president, and evidently, some people in this class need one."

He walked to the window and looked down on Spriggs who was directing traffic and guiding the latecomers across the street.

"I want to apologize to those of you this scolding doesn't apply to … for taking up your time with this. And, of course, what Kaseem did can't be lauded enough. It was courageous and noble. If this's the kind of thing young people're capable of, there's hope for this world yet."

A few *sotto voce* groans stopped at the teacher's whirl.

"You have to be kidding," he growled.

The day actually came. That morning she and her mother took special pains to see to it that Kaseem had a good breakfast, not that they didn't always do this for the youth. Still, on this day, a day both women had dreamed of for such a long time, their baby would show the world that he had turned a corner. Sliced grape fruit, scrambled eggs, crisp bacon and golden brown pancakes would communicate their deep happiness on this day. Unfortunately, Mrs. MacNeil was on the day shift and would have to depend on hearing about the event from her daughter.

The two women eagerly chatted with each other as they watched the youth eat his breakfast.

Later that morning, she parked her vehicle across the street from the school and, as she got out and crossed the street, nodded warmly to Officer Spriggs who silently returned the greeting. The entrance to the auditorium was across the lobby from the main entrance. Mr. Hanley was there to greet her and solicitously usher her into the assembly. Mr. Chaney smiled and walked to her from the side.

Julia, in a seldom-worn, snug, dark blue, one-piece velour dress, stood in the rear of the auditorium and fought tears of deep pride as she watched her son being called up to the stage to receive the "most improved student" award. The audience applauded vigorously, though there were a few sneaky boos. Fox punched the air with his fist in a victory gesture. A few students turned around in their seats to glimpse with vicarious enjoyment the mother standing next to her son's teacher.

Spriggs applauded and punched Earl's shoulder, the latter nodding and making the victory gesture with his fist. Mrs. Stanton, near the front, smiled. Mr. Devonshire, standing in the aisle on the far side of the auditorium, gave Earl a thumbs-up.

Ingram ambled over to Earl and pushed his hands idly into his pockets. "Well, well, well," he said. "Our own Svengali and Father Duffy all rolled into one. I coulda used you five years ago with my own wastrel of a son. You can come teach in my school anytime."

Somewhat clumsily, Kaseem walked up the stairs to the stage. A chill crept up the back of his neck, and he swallowed. The euphoric feeling in him, however, was tempered by the fact that he didn't completely deserve it. He was briefly tempted to turn to the audience and shout out that fact, to confess all, but he held to the good things he'd done. He held to the happiness and pride his mother must have been feeling and the esteem he must have been giving to Mr. Chaney.

Mr. Rako placed the gold-embossed scroll into Earl's left hand and shook the other, slapping the youth's shoulder as well. A volcanic eruption of applause accompanied it as the humbled boy turned toward the audience, dipped his head slightly, and walked off the stage. Teachers and students all applauded. A few students stood up. Even the thin sunbeams that stabbed through the slits of the drawn auditorium window curtain seemed to contribute to the feeling.

Julia embraced her son and then turned to Mr. Chaney, whose hand she grabbed in both of hers. "I'll never forget you for this," she said, seeming on the verge of kissing him but inhibited by the myriad of eyes on them and her innate reserve. All too soon, her head swirling with exhilaration, she was on her way back to work. She would change into her nurse's uniform at the office.

After the assembly period, Earl caught up to Spriggs in the corridor

Rudy Gray

outside the general office. The pupils were filing back to their classes, and the other two grades were changing their classes as well.

The two men went to the unoccupied nurse's anteoffice nearby. It was an empty chamber with three chairs sitting about idly and an old scale in the corner.

Spriggs looked somewhat harassed, tired, the lines deepening in his face. The problems both inside the school and out seemed to be getting to him. There'd been a rash of copycat, gold-chain snatchings, muggings, and burglaries in the neighborhood and immediately outside it, and pressure had been put on him to look more closely at his population of early teens. He'd been doing so but coming up blank, except for a suspicion or two here and there.

"Can anything be done for Vinny?" Earl asked.

Spriggs shook his head. "Caught dead to rights. All up to whatever the lieutenant decides and what the disposition of the case is. I'd say right now Vinny's in deep doo-doo."

"There's no possibility a mistake was made?" asked Earl, trying not to let despair spoil his exhilaration.

Spriggs gave Earl a look. "Come on, brother, what is this? You sounding like you in your first year in this business. The boy is wrong. These young boys today into *heavy* wrongdoing. No more lifting pens and cookie change. Some of these little motherfuckers just as soon take off an old lady as clean your board. But that don't take nothing from you as a teacher now. See what I'm saying? Street out there a different classroom. And different classroom, different rules. Some boys in this school already dealing. Come in every day with their homework all neat and complete. Your boy Kaseem. I gave'm a pound before, and I meant it. I was proud. But I still got my eye on'm."

Earl put on a jovial air, concealing the sense of something sinking inside him. He didn't want this man, who, he knew, must have experienced the worst, to detect any hint in him of his cursed self-pity. "If everything you say is true, I might as well bring in the *New York Times* crossword puzzle and spend the day doing that."

"Hey, I'm a policeman. What can I tell you? Keep your pencil sharpened and have a big eraser, y'know."

Earl stared at him. Something was in the air, bothering him.

Spriggs continued. "What you did with that boy is more important than I think even you know. We got to have what you do in that classroom. We can't wait till it gets to me, or it's back to one million BC, homeboy. And you better believe me when I tell you my right pinky toe's there already. Hey, we both know lotta these teachers around here're bu'shittin'. But teachers like you ain't. So you gotta hold the line."

"It's all right," said Earl, going. "I don't need to be stroked."

As he passed Kaseem in the corridor, he informed the young man that the woods excursion was on for the coming weekend. He then slapped the youth on his shoulder.

The youth watched his teacher walk away from him and allowed thoughts of admiration, pride and guilt to swirl briefly around inside his head until a passing fellow student slapped him five and a teacher said to him, "Let's go, star. Don't be late for class," bringing him out of himself.

After lunch, Kaseem sat in Mrs. Stanton's class, trying with minimal success to focus on the lesson. His head was still swirling, and he was beginning to feel for the first time that maybe he belonged in this world and its human family. Yet, a malaise nudged him on the edges of his consciousness.

A soft tap on the rear window came to his ears. He turned and saw, to his surprise, Michellene's face looking at him, signalling for him to come outside.

The corridor was empty now, and Michellene looked seductive as she beckoned to him. Though enticed by her, he felt uneasy as he approached her. They were now out of earshot of any classroom with a class or teacher in it.

"I just wanted to congratulate you on winning that award today," she said. "That was terrific. And you were fantastic yesterday. Superman to the rescue and all that. Impressive. When're you gonna ask me out again?"

"That's up to you."

"Don't make it up to me. Make it up to you. Assert yourself."

"Well, I—" he started.

"Don't worry about that last time with us. Water down the drain. And I understand. When you guys get turned on, sometimes you get carried away."

He stared at her, feeling something deep inside him tightening, screaming surrender.

"So let's make it soon, huh?" she said, almost purring. "Catch another flick and grab a bite at Wendy's or something. Check out the scene, y'know what I mean?"

"I hear ya."

"Good. Now soon, huh?" She started to move away but then stopped. "Oh, interesting thing," she said, reaching into her handbag and extracting a composite drawing cut out from a newspaper, looking at it and then at Kaseem. "You know, I'll be damned if you don't have a twin brother out there somewhere. Spittin' image of you. This's the guy who's been snatching gold chains off people." She showed it to him.

It wasn't quite his face, but it was enough to make his throat tighten still more as he looked at it and handed it back to Michellene, who studied his eyes. A bubble had burst inside him.

"Brother man," she continued, "this drawing favors you so much that if I was a policeman, I'd arrest your butt."

"What is this?"

"See, this dude here pushed this woman into the street at a bus stop. Right before school. Injured her hip. Almost got her killed. Terrible thing, tsk, tsk. Dude and his accomplice—and, boy, does Fox ever fit that description—were chased by a small crowd of people, but they didn't catch'm. You know how these eighth graders can haul butt when they have to. Another crowd chased these same two guys after they did a woman at this small shopping mall east of here. All I can say is you'd better watch out. See, the way I found out about all this was they put Vinny in a line up 'cause they thought one of them mighta been him. But it wasn't. Just like it wasn't him took Mario's chain."

"You fixing to start something?" Kaseem asked, curious.

"Start something? Start what? What could I start?"

"You trying it?"

"Vinny says he thought he saw you near Mario's books in the lockers."

"Everybody's near everybody's books in the lockers. So what?"

A faint ringing came to his ears.

"Hey, Kaseem," she said. "This's me you're talking to. We know you always been jealous of Vinny."

"Jealous of what?"

"He's got what it takes. You don't. If you catch my drift."

"That your excuse for being a scrufty ho', spreading your legs like the curtains in a theater every time he crooks his finger at you?" he said to her.

"You could ring the Liberty Bell. It ain't never gon' happen with you. You get to that."

He started toward her, she backing away.

"Don't you put your hand on me, nigger," she said. "You done used up your last time you lay a hand on me."

He checked himself. Something was up, and he had to watch his movements.

Suddenly, her face lit up with a smile. "Well, hi, stranger!" she said to someone behind Kaseem. "Welcome back!"

Kaseem turned.

Vinny had returned to school.

CHAPTER 20

Apparently, after they had looked at Vinny's record and after subsequent questioning, the precinct plainclothesmen had determined that a boy of his caliber and intelligence would not steal someone's gold chain and stick it inside his own textbook, which it appeared he was going to leave in school overnight. It just didn't make sense. So Vinny told Kaseem.

Kaseem, keeping himself under control, welcomed Vinny back to school, focused on Vinny's smiling, staring eyes while aware that Michellene's were on him, too.

Then she wrapped her arms around Vinny, and they kissed long and passionately. Kaseem averted his eyes and looked through a window at a distant, dark green, thatched rooftop. He wanted to escape this scene but instead stood frozen, not knowing what to do.

Then one of her eyes opened and looked at him. They unravelled, and she turned around and pressed her back, mainly buttocks, into Vinny, grabbing his hands and rubbing her stomach with them.

"Hey, brother," said Vinny. "Whaddya say about a little privacy, huh?"

"Yeah, you can go now," added Michellene.

As Kaseem walked away, he could hear subdued giggles behind him. He had to admit to himself that, under these circumstances, he was behaving quite well.

He was also thinking of that drawing.

Feeling the floor under him continuously opening, he went to Mr. Chaney to tell him that maybe he wouldn't be able to make it that weekend.

"Nonsense," said the teacher. "It's all set. It'll be a very important experience for us. Didn't you enjoy yourself with us at the basketball game?"

"Yes, I did. But—"

"Don't you want to go?" Earl inquired.

"Yes, but—"

"Do you have reason to feel we really don't want you to go?"

"No," Kaseem said.

"Then what is this? There's been something going on with you lately. Is there something wrong?"

"No, sir." The subdued student met the teacher's eyes.

"You're okay?"

"Yeah, I'm okay."

"Good. Then we're going. It'll be a beautiful, invigorating experience for you. Cap everything that's happened up to now. Put some hair on your chest."

Earl slapped Kaseem's shoulder and walked on. Kaseem stared after him, shrugged his shoulders, and started to walk back to his subject classroom when he saw Spriggs emerge at the end of the corridor and beckon to him.

His stomach caught. Something ominous, nightmarish was stalking him from somewhere in the surrounding air. As he approached the policeman, he took a deep breath to relax himself. Perhaps Spriggs wanted only to congratulate him on his award. The patrolman took the youth into a nearby empty office.

"Would you be willing to go with me to the station house so that a lady and a man can take a look at you?" he asked.

Kaseem tried to keep his eyes from blinking as he looked at the officer.

"How'm I supposed to answer that?" he said.

"Yes or no," said the officer, stabbing him with his eyes.

"What is it about me you don't like?" asked the youth, a faint ringing in his ears.

"You getting into personalities now?"

"Ever since I can remember. If you don't like me, hey, the way it be's, y'know. I just don't think it's fair that you keep me tense alla time with your insinuations and stuff. Now I'm tired of it, all right? Tired of it. If this crap keeps up, I'm gonna have to go to your commanding officer and put in a complaint of police harassment."

His heart was now pounding in his chest as he watched the policeman lean back, an expression of wide enthusiasm on his face.

"Oooooooh, get back," he said. "Okay, youngblood, you said your piece. You laid my behind to rest six ways from Sunday. You all right. You got heart. And, about this, don't worry with it. Woman's dead anyhow. Heart attack."

Kaseem's heart jumped. His guts dropped to his knees, and he strained to conceal it.

"Whoa!" went on the officer. "Look at that face. Hey, when you gotta go, you gotta go, you know? You take a woman her age off, she ain't exactly gonna take to the experience. But she couldn't identify a soul. Besides, Fox already confessed."

Kaseem swallowed a mouthful of molten lava.

Spriggs slapped him on his shoulder. "Only joshing with you," he said finally. "I'm misbehaving. I need to stop."

The young man smiled wanly and walked out of the office. He decided he would stay home from school the next day, "suffering from a headache." Still, he would have to get through the rest of this day.

Later, while he was in Mr. Chaney's classroom, dwelling on the knot in his stomach, Spriggs appeared at the front doorway. Despite their last exchange and perhaps because of it, the youth still groaned inside. Was there to be more? Mr. Chaney walked to the policeman, who whispered something to him.

Then, feeling eyes looking in his direction, the youth turned to the rear window. His neck squeezed.

The face of a young girl was there, her eyes searching the classroom. She was light-skinned, a beauty mark on her right nostril, and her eyes were large and doleful. She was also a girl he'd once snatched a gold chain from.

He snapped his face front, leaned forward on his desk, and put his face between his fists. Spriggs was now scrutinizing him. So was a now-confused Mr. Chaney.

Suddenly, Kaseem heard an outcry in the corridor near the rear door, the voice of a young girl in great anguish. Students got up to go to the rear door.

"Back to your seats," ordered Mr. Chaney, freezing everybody.

Spriggs had returned to the corridor, Mr. Chaney following him. The voices outside were animated, emotional, but there was a certainty and pointedness about them that made Kaseem grow even tenser, because they somehow seemed to have him focused in the center. Or was it his paranoia?

Numbness had gripped Earl as he walked into the corridor. The teacher was trying to catch up to what was happening so that he could lay hold of it and gain an understanding. But events were moving too fast, staying ahead of him. He found himself partially groping in the dark. Still, at the same time, another part of him was making sure he didn't catch up, slowing him down when he appeared to be getting near.

Spriggs was calming the hysterical girl, holding her in his arms, talking soothingly to her. Her tears were dotting the chest area of his uniform, though they vanished into the dark blue of the cloth. A fist was lightly but firmly pounding his shoulder.

"Let's get the young man out here," the policeman said to the teacher.

Earl returned to his classroom and stared into space for a brief moment. Then his eyes turned to anger as they moved toward Kaseem, who dropped his to his desk.

"Kaseem," he said. "Outside please."

Maria turned in her seat and stared, aghast, at the young man as he rose and started toward the front door. The rest of the class was silent.

Spriggs stepped back into the classroom, but by then, Kaseem, his eyes avoiding Earl's, was nearing the front of the classroom.

"Let's go, blood," snapped the policeman, who disappeared into the corridor again.

Fox was there, having just been brought by a monitor. His hands were in his pockets, and as he was staring down at his shoes, he was leaning against the wall. The fuming girl was kept apart from him. Faces, every now and then, appeared at the door windows of surrounding classrooms.

Kaseem watched himself from some great distance walking into the corridor, being pointed out by an enraged, livid girl who had to be prevented by the policeman from inflicting some terrible violence on him. "You pieces of scumbags!" she hissed as the policeman gently placed his finger onto her lips.

The general office staff was standing around in small groups and whispering to each other when Spriggs, Kaseem, and Fox entered. The stunned ladies stopped and, with their eyes, followed the three into Mr. Hanley's office. The livid girl, Nancy was her name, Detective Wenders were waiting for them.

Mr. Hanley ushered them into the anteoffice to join Mr. Rako, and the door was shut. The office secretaries were told there were to be no interruptions.

Nancy was given a seat along the wall, and the two boys were given seats facing her at the table. Everyone else stood.

"Mrs. Wilson's been contacted," said Mr. Hanley. "No one answers the phone for this one."

"You the one won the Most Improved Student Award?" asked Wenders of Kaseem who nodded. "Big joke on us, right? Now, Nancy, I want you to answer yes or no. Are these the boys who took your gold chain?"

Glaring at them, she nodded.

"She's lying," said Kaseem.

"She know you?" asked Wenders.

"I wouldn't know a piece of garbage like that," she hissed.

"Kaseem, she know you?" Wenders signalled for Nancy to calm down.

"No," the youth answered.

"Then why would she lie about you?" asked the detective, glancing around the office at the other adults. Finally his eyes rested on Fox.

"I dunno. Well, maybe what I meant was she made a mistake," Kaseem answered.

"Maybe you meant?" persisted Wenders, seeming to stab the silence of the office with his words.

"I meant." Kaseem held tight to himself.

"Nothing to say, Fox?" Wenders asked.

"I didn't make no mistake," said Nancy before Spriggs placed his hand on her shoulder.

"All that aside," Wenders injected. "How do you explain, Kaseem and Fox, the phone call from somebody who sounded pretty sure about you, somebody who seemed to know you? Oh, yes, there was a call. These drawings from *The Bronx Home News*. The descriptions given to us from a pretty wide variety of mugging victims and witnesses. And, if you want, we can take you to a lady recently home from the hospital, face her husband, who's ready to string you up."

"Not us," sputtered Kaseem.

Wenders looked at him. "Oh, you're speaking for your friend, too? You know, for a fact, everything he's done in his life? What do you say, Fox? Does he?"

Fox stared down at the table mahogany.

Michellene and Vinny must be laughing their heads off, thought Kaseem.

"Okay. Whaddya say you empty your pockets and wallets out on the table."

Kaseem managed not to feel the humiliation of it too much. Fox did not have much money, but he did have an expensive looking wallet. Still, Kaseem had over one hundred dollars he'd planned to buy some camping equipment with.

Spriggs's eyes flashed. "Damn, bro, I gotta look you up when I get tight."

"Where'd you get that kind of money, son?" Wenders asked.

"Saved it up from my allowance," answered Kaseem, clearing his throat.

Wenders turned to Spriggs. "Tell you, being single sure has its points. I can't put together five bucks from my paycheck."

"What do you do to earn that salary?" asked Spriggs.

"Mow the lawn," Kaseem said in a businesslike tone. "Shovel the front walk. Tend the garden out back."

"You live in a private house then," said Wenders.

Kaseem nodded.

"And you do this?" The plainclothesman stared at Kaseem for a few moments before he turned to Fox. "What about you, Fox?"

"I live in the projects," he said.

"Projects" said Wenders as if he hadn't known that. "How'd you get the fancy wallet?"

"He mowed the lawn, too," quipped Spriggs, and the two policemen sniggered.

"How long'd you have to mow the lawn and tend to the tulips to accumulate that kind of cash?" Wenders asked Kaseem.

The youth swallowed. "I'm not answering anymore questions until I see a lawyer."

Wenders and Spriggs exchanged impressed looks. "Well," said the plainclothesman, "it's nice to know he's home some nights watching television."

In a tight squeezing vice, Earl's head was very slowly turning, and his ears were hot. He tried to get his bearings. Because he was not completely there, he could hear his voice in some distant chamber giving instructions to his students, and he saw their faces as they eyed him, most with sympathy, some without. None of it connected to him, however, or anything else having to do with him. He was clearly off balance, off his classroom rhythm, and he struggled mightily to conceal his state of inner disarray.

At the class's dismissal, Maria lightly patted him on his back, and Vinny donned a mask of stern seriousness that seemed barely to contain a volcanic eruption of guffaws. Still, he managed to bring his fist down on Earl's half-consciously offered fist and, shaking his head in bogus disappointment, proceeded down the corridor to his next class.

When they were out of sight, Earl raced down to the general office. He did not want to wait for Ingram to appear in his face and "unconsciously" rub salt into his wound. He would do that soon enough.

When he burst into the office, every pair of eyes, it seemed, either snapped down to the shaft of papers on the desk or looked out to the street. One secretary, his "monthly attendance form" friend, stepped up to the counter. "I don't think this's a good time to see Mr. Hanley," she said, not unsympathetically.

"Are they still here?" he asked, a coldness swelling in his voice.

"Yes, they're still here, waiting for Mrs. Wilson to arrive."

He fixed his eyes on her like two brandished bowie knives. "Tell Mr. Hanley," he said through clenched teeth and what must have resembled a smile, "that Mr. Chaney is here."

She wilted under his glare and walked to the principal's door, which she tapped on with her well-manicured nails. Mr. Hanley opened the door and, seeing Earl standing on the outside of the counter and the ice-cold rage on his face, reluctantly gestured for him to enter.

It was as if he'd stepped into a *Twilight Zone* replication of the world he lived in. There they were, Kaseem and Fox, at the table facing the girl, Nancy. Fox focused on his folded hands on the table. Kaseem stared blankly into space. Earl's eyes stared confusedly at him for a moment. Then he turned to Mr. Hanley. "I'd like a word with Kaseem if you don't mind."

Mr. Hanley looked at him. "Mr. Chaney—"

Spriggs stepped in front of the principal and urgently whispered something in his ear. Mr. Hanley relented and signaled for everybody to leave Earl and Kaseem alone in the anteoffice.

For a long while, teacher and pupil gazed at each other. Then the pupil looked down at his lap.

"There's something I'd like to know," Earl said, swallowing his words, still not completely sure this wasn't some nightmare from which he would jump to wakefulness and sweat-soaked sheets. "All those good things you did. Were they sincere?"

The teacher wished, in the ensuing silence, that he could call the words back. He was already handling this badly, his sense of accomplishment and magic having vanished.

"I wasn't insincere," answered Kaseem finally. "I really meant what I did."

"Then why?" Earl checked himself. Everything coming from him now seemed inappropriate. He no longer trusted his reflexes around this youth, who, he felt, had so profoundly betrayed him. "And your mother?"

"Yeah, that's right, my moms," the young man snapped. "See, that's it. It's my moms, you, the school—everybody but me. What about me? Well, nothing, naturally, because 'me' never really counted, right? It was everybody else, making brownie points with somebody or other and using me as the tool."

"That's what it's been, huh?"

"Hey, with us nigger hoodlums, that's the way it'll always be," Kaseem said.

"So you're not responsible for what you did?"

"Now I'm gonna hear about responsibility. Like that word's supposed to mean something important to me. Well, check this out. We been working with two different dictionaries."

Earl stared at him.

Suddenly, there was a faint commotion heard by them through the closed door, first in the general office and then in Mr. Hanley's office. There were muffled but animated voices. Then someone shouted, "Wait!" before the anteoffice door swung open and a livid, suddenly aged Julia Wilson marched in and up to Kaseem. Immediately, she began pounding him with her fists on his head and shoulders, he having turned his back to her and hunching himself over, and threw a couple of hard punches on his back.

Had the scene not been so horrific, Earl might almost have thought it comic. The violence of it not only didn't abate, it escalated. Now certain she would do something unthinkable to him soon, he started to move toward them, but a hand on his arm stayed him. It was Spriggs. "She needs to get to his bones," he said.

But Earl broke free, rushed to her, and pulled her, now weeping profusely, off him.

"Get off me," she said through her gritted teeth as he pulled her away. "Get off me."

"Think of what you'd do," he said. "Think of what you'd do."

"I don't care!"

By now, the anteoffice doorway was filled with shocked onlookers as Mrs. Wilson struggled against Earl's hold. At length, he felt her relax and released her, holding his hands ready to grab her again.

She leaned forward on two stiff arms, punching two fists into the tabletop, and dropped her head as she continued to weep.

Kaseem was, by now, unravelling himself from the ball he'd become. Straightened up and visibly trembling, he stared through tear-filled eyes at the blank wall to his left.

She jabbed a finger toward him. "If I go before my time, it's on your head! Do you hear me? If I go before my time, it's on your head!"

"Take it easy, Mrs. Wilson," said Mr. Hanley. "It won't help to get yourself so worked up."

"What am I gonna tell my mother? How'm I gonna tell her without breaking her heart?"

She turned to her son again. "That's it, buddy! When the law gets finished with you—if it ever finishes with you—I'm putting your behind away! I'm washing my hands of you! I could care less what becomes of you!"

"Is that how you did it with Daddy, too?" Kaseem's quavering voice cut through the air, leaving in its wake a staggering silence, his mother's eyes blinking as they gaped at him.

Suddenly, she was upon her son again and whipping her palm with savage fury across his face. She stared at him for a few moments more before she turned to Spriggs and Wenders and said, "He's all yours!"

As she started to leave, her eyes met Earl's, an intercourse of pain, helplessness, and apology bursting between them. Then she stormed out.

The anteoffice became silent as everyone stared at the boy. Detective Wenders returned with Fox. An uncle took Nancy home, her trembling hand covering her mouth and her eyes bloodshot.

"I'm placing the both of you under arrest," Wenders said, Mirandizing them, and then he and Officer Spriggs took the two boys away.

Earl stood behind one of the chairs and stared ahead.

"Don't forget your other students," said Mr. Hanley.

"I'm free this period," the teacher said absently.

"I'm sorry about all this," the principal lamented. "I was really pulling for'm."

"What happens now? We just file'm away, dust off our hands, and go on?"

"Yes, as a matter of fact, that's exactly what we do. Hey, am I supposed to go on the defensive here? I'm not about to go on the defensive. Doesn't change our jobs or the world. I have twenty-eight hundred other students to worry about."

"Of course you do," Earl responded.

"No, I'm not going to get into a tiresome debate with you on our social ills and personal responsibility. Whatever is … is. I'm going to rejoice that a large number of people out there will now not become mugging victims and an innocent boy did not go to jail. I will pull my troops back to the next line of demarcation and regroup for the next defeat."

"Just like that?"

"Just like that," the principal said as he glanced at his watch.

"At the risk of seeming insubordinate, I want to ask you something," came out of the teacher's mouth like thrust daggers.

"At the risk of seeming rude, I will ignore the question. Man, for Chist's sake, give it up! The mission's over! I put my neck on the line, too."

"Well!" Earl said. "That's a chastening piece of information. May I cling to that? Makes the emotional, physical, and spiritual energy I expended on that boy pale by comparison. I don't feel so bad now."

"Good for you! But also bleed for the victims, Mr. Chaney. Nancy out there. The woman who had to go to the hospital. God knows what others whose meeting with Kaseem and Fox was not as pleasant as yours was, who haven't even come to light. And never will, God help them. Let's get back to thinking about the guy who doesn't resort to a switchblade to solve his problems."

"And close our minds to the guy who was never given anything else but the switchblade."

"You can't be talking about Kaseem," the principal responded. "With the mother he has. Teachers bending over backward to work with'm. How does he repay us after what we did for'm? That's a specious argument at best. Look, you're understandably upset about all this. But meanwhile, I have another concern. You're down here giving me a hard time. You're sure there's no class upstairs waiting for you."

"I'm free this period. But, you see, you still had to say that. After all that's transpired. And that's what this argument's really about."

He almost knocked Mr. Rako over as he marched by him on his way back upstairs. He had time before his next class, yet he had to get up to his room for fear he would burst.

He sat alone at his desk, trying to put everything in perspective, trying to be mature, trying to see things clearly. No dice. He was too far inside his limitations. Who was this boy Kaseem? Was he truly an evil person? A bad seed? Or just a misguided youth acting on errant reflex? Who was he in response to all this? And why hadn't he seen this coming?

During homeroom at the end of the day, Maria took over. His students closed the windows, pulled the shades down to half-mast, put their chairs up on their desks for the custodial assistant who would have to sweep, got their clothing and books, and got in line. A few students policed the room for balled-up pieces of paper and checked the rear cabinets for any closeted "renegade" textbooks. Others just waited quietly.

Vinny was subdued, and a few other students whispered animatedly among themselves. It was business as usual.

One student hesitantly approached Earl. "Excuse me, Mr. Chaney. I just wanna say I'm sorry. I know he was your favorite student."

"He wasn't my favorite student!" Earl exclaimed. "You're all my favorite students! That's what a good class is! Let's get that understood!"

The student blinked at Earl. "Oh, well, I hope it turns out okay." The student then started to move away.

"Hey," said Earl. "Pay me no mind."

Mr. Rako walked in on the class as they were moving toward the door. "I would like to speak to the class for one moment before you leave."

A faint groan reverberated through the class.

"We can do better than this, can't we class?" said Earl.

Mrs. Stanton went by with her class. She briefly looked at Earl, pressed her lips tightly together in sympathy, and then moved on.

With Earl's class hushed, Mr. Rako proceeded, "I just want to make sure you understand what happened today. When Kaseem was transferred to your class, he was already on borrowed time. Yes, he improved greatly with you, and you should take credit for that. He did a remarkable turnaround in here that should go down in the annals of our school. And he did commendable, quite admirable things. But there's a lesson to be learned here. You can't go to one teacher, be a model student, and then turn around and be an absolute hellion with another. You can't make such strides in marks and character development in school and then put a woman in the hospital outside. Being selectively good doesn't wash. The way the world is, ladies and gentlemen, the effect is that the bad ends up counting and the good fades off into nothing and is forgotten. The boy couldn't've asked for a greater opportunity than was given'm. We put'm under the charge of the best, most sympathetic teacher he could have gotten. No one can say we didn't give him his chance."

He turned to Earl and asked him to step into the corridor. The other classes were still filing to the stairwell.

"Look," the administrator said to the dour teacher. "You can't take this personally. I shouldn't have to tell you that this profession is mostly defeat with occasional victory. You are, after all, a professional."

"Oh, am I?" the teacher returned. "I punch a time clock every morning and afternoon. How does that make me a professional?"

"Aw, for Christ's sake."

Earl bristled but contained it.

Chapter 21

He drove to the Orchard Beach parking lot and sat in his car. Though spring was well underway, the beach season had not yet really started. Most early beachgoers had long since gone home in this relatively cool early evening, leaving only a few scattered parked cars and their passionate inhabitants as well as the distant staccato sound of paddle ball players on the handball courts. Occasionally, a patrol car would cruise around to make sure no drug trafficking or other nefarious activities were taking place. Otherwise, it was a good place for solitude and self-collection.

Had he become so involved in his personal problems and inadequacies that he'd rendered himself blind to the hundreds of tiny perceptions? Was this what happened to men of his age, losing their sensitivities and acuity, a sort of pre-senility? Had he simply not wanted to attend to what he'd sensed?

The house of cards had crumbled around him. The fall of the house of Earl Chaney, doomed to a poignant finiteness and mediocrity, the very idea Dionne had been railing against and Ida seemed to accept as a mere inevitable fact of life? The flickering candles had replaced the floodlights preceding them. Only his candle had never gotten lit.

The crumbling of his marriage. The fine human being Anthony had become, most likely not to the credit of him but to Ida and whatever worthy boyfriends she'd managed to entice between her legs. His acceptance of weak excuses for wrongdoing, lapses, or disappointments. His iron containment of his rage that would probably put him in his grave someday. His spiritual paralysis. A teaching career that had gone nowhere. The students arrived to his class poor writers and thinkers, uninterested in quality literature, and left unchanged. He had to look upon the Ingrams and Rakoes as either superiors or at least equals though he knew in his heart they were neither. The contempt his colleagues had for him and he for them.

His mother and father, who looked at him with ill-concealed disappointment. They tried to wear masks of satisfaction, but it showed through like melting ice in a paper bag. Did he ever give them reason to react otherwise? Ida was a nice person, they often said to him. You should've held onto her. Dionne had class. Brash on the edges maybe. Got carried away at times. But feisty. You should bring her around more. Unless it doesn't matter to you since you'll probably soon be rid of her, too. We don't see enough of our grandson, though he does call, which is not enough. Why couldn't you have put forth a little more effort and gotten yourself a law degree? More money, you know, more prestige. Schoolteachers're nothing in this society. They're the niggers of the professions. And for the life of us, we can't see why you wanna waste time with that hoodlum. A leopard doesn't change its spots. When you're no good, you're no good, and that's that. Just like all your life. Putting all your apples in the wrong basket.

But there were those good things the boy did. His incredible improvement in school behavior and academics. His monitorial work. The heroic stand he took for Mario. What about that? Then again, was it all a front, a ruse to sucker all the satraps he had to deal with? To put everybody in his place, his ultimate wickedness?

He pulled the car out of the lot and started for Manhattan. By now, he'd begun to feel a heaviness in his stomach. It was said that facing the worst wasn't supposed to be as bad as it seemed. His stomach disagreed.

He had to be careful on the Cross Bronx Expressway. His mind was swirling, making concentration difficult. The rigs were out in full force this evening, westward bound. Other vehicles whipped by, their drivers lost in their own troubled worlds ... or escaping from them.

He swung off at the Amsterdam Avenue exit and worked his way over to the west side of Upper Washington Heights, where he cruised around aimlessly, anxious, hungry for something, anything, not knowing what.

What did all of this say of him as a teacher ... as a man? Was this how he struck his students? Was this his effect? And, worse, what did it now make him in the eyes of his colleagues and acquaintances? He felt like such a fool.

He thought first to go to a bar and get drunk but decided to go home instead. There, he made himself a strong rum and coke and lay down on his bed. He stared at the faint, street-created shadows on the ceiling, pale yellows mixing with pale blues, exchanging places like the glows from dying neon signs.

Soon, it all blurred, and a faint buzz came to his head. He closed his eyes, hoping sleep would rush in and whisk him away from his anguish, but it didn't come. Could he perhaps have saved Kaseem?

He plowed into his mind, seeking the unanswerable, perhaps the unthinkable. His thoughts banked to Kaseem's resemblance to Ray. Could it have been that he'd really hated the boy for this, suppressed this, and blinded himself to the danger signals in the unconscious hope that the boy would meet with disaster?

He sat up in bed. God, if that were true—

The phone rang, snatching him from his thoughts. He glanced at the clock. Six thirty!

It had to be Dionne. They were supposed to go to another Black Resurrection meeting that night. Still no opposing candidate to Shehab, who was about to take over by default. Time was running out on them. Dionne was growing more uptight.

No, he was in no frame of mind to deal with her tonight. He couldn't care less if Charles Manson took over the Black Resurrection organization. That was another mess he was going to push to the side.

He jammed his hands into his pockets and backed away from the phone, almost ringing off its cradle.

Then it stopped, though he thought he could still hear its ringing. He started for the front door.

Dionne! What was the matter with that woman? She could do so much better than him. She was so together. He was muddling his way through life, muddling because he'd been too fearful of organizing the group that it might lead him to other truths about himself. Safety in confused cursoriness was preferable.

He finally drove to Fort Tryon Park, where he sat in the car and stared out over the Hudson River. He struggled to turn his mind in another direction.

The pinewood pews were always so shiny, it seemed like God wouldn't allow a single fly to land on anything. Why couldn't her life be this clean of trouble? Julia knelt and briefly chastised herself for such an immature wish. She also begged to be forgiven for her behaviour in the office and hoped the girl would not grow up to hate men so that she could be a happy woman. If she only understood what inside her drove her to make the choices in bringing her son up that made him come to this.

Julia prayed for her son's soul, and she prayed for strength. Though she no longer wanted to pulverize him, her fury at him persisted, and every inch of her was still trembling. The thing for her to do now was separate from her crazed frame of mind and her personal hurt and deal with practical considerations, mainly how to get the best possible deal for Rodney.

Reverend Boston slid into the pew and took her hand. "Are you all right?" he asked.

She nodded and thanked him for asking.

"I have coffee in the rectory if you want some. Even something a little more ... medicinal."

"Don't fuss over me, Reverend. I'll be all right." She wondered what his mother had done that was obviously so right.

"I know you will, because you're a strong woman. Still, even the strongest bridges need shoring up at times."

"I'm not exactly that right now but I'll get by," she said.

He smiled at her and inhaled. "And be assured, everything's been taken care of. The lawyer we got will get the boy the best possible deal for'm."

Tears came to her eyes, so she turned away and covered them with her hand.

"No need to hide your sorrows, sister," he said.

"It's just that I don't know how this came about. There was something somewhere along the line that I did absolutely wrong to'm. When his father and I broke up, I had to do it alone. My mother'n I. Well, it never worked for me. I was never able to get his acceptance and devotion to me."

"Did his father ever see Rodney after the break up?" he asked.

She hesitated. "I wouldn't let that lying hypocrite near the boy. Not if he gave me a year's rent, which he never did, of course. He couldn't. Well, maybe I was wrong."

"It may've been a serious mistake not to let boy and man have their time."

"But I made it up to'm. There's no man in my life. Never has been, except for company one or two times. There's been no life of my own to speak of. There was only Rodney. Got these little pieces of jobs. Got'm a home in this neighborhood. Worked as hard as I could. Called myself doing for'm. So what great wrong did I do'm? That he should turn around and pound everything in my life to dust?"

"It's not for me to take that on. The answers are deep within you. But I can tell you. Condemnation will only keep the answers hidden. How did your mother take this?" he asked.

"She was amazing. Took it like I'd just told her what was on TV tonight and went into the kitchen. I know she's there, crying."

"She should come see me as soon as she can."

"Yes," Julia admitted.

"The thing to think about now is the boy's welfare."

"Of course."

"He should've had some man in his life," the reverend said again. "You, too."

"I've just never trusted anybody enough to—"

"It's yourself you have to trust."

Her ex-husband had actually crossed her mind on this day, and certain forgotten and lost feelings began to make themselves known again. She'd see him on occasion, only because the relentless, investigating side of her had led her to him, unbeknownst to him.

She cruised up to the corner, sat in her double-parked car, and looked across St. Nicholas Avenue to St. Nicholas Park, where Kevin and some of his friends were congregated around a park bench, sharing a bottle wrapped in a brown bag.

Watching him, she no longer hated him, no longer loved him, but did feel a profound sorrow for him and what they had lost. Like his friends, he had gone to great seed. The first thing she noticed was his jacket, filthy beyond words, torn at the elbows, and frayed at the sleeves. The same was true of his chinos that were five shades darker from soot than they should have been. His sneakers had openings on their edges, where the toes showed through and looked like they'd been walked in oil slick for years.

Revulsion gripped her.

He was passing the brown-bagged bottle to a buddy after he had taken a long pull on it, causing another buddy to comment, which precipitated animated arguing between them, joined in by others while still another cut the fool on the sidewalk. They were like pitiful clowns going through a raucous pantomime of absurdity, folly, and self-degradation. They barely seemed to notice the two attractive women who walked disdainfully by them. The only serious figure in that pageant, in fact, was the bottle passing from one pair of lips to another.

She wanted badly to get out of her car, walk across the street, and pull Kevin from his friends so that she could tell him about Rodney. Instead, she remained immobile. She just could not bring herself to do it. She could only fight tears of fright and anger as, shaking her head forlornly, she started her ignition and drove away.

———

Washington! The name crashed into Earl's mind, bringing with it a still-poignant sorrow. It seemed to him that many of his troubles stemmed from his unresolved relationship with this man. So many of his relationships were sloppy and immature. If only his tortured emotions could climb up to whatever intellectual understanding he had of his circumstances. But that kind of marriage always eluded him.

He reached into his glove compartment and rummaged around in the back of it with his fingers, knocking old ticket stubs and crumbled sales slips aside. He was sure the paper with his number would be here, if somewhat less readable.

He found it beneath a rag he used to wipe his side windows with. Almost in tatters, it was amazingly still readable even in the dim flashlight glow. His memory brought it forth all the more clearly.

He drove to the block where Washington had lived only to learn that he had moved away two years earlier. Now his heart was pounding.

He went to a candy store to look him up in the phone book. In no time, his trembling finger found the number, so all escape routes had been blocked.

Washington lived on a brownstone side street off Broadway in an area just north of Lincoln Center. Because he wasn't home, Earl decided to sit in his car and wait. He didn't have to wait long.

The eyes were unmistakable, still piercing, still evincing a great strength behind them. This was evident to Earl even through the beard and the slightly increased beefiness of the man just entering the block with groceries. Evidently, also, an increased fatigue had set in, and the sideburns had begun to go gray.

Earl watched him go upstairs and then paused, monitoring his heartbeats. Finally, he took a deep breath and got out of the car.

"Yes?" came the voice inside the apartment.

"It's me," said Earl, voice quavering. "Chaney. Earl the Pearl Chaney."

There was a long pause before the click of the lock stabbed the hallway silence and the door opened, revealing a flabbergasted Washington.

"I'll be goddamned," he said, gaping at the teacher. "Nigger, what in the hell's your story? You'd better get your butt in here before I have to kick me some ass all up and down this hallway." He pulled Earl in and wrapped his arms around him in a tight embrace. Earl followed suit. Then he pushed Earl away. "If you ain't something else. How long's it been?"

"Fifteen and change." He eyed a photo of Washington on a hall table.

"And you don't look like you aged a minute," Washington said. "You must not be getting much pussy."

"Well, it's more qualitative now rather than quantitative."

"Sheeeeit. Come on. Come on. Sit down."

He pulled Earl into a spacious living room nicely but modestly furnished, comfortable; Earl figured six grand had been thrown into this apartment, its center a photo of a stunning black woman on the mantel of an unused fireplace.

"Your woman?"

"Wife." He shrugged. "Donna's her name."

"She's a knockout."

"Thanks. Teaches accounting at Bronx Community. I'm a research assistant for CBS. We managed to scrape a few pennies together. Splurge on a Big Mac from time to time."

"A few pennies, huh?" Earl said.

"Uh-oh. Gonna run that soldier-of-fortune-gone-bourgie-on me?"

"No, no, nothing like that."

"What're you drinking?" Washington asked.

"Scotch. Just enough soda to make the alcohol get upstairs faster."

"I hear ya." He went to a fancy, rather elaborate mirrored bar in the corner. "Where you been keeping yourself?"

Earl paused and looked off before the drink being placed in his hand snapped him to. They toasted, and he drained his glass.

Washington regarded him. "Don't tell me you're gonna jump out ahead of me."

"Donna due home?"

"Not for another hour. Want me to throw a Swanson in the oven for you? Won't fill ya to the gills but keeps the paunch reasonably down. My nutrition, nights she's working."

"No, you go ahead."

Washington disappeared into the kitchen. "What's up?"

A faint buzz had started in his head as he followed his friend.

"Look, man," he said. "There's an unresolved issue between us."

Washington slammed the oven door and faced Earl, now leaning against the kitchen doorjamb. He said nothing.

"After that Civil Rights demonstration in that town, we sat in that bus terminal bar and promised to keep in touch. I didn't keep my promise. I didn't call and dropped out of sight." He stopped and stared at Washington.

"And so?"

"So don't be so hail-fellow-well-met with me with this between us."

"We can at least be civil. Goddammit, man, we haven't seen each other in fifteen years, and I'm about to eat," Washington said. "Why the hell'm I gonna involve myself in stomach-wrenching recriminations and wrangling?"

"I'm not here to wrangle with you."

"Then let's deal with it without the edges in our voices."

"Okay, look, you're right. Why don't you sit down and let me speak my piece, and then I'll be gone, because you'll want to kick me out of here by then."

"You're gonna keep it on that level?"

"If I spoil your appetite, I'll buy you a four-star dinner," Earl offered.

"Chill, brother."

"Please don't weaken my resolve. I have to push this. All right, here goes. You know why I disappeared? Because I was ashamed. You were out there in that street getting the shit kicked out of you, and I was cringing in an alley watching. I didn't run out there to help you. I just watched. And you know what? Part of me even enjoyed watching."

"C'mon."

"Because the truth is I thought I didn't like you! Because you reminded me of the sonovabitch who was screwing Ida while I was at work."

"How're the kids treating you at school?"

"Fine, fine. No problems there."

"I still dunno how you guys do it," Washington said, changing directions. "I mean, the way—"

"Hold up!" The kitchen became momentarily silent. "Now you got to know that was stupid! But I still kept getting those pictures in my mind of you fucking my wife. Which may've been my rationalization. See, the worst thing about it was if it *were* true, my reaction in that town still would've been despicable. But it wasn't even true. I barely made it in that bar. So I pulled up my stakes and faded into the background, where I've been ever since."

Washington stared at him for a long time.

"Well, say something," said Earl.

"You want me to whip you? Beat you over your head? Put you on the rack and turn the wheel? I can't. It's been too long a time. It happened in another century to some other guys on some other planet. And I didn't find out about it till just now. I mean, you whip all this on me. How'm I supposed to react? And that couldn't've been all of it, because you're here in my apartment right now. Brother man, I'm tickled to death to see you. I just can't relate to this other shit."

Earl gaped at him. Instead of relief, frustration rose in him.

"Hey, I'm not trying to make light of this," Washington said with nonchalance. "But I hope it's not gonna be the cause of us not ever being friends again."

"It's an issue between us that's got to be dealt with."

"I don't wanna deal with it, okay? What's there to deal with? I wanna sip my wine, greeze on this TV dinner heating in the oven, and goof with you. You were a pretty good buddy. But I knew something was there. I always knew. I wasn't exactly a block of cement, you know? But I accepted it, because

I dug you. And, yes, I was hurt when you boogied on me. I hear what you're saying, too. Hey, I woulda reacted the same way. Dude gruggin' with my woman behind my back, I'd go to nut city, too. Regarding that other thing, I'm not gonna judge you."

"Bullshit!" Earl exclaimed. "There's no way you're not judging me!"

"All right, I judge you. I condemn you to a lifetime of pushing that stone up that hill. Or would you prefer crucifixion?"

Earl grabbed Washington's shirt. "Don't make fun of me, goddammit!"

"Take your hands off me, brother. You ain't gon' get any absolution this way. You going a little bit off the deep end here. If you really wanna know."

Clinging to Washington's shirt, Earl shoved him backward. Washington suddenly whipped his hand across Earl's face, knocking him against the coffee table. As he rubbed his face, the teacher recovered and then went for the other, who blocked his blow with his arm, and then the two were wrestling against the kitchen doorjamb. They fell onto the dining room floor, where they found themselves in a struggling standoff.

Suddenly, Washington broke wind that caused the two, after a brief moment of abashment, to break down in laughter that was at once maniacal and fervid.

"Damn, bro," said Earl. "You about a cold sonovabitch."

"Gotta use every means possible to win."

They guffawed again.

"Happens when I get hungry."

"You'd better turn that oven up a notch."

They fell into insane laughter again.

Then it all hit Earl. The risibility turned into such a deep melancholy that the tears of his laughter became tears of sorrow.

"Hey man, this's fucking ridiculous," said Washington. "Who cares about what happened way back when. I'm just glad you here and our wrestling match is over and my TV dinner's about ready. 'Cept I'm not sharing it with you."

"I'd better go," said Earl. "I got a lotta garbage in me to deal with. And you're doing it to me again. I look like dog doo. You look like the goddamned burning spear."

"You don't look like dog doo. Maybe like the cuckoo bird but not dog doo."

"Do me a favor, please. Stop being so damned understanding. It grates me." He helped Washington straighten out some of the furniture.

"Look, I got the stew beans kicked outa me that day," Washington started. "Some dogs turned my elbows into Alpo, and I'd been threatened, spat on, scared outa my wits. And did we accomplish anything? Maybe. I like to think so. More soul folks vote now. More mayors. Splivs look the man in his eye more boldly now. And my woman's teaching college. Not bad. We take it from there. Coulda been better. Coulda been worse. I know that's not enough. 'Specially for guys like you affected more by it. But ya make do. Then again, it comes to me you been away these fifteen years. How come today you crash back into my life? What happened to you today?"

Earl burned his eyes into Washington's chin and fought more tears. "Go get your dinner, man. Before you fart us into oblivion."

"Maybe I can help."

The teacher strode to the door.

"This gonna be another fifteen years?" pled Washington.

Earl regarded him for a few seconds and said, "I'll see ya," before he left.

When he got to the Black Resurrection hall, the meeting had ended, and everyone had gone home. A few of the guards were still standing around, one or two eyeing him curiously and with a little hostility as he pumped himself up the stairs and turned into the dimly lit hall. He noticed a sliver of light in the back, meaning the office was still open.

He interrupted a conference that Shehab was holding at his desk with a few of his guards. They looked up quickly as if surprised in some conspiracy.

"Little early for the next meeting, ain't you?" said Shehab. "Tonight's ended over an hour ago."

"Your woman was looking for you," said one of the guards. "We couldn't cover for you, 'cause we didn't know the situation, know what I mean?"

"But she didn't look too happy," said another.

"So what can I do you for?" Shehab finally asked.

From some great distance, Earl watched himself fix his eyes on Shehab. "You get that opposing candidate yet?"

"No, and can't say we didn't try."

"I can."

Though the guards didn't move, Earl could sense them tensing. A slight ringing came to his ears, which was accompanied by a warmth in his cheeks. It was evident to part of him that the drinks he'd had earlier that evening were definitely doing their work on him. "May I ask you something?" he said, drawing no reply. "Why did you have Iggy beat up?"

Shehab stood up. "Brother, I think you've been hitting the sauce."

"I didn't ask you that."

"Would you please leave?"

"What?" Earl said. "You're going to have your boys help me to the door?"

"I'm sorry you have that image of us," Shehab said. "Because you're an educated man, and we coulda used you in our organization."

"Was Iggy going to run against you?"

The guards burst out laughing as Shehab looked down to conceal his amusement.

"I say something funny? Y'know, one thing I never quite understood. What *is* your program?"

"Why don't you go home, sober up, and come back tomorrow night when I announce that I'm taking over for lack of an opposing candidate. Then you'll hear about my program."

"Y'know," interjected a guard. "You shouldn't listen to Dionne so much. She thinks too much with her twat."

Earl stared at him for a few seconds. "You know, I think I just got a glimpse of your program, Shehab. In fact, I think I just got a glimpse of what Black Resurrection's all about." Then he turned to Shehab. "Well, I'm announcing my candidacy."

Now they burst out in loud guffaws, giving each other five, strutting around the desk.

"All right, guys. Let's get serious now," said Shehab, recovering. "You can't do that. You declined when Dionne nominated you. The nominations're now closed."

"How can they be closed when no one's been nominated to oppose you?"

Silence answered him.

"Do you have a program?" asked Shehab.

"Yes, and it'll be more fully developed by tomorrow. Unlike yours."

"Why you so hostile, brother?" asked one of the guards.

"Don't patronize me."

"Patronize you?" Shehab started. "You come in here half-bombed, telling us about some half-assed intention of taking on the heavy responsibility of running for office here—after first declining when you were nominated—as if this was some jive organization. And you got the audacity to tell us not to patronize you? What's your name? You think because you come from the Civil Rights Movement, you got all the goodies we need? Take a good look around you, and you'll notice that don't mean a thing. Not a thing. Okay. You come in here tomorrow evening, let Dionne nominate you, present your program to the folks, and we're holding our election. Sometime early next week. We can't wait any longer if we're to qualify for any funds. Maybe it's just as well. You know what you'll accomplish? I'll end up getting such a heavy vote—much of it to put you in your place—that it'll come off a mandate for me."

"Do you need a mandate?"

"Not really, but I'm not gonna stand here and discuss my political needs with you."

"Of course, you're right. Forgive my impudence." He went to the door, stopped, turned back to them, chuckled to himself, and went down the lonely flight of stairs. Outside, he realized he was trembling and that the drinks he'd had at Washington's place were wearing off. He still needed to drive carefully as he'd been doing all night. To clear his head, he took the long route to his car. He walked vigorously and took deep breaths.

Maybe this would make up for Kaseem and Washington, he thought. A kind of peace settling over him as he turned a corner to his parked car.

He stopped.

Three men were leaning against the vehicle.

Someone behind him with whiskey breath said, "Your short, ain't it, bro?" He gave Earl a gentle push, and they joined the trio, none of whom Earl recognized. They wore various types of worn, dark-colored sweaters and jeans.

"Aw, fellas," said Earl, now very alert. "What's this?"

"You an educator, right?" said whiskey-breath, obviously the leader. "You impart that knowledge to our youth."

Earl noted that the street was empty and that he was a distance from the nearest lamppost light.

He clamped down on his impulse to run, because he was too far from any escape route. He was in no condition, and most important, being caught somewhere else and knocked down to the pavement would be both undignified and unmanly. He became merely watchful.

"Now why you wanna get yourself involved with that jive Black Resurrection group?" continued the baleful leader. "They ain't gon' do nothing 'cept waste people's time and energy."

"And money," said another.

"And money. Yeah. Check it out." Whiskey-breath drew closer as did the others. "Look, bro. Lemme clue you in to something. Shehab ain't nothing but a CIA agent, all right, vampin' on the community. The skank's collectin' money from them to keep the community tied up in nonviable activities, y'understand what I'm sayin' to you? You run against'm in the elections, you gonna legitimize the group, and that'd be helpin' the CIA pigs. Now I know you don't wanna do that, do you?"

His heart now pounding, Earl eyed his antagonist and then glanced at the others.

"I don't hear your answer," said another.

The third jabbed his fist into Earl's stomach, doubling him over. Another elbowed his shoulder.

"Be cool, y'all," said whiskey-breath. "And don't hit'm in the face, 'cause he gotta present that Ivory Snow image to the students. Am I right or wrong?" He slammed his open palm against Earl's chest. "Huh? Huh?"

Another hand came down hard on his back just before an iron fist hammered his shoulder, knocking him slightly to the side.

"You know, you get carried away," he heard one say to another.

"Shut the fuck up," said the other, and Earl's other shoulder took a rocket blow from steel knuckles.

Then whiskey-breath filled his nostrils. "Do yourself and us a favor. Don't run against the scumbag, huh? Mess everybody up." Then there were rapid footsteps and silence broken only by a distant car horn before someone said, "You all right, mister?"

For a long time, he soaked in his bathtub with steaming hot water filled with Epsom salts while the phone rang off the hook. There was something about that beating that brought home to him the unresponsive, victimized nature of his life. The things done to him with no retaliation from him.

Shehab and the CIA? The thought made Earl burst out laughing, causing waves and splashing. What on earth would they want with him? To sabotage Black Resurrection? It's like giving a hotfoot to a statue. And so incorrect.

His body still smarting, he went to bed, not before he called the district registry at the board of education to inform them that he would not be in the next day. He felt sorry for momentarily deserting his students, but he was in no state of mind to give them what they had a right to expect from their teacher.

He decided he would not cancel the weekend trip to the woods. He would merely replace Kaseem and keep to his plans.

After a restless night's sleep and breakfast, he felt a little better, enough to venture from his apartment and take a drive in the country. Though the scenery was beautiful, it soon began to bore him, so he headed back to the city. Gnawing at him was the desire to take something in his fist and smash it or take charge of it. Strangely, he felt no resentment toward his attackers. It went beyond them to something else in his life, something still plaguing his deepest recesses.

He knew now he wasn't going to return to Black Resurrection. The fear had now gripped him too firmly. If he could only wrench himself and his intentions from his coward's shell—

What about Dionne? Would he see her again? Could he ever be the man she deserved? He did love her. But he did not want to foist onto her life an unsettled and tormented soul any more than he already had.

And what about Washington? The man certainly did not deserve the treatment he'd given him. The simple solution, he considered, would be to slink away again and to slink away from Dionne. Better to do that than to turn her beauty into a premature harridan.

He found himself right back at the beginning of the circle, trapped into making an evaluation, a choice, a decision, when he had no real answers. If he'd only had another chance in that alley in that southern town. Perhaps he could turn things inside out.

Then maybe any future Kaseems put in his charge would respond in a different way to him or at least be honest. If he ever bothered again.

Chapter 22

Kascem still had difficulty believing all this had happened to him, though something deep inside him had known it was inevitable. He distantly watched a cell mate go to the bathroom in their one toilet (unconcealed and serving four young men) and was surprised to note that he wasn't as revolted as he had thought he would have been. Still, he had yet to move his bowels.

He leaned against the bars and maintained an attitude of nonchalance, though not so much that it would call attention to him. He kept a blank expression on his face and mainly kept to himself, frugally doling out occasional "what's up, bros" and liberation handshakes. It was not as bad as he had thought.

What he really did have difficulty adjusting to was the continuous din, punctuated by eardrum shattering outbursts of atonal violence. The noise always seemed drenched in rage, resignation, frenzy, desperation, and sorrow.

This latter always brought him back to his own melancholy. His rancor toward his mother considerably dampened now, it cleared his mind for acknowledgment of what he'd done to her and his grandmother. He felt true remorse for that and what he must have done to Mr. Chaney, Mrs. Stanton, and Reverend Boston. He'd hurt a lot of people close to him, important to him.

Spriggs must have been laughing. Vinny and Michellene, too. And he wondered just how much they'd had to do with what had happened to him. Some of those teachers he'd noticed applauding unenthusiastically when he received the award.

Though he tried not to think of his mugging victims, when he did, he found he felt little remorse. This was problematic for him, for, objectively, he knew there should have been more. The victims, though, seemed so remote and foggy in his consciousness, except that girl, Nancy, whom he'd come face to face with in the hallway and anteoffice, whose tears had been a harsh reality for him, superseding even the subsequent events.

"Wilson!" woke him up with a start one early afternoon. "Visitors!" He'd been restively napping on his bunk, chow not being quite ready yet. Most of the inmates were out in the yard, playing basketball, lifting weights, and generally hanging around, some conspiring to commit this or that malfeasance. He hadn't felt like being bothered with experiencing any of it, directly or indirectly. Nor had he felt like hanging by the walls like a wallflower that might draw unwanted attention to him.

The tall corrections officer with rolls in the back of his neck led him through a long corridor to the visitor's room, an elongated, oblong chamber with tables arranged in two zigzag formations, with two guards patrolling among them and one at the entrance. The chamber was almost empty at this time, the bulk of the visitors not having arrived yet.

Julia was there, along with a neatly dressed young black man with a small goatee. The correction officer sat Kaseem down and then disappeared.

Julia's eyes bore into her son, who looked down. Her face was of stone, and she seemed older.

"Rodney," said the gentleman, extending his hand to the youth and shaking it. "I'm Ezra Horne, your representative." He began to open up his valise as Kaseem nodded to him.

"How are you, Rodney?" Julia asked.

"Okay," said Kaseem, sitting stiffly in his seat.

"Are they treating you all right?"

"Yes."

Ezra then spoke. "And you'd let us know if they don't, you hear?"

"Where's Grandma?" Kaseem asked.

There was a long pause.

Ezra cleared his throat. "Wear your Sunday best your mother gives you when your date comes up, which'll be very soon. Stand up straight and look the judge in the eye when you come before'm. Answer respectfully and directly when spoken to and speak up. Don't mumble. What you have on your side is your recent record in school, your award, your turnaround. Are you following what I'm saying to you?"

"Yes, sir," said Kaseem.

"Good, like that. Soft but not so soft we can't hear you."

"Grandma couldn't come?"

Julia stared at him. He could see the red outlining her eyes now. "I told her not to come. I'm not punishing you. I just wanna make sure not to subject her to any undue stress."

Kaseem looked down and choked back his tears. "I guess I understand," he said with a quavering voice.

"There's something else you have to understand," added Ezra. "Our judge, Judge Hyrniak, is somewhat of a hard nose, I'm afraid. He's for grounding the youth of the world till they're thirty. All I can say is put your best foot forward and hope he doesn't stomp on it. If things go as planned, we can get you one—at most three—with two for good behavior."

"What if things don't go as planned?" the youth asked.

"Throw such thoughts from your head for all our sakes."

The two adults stood up. Julia bent down and tenderly kissed her son on his forehead. "Take care of yourself, son," she said, scrutinizing him momentarily before leading Horne out of the room.

He sat and stared ahead into space for a few moments until his corrections officer escort returned and took him to the cafeteria. He was not hungry, so he snatched a muffin off the tray and absently munched on it as he strolled along the lower level corridor toward the rear of the building. Amidst the caged, bulbous boilers, there was usually very little activity, and few correction officers came around.

He sat on a metal step and surveyed the goliath machine works around him with their pythonlike pipes and myriad of exhausts and meters, all caged in a kind of metallic rainforest. The inmate din was still prevalent but less pronounced now, more distant. He imagined that all kinds of secretive negotiations must take place in this lonely area.

Presently, a new sound came to his ears, one mixed in with all the others, a continual grunting sound punctuated by skin being slapped and accompanied by *sotto voce* but excited human exclamations: "My man tearing it up!" and "Hurry up, Hog. This ain't no damn honeymoon!" When he focused on the sound, he perceived that the grunting was colored by pain and anguish. Was somebody in difficulty somewhere and calling for help? Not able to determine what it was, something inside him propelled him to investigate.

He stole along a lower catwalk and around one of the larger boilers.

He froze and ducked back. Then he carefully leaned forward and observed four young men, bare-legged with their briefs pulled off, standing around a fifth who had mounted a single person on his hands and knees, crying out and grunting. As the others cheered him on, the "piggyback rider" was thrusting his haunches violently at the bare behind of the other, a male dog on a female. Each time the "mounted" cried out, the one atop him would smack him on the back of his head and shoulders, telling him to "shut up, bitch."

The others laughed cruelly.

Sickened, Kaseem backed away from this scene and turned to rush out only to bump into the pointing stick of a corrections officer saying, "What the hell're you doing here? What're you doing here, Wilson?"

Kaseem couldn't answer. The officer backed him against the gate.

"Listen closely to me, asshole. You don't belong here. You're gonna wind up cleaning every toilet on the top floor. How'd you like that? Huh? How'd you like to get transferred to Rikers? Keep outa places you don't belong. He's a creep. Did an eight-year-old girl. He's lucky this's all that's happening to'm. So if you know what's good for you, you get your black ass the fuck outa here right now. And don't you dare open your yap. Understand me?"

Kaseem rushed to the yard, loitered confusedly for a while, and then went to the dayroom, where ping-pong was being played and various minds concentrated on chess, checkers, double solitaire, coon-can, and an unremarkable TV screen. A few corrections officers, one female, stood around studying the inmates. One of the corrections officers looked like a supervisor.

Kaseem sat down at one corner table and folded his hands on it. Who the hell'd that hack think he was talking to that way? He had a good mind to report this whole thing.

He could have been that victim, the creep. After all, had he not snatched a gold chain from that sixth-grade girl in his desperation to do as many chain snatchings as possible? He imagined it was he being mounted, gang-raped, and ridiculed by those boys. The thought filled him with terror and disgust.

Suppose they found out? How would he defend himself? He'd seen some of the detainees look at him as if he was a piece of meat, and it made him uncomfortable. He made it his business never to find himself in any isolated situation, nor to allow himself to be pulled into the midst of any of the groups he'd been warned about.

Suddenly, a pungent indignation gripped him, and his eyes turned toward the supervising corrections officer in the dayroom, watching a near-violent ping-pong game. How dare that hack talk to him that way? He swallowed a mouthful of air and saliva and stood up. Admittedly, he knew that if he told, it might bring untold repercussions upon his head, but it was only right. So what? What they had been doing to that guy was unforgivable.

Still, could he trust his luck now? Things had backfired on him so fast, could he ever trust his life to go along predictable paths again? For the first time, he was beginning to wrestle with matters of right or wrong. His mother? His grandmother? What he'd done to Vinny was wrong, of course. Michellene? Did they cause what happened to Fox and him? It mattered and then didn't. His victrims. Did they really not matter? And what about Mr. Chaney?

He was about to take a step toward that supervisor when somebody tugged him on his sleeve. He tensed, inhaled, balled his fist, and turned around, ready to swing out with all his might. They could put him into the deepest bin after for all he cared.

It was a young man, terror filling his face. "Can I talk to you?" he said in a trembling voice.

For the longest time, Kaseem suspiciously regarded him until it dawned on him that this had been the victim of the gang-rape earlier. He jerked his arm from the other's grip. "Couldja come with me please?" the terrified young man pleaded.

"I ain't going no place alone with you," shot back Kaseem.

"Just over here to the corner of this room."

Kaseem looked at the far end of the room, where a few detainees were napping on a large sofa and one sat pensively with his face between his fists. He reluctantly moved to that area but remained standing as did his "companion." They spoke in low voices.

The "victim" looked down. "They ganged up on me and—"

"I know," Kaseem said. "So?"

"They said they were gonna do something to you if you told."

"Think that means a fiddly fuck to me?" He gestured toward the perceived supervisor. "That's the big cheese over there, right? I'll walk right over there, and any mothafucker comes near me, I go to nut city. And that includes you."

The "vic" turned away. "Okay. They said if you say anything, they're gonna ice me and tell my family about—"

Kaseem glared at him. *Goddammit. Why'd I have to go down there anyhow? Why'd I have to go down there?*

"Something the matter?" he heard a female voice say behind him. He turned to face a decade younger version of his mother, spruce in her uniform as his mother was as a nurse.

"Nothing," he said. "He owes me some money, that's all." Oddly, at this moment, thoughts of Fox came to mind, how he was faring.

She looked at the other youth. "What's the matter with you?"

"I don't have his money right now," he answered.

She regarded him momentarily before she looked again at Kaseem.

"Don't make loans, hear? That's where a lot of our trouble comes from. We don't need that kind of trouble." Then she strolled away to another side of the room.

Kaseem looked at his "new homie," sucked his teeth, and went to the library, where he took out a copy of W. E. B. Du Bois's *The Souls of Black Folk*, which he'd been sampling on and off. He sat at a lonely table and stared into the pages, trying to decode the ideas that stabbed up at him.

CHAPTER 23

Earl called Dionne on her job. (She worked as an editor's assistant for a fashion magazine.) She seemed almost to come through the phone.

"Where the hell've you been?" she almost screamed. "I've been out of my mind trying to call you."

"Look, I'm sorry. I've been going through some changes."

"When I didn't hear from you, I thought maybe … we were through."

"No, hon. C'mon. Is that the kind of guy you think I am? A creep who slinks off in the night?"

"That's how crazy I got," she said. "Sorry. I didn't mean that. But you didn't call and— What happened?"

"Everything fell apart on me yesterday. A million things went every which way. You could say I bumped into myself and met with a total disaster of a life."

"Oh, Earl."

"I won't bore you with the details," he said. "But I'll tell you I'm scrambling."

"Please don't go on like that."

"Look. They're having that meeting tonight, right?"

"Meeting?" Dionne said. "Shehab's travesty? Yes, he makes his announcement, with great pretended regret, to take over."

"Okay. Nominate me again. I'm running against'm."

There was a pause at the other end. "Oh, darling, I'll work with you. I'll stay with you every step of the way."

"I hope so," he said. "Because you have a babe in the woods on your hands now."

Earl reentered a strange new world, a world from the past. He'd impulsively taken a Delta Airlines hop back to that southern state, to that southern town. There, he took a bus from the airport and soon debarked at the bus terminal of that town now called Jason's Point, named posthumously after a black Viet Nam war hero.

The terminal seemed the same, except for the video games being played by teenagers who should have been in school at this time (possibly on the verge of "escaping" to New York City) and the giant-sized photos of Dolly Parton, President Reagan, Jerry Lee Lewis, and Magic Johnson. A few would-be roustabouts stood around, and people sat on the hardwood benches, waiting with their meager belongings, on their way to some vital destination.

He took a cab into the town proper and noted how similar it was to that mysterious, distant place of his tortured remembrances. New stores were there—Rexall Drugs, K-mart, Sporting equipment/hunting gear/fishing tackle stores, florists, housewares, health and beauty aid stores, and those selling stationery, office equipment, doodads, and other thingamajigs. A few stores from old were still there—the haberdasheries and antiques shops, the hardware store with its farm equipment supplies, and the one bowling alley. It was all very familiar but so foreign to Earl.

His ears began to warm as the cab turned into the main street, where it'd all happened, relatively unchanged, a few up-to-date touches here and there, more traffic lights, more pavements, more vehicles.

"Visitin' relatives?" snapped his attention to the driver. For the first time, he noticed the man, sunglasses, graying temples, slightly tanned back of the ruddy, rough-hewn neck.

"No, just stopping by. Going back to New York in an hour," he answered, studying the man.

"You a schoolteacher or lawyer?"

"Teacher," Earl said.

At a red light, the man turned around in his seat and faced Earl. The face! It looked so familiar! It couldn't have been the face of one of those men who'd menaced him in that alley! He studied the nose, the turn of the jaw, the faint hint of piercing eyes behind those sunglasses. Possibly, was it the trickery of an imagination desperately seeking some sort of closure?

"More power to you," he said to Earl and turned back around in his seat.

A car horn honked next to them, and the cabby turned toward the vehicle.

It was a black cab driver who pointed to Earl's driver with mock menace. The latter returned the gesture, and both laughed and honked at each other before the black driver took his passenger down a side street to the right.

Earl's driver made a leftward arc past the municipal building and around the town square with its nicely manicured lawns and artfully arranged flower beds of black-eyed Susans. Then they were approaching the alley.

His heart now pounding, Earl got off and paid the cabby, who offered to drive him back to the airport at a discount. Earl smiled at him and offered that he had limited funds and would go with the bus. He thanked the cabby, who gave him his card before he drove off.

Now he turned toward that alley and started slowly to walk toward it. It was different now, a small apartment house on one side and a furniture store on the other. The surrounding world seemed to get darker as he stepped to the opening and looked into the alley along the faded, rusty walls and at the minimal piled-up debris.

Was he seeking out the ghost of another Earl or merely the reflection of something still very much present inside him? Who was there in that alley? What was causing the terror still filling his insides? Who had been that stranger who had cringed before the threatened onslaught of those three men? And why hadn't he swallowed his terror and flown at them with all the rage he had? When one of them spat on his shoe, why hadn't he at least just kicked the air at them and screamed imprecations? Why couldn't he have chosen one of those actions rather than the one he had? Would it have made a difference? Would it have mattered in the scheme of things? When they subsequently threw him into the jail cell with his fellow demonstrators, would he have felt less poignant shame? Would he have lived thereafter with as much rage, cynicism, and self-loathing? Was this place forever to be the synecdoche of all his personal failures?

"See a rat in there or something?" someone asked behind him. He turned to see a dark-skinned young man with large lips and wide nostrils whose broad shoulders gave him the appearance of considerable strength.

"No," Earl replied, noting his sheriff's deputy uniform with its sharp creases. "Just staring into the alley."

"Sure everything's cool? You see any monsters in there, lemme know so I can book."

Earl smiled and nodded, and the deputy started away.

"There is one thing," blurted the teacher, bringing the deputy's attention back to him. "There was a voter registration demonstration years ago."

"In front of city hall?"

"Yes."

"I wasn't old enough to participate in it, the deputy said. "My grandmother made me stay home with my aunt. Said she would whup my butt to a fair-thee-well if she saw my face anywhere near this town that day. And yet she herself went to jail. Some kinda woman, my gran. Stayed on my butt something fierce."

"That couldn't've been Annabelle, could it?"

The deputy's face lit up. "Were you one of the demonstrators?"

Earl nodded and looked down.

"Your name is—"

"Chaney. Earl Chaney."

"The schoolteacher? Get outa here! Gran used to talk about you alla time. How you and that other fella—"

"Washington," Earl said.

"Yeah, Washington. Came down here from New York and turned it out. I mean, the stories she useta tell us. My gran had so much admiration for y'all. She'd get all weepy-eyed every time she mentioned you. Thought y'all dropped down to us from the heavens above. And I finally get to meet you. My name's Gus."

"Thank you," said Earl as he shook hands with Gus. "How is Annabelle?"

"Oh, she passed. Seven years ago. The jail. Crackers throwing stuff at the house. Whole buncha nonsense. Finally was too much for her. But this town got a lotta things to thank her for. Lotta changes."

"I'm sorry," Earl said, regarding Gus.

"Our history, man. Hey, follow me." The deputy suddenly walked into the furniture store. "Hey, Mr. Zee!"

A short black man, balding, with a paunch, came forward from the rear of the store. The deputy gestured toward Earl. "Know this guy?"

Mr. Zabroman looked at Earl and smiled. "Do I know this man? Of course, I know'm. One of our great heroes." He wrapped his arms around Earl, who by now was totally baffled but deeply moved.

He held Earl at arm's length and looked at him with deeply admiring, watery eyes. "Earl Chaney, the teacher. You turned things around, man. You'n Washington and the others. Things're different now. You may've noticed. Oh, yeah, some things haven't changed all that much. Never will. Some areas you still best stay out of. Don't need to draw you a picture there. Got this business here though. Doing pretty damn good. Even got some peckerwood customers ... good customers, too, once they learn to trust you. All that's on y'all. For what y'all did, we'll be forever grateful."

To tell them the truth, to remind them, to clear up a vague romanticized memory, to confess would do more harm than good. These folks and others like them lived inside this new reality. He was not going to achieve any kind of absolution by smashing it. Ultimately, the whole issue—his cowardice that fateful day, historical memory making the event an act of bravery, partly the catalyst for major social change here, was not about him. It was about them. Whether it was another coward's way out for him or not, it would have to do.

"Thank you," he barely whispered.

"I wanna take you to see my Aunt Geraldine," said Gus, ushering Earl into the car. "Come on. Won't take long."

Gus drove him to the edge of town, now bigger, longer. Certainly, the streets were smoother, and there were more sidewalks. One and two family houses had replaced woodsy areas. Still, the country feel remained.

Gus wheeled the vehicle up a slight backward C driveway to a modest, rust red, wood-framed, two-floor building with a short porch in front. The driveway sliced through an almost perfectly neat front lawn, with multicolored roses, daisies, lilies, azaleas and lilacs.

She sat on the porch, a stout, regal, brown-skinned woman, her hair graying, her face a kindly whisper in a breeze. A warm smile filled that face.

The young deputy led Earl to the short front stairs. "Auntie Ger. I present to you the teacher who came down here and marched with Gramma."

Aunt Geraldine's eyes fell on Earl with contained exhilaration.

"Mercy me," she said while Earl later munched on half of a delicious cucumber sandwich. "Used to be you couldn't look sideways at nobody without finding your butt in trouble. I tell you, Mr. Charley, something else. Every time you turned around, somebody else was hanging from a tree or putting out a fire in his house. Terrible. Terrible. Then y'all came. Lot of ruction, I tell you. And because Mamma was in it, they gave her what-for after. Rocks through the windows. Messed up her garden. Those awful telephone calls. Finally, heart couldn't take it no more. But things changed. After Mamma's funeral, Jamie Wallace came to me and apologized for throwing the rock through the window. Asked my forgiveness, which I gave'm. I'm a Christian woman. No need giving the Devil anymore due. Come do my garden and lawn real nice every month and dare somebody to comment about it. That a fact, Earl. Come do my garden every month. Without fail."

He couldn't believe the tears that poured forth from his eyes on the flight back. As he hid them with his cupped hand, he stared out the window at the passing scene below. The regal clouds below blanketed the many-colored dots that were houses. Was this what heaven looked like as described to him from the time he was a babe? It was true; all was not as it appeared. The answers came to him from strange angles. So he might as well plunge forth, and the devil take the hindmost. This emboldened him as New York City loomed ahead.

Chapter 24

There were two guards standing at the doorway of the Black Resurrection headquarters. They were looking from side to side like two Dobermans, a two-headed Cerberus. For Earl, there were no signs of his assailants.

The security guards' eyes flashed as he approached them and the doorway, and they tried subtly to close their ranks. This didn't work, because there were many others entering the building as well. So they parted again, letting all in.

A few more of them lined the long flight of stairs, but again, they could do no more than balefully eye the teacher as he ascended. Shehab's eyes flashed when Earl entered and clasped hands with Dionne.

All settled down. Earl was nominated, and it was seconded with applause. Shehab invited him to the front, but he chose to stay next to Dionne. He was then asked to stand and give the audience his platform.

Thinking fast, he regarded the guards around the hall and then briefly locked glares with Shehab, who cut his off with a smile.

"I intend to bring the issues we must deal with to the people," Earl started. "No elitism. No I'm-in-the-know-and-you-out-there-don't-know-what-it's-all-about attitudes. The operative word here is 'we,' you and I. We're in this situation together, and we'll work with each other to improve this situation. We'll make ourselves heard whenever opposition to affirmative action programs rears its ugly head. We'll work on voter registration, fundraising, and general all-around community organizing. We'll work on unity in the community and the disunifying effect of crime. We'll interfere with the drug traffic as much as we can without putting anyone in harm's way and closely monitor the housing situation. We'll seek to strengthen the role of our religious institutions. And our families. We'll establish and maintain liaisons with the private sector, white and black. And we'll look over the shoulders of the schools where our children're being introduced to the world outside of the immediate surrounding world of the streets. And we'll get behind our disruptive students. Because they're sending messages to us, ladies and gentlemen, that we're not heeding. We'll be a positive force in the community."

"That was a very nice speech," said Shehab. "Very impressive. I'd like to ask you a question, if I may. How exactly do you propose to do all this?"

"Are we having a debate?" Earl responded.

"Do you have an objection?"

"No objection. I'd just like to know what your game plan here is."

"Let's call it a mutual review."

"Mutual?" Earl said. "You sure that's what this is? No secret rules and riggings and cryptic definitions?"

"I have no fear of anything you have to say. Work it out whatever way you want."

"Good. Because the second I smell any sneaky games in the air, I step out of this dialogue, and the devil take the hindmost." There was vengeful threat in Earl's tone.

"You're assassinating me on the sly," Shehab argued.

"I apologize. I didn't mean to be on the sly. Now, I'll answer your question. I'll use the natural resources in our community. Our youth. People who want to get involved in a worthwhile process. Set up a committee that'll keep its fingers on the pulse of the community. Find out where the talents and passions lie, which I have to do in my classroom every working day of my life. Tap the wealth of that and use it for the benefit of all."

"Again, my worthy opponent gives us dynamite ideas, beautiful sounding calls to action. Makes me wanna get on that phone and call my cousin Brooks in Glendale, where he escaped four years ago. Tell'm c'mon back, cuz. The man is here to make everything right again."

A few chuckles bubbled through the audience.

"I'm glad you're being so entertaining to our audience," Earl said. "But since this is, in your words, a mutual review, perhaps you can entertain us some more with a few answers to my questions. Of course, if you'd rather not—"

"I'll answer any questions you have to throw at me," said Shehab, slightly discomforted.

"Well, I won't exactly be throwing them at you. I'll be more like … putting them to you in the spirit of honest inquiry."

"Okay, I've been over this before, and you were present. My program is to—"

"Hold up, brother. Hold up," Earl said. "That's not what I was going to ask you. I've heard your program for the community. Seen it in action, too."

Shehab stiffened slightly. "What do you mean by that?"

"No, we're sticking to the point, all right? You're not going to lead this inquiry where you want it to go. I'm asking the question. Now, I want to know about Iggy."

Shehab squirmed. "Who?"

"Iggy. Ignatius, if you want."

The leader glared at the teacher before a moue flashed onto his face. "Oh, him. The ninth horseman of the apocalypse. The man was jockeying to take over Black Resurrection without an election. Now that wouldn't've done us much good, would it? He was out for himself."

"Did you have him worked over?"

The audience gasped as one of the guards moved down the side aisle to near him.

Earl stabbed his finger at him. "You'd better stay over there, brother man, if you know what's good for you."

Panicked, Shehab quickly signalled the guard to stop. "Now why would you wanna say a thing like that? What kinda politics do you think we do around here?"

"You don't really want me to answer that question, do you? For instance, I happen to know what that little adventure last night was really all about." He glared back at the guard. "And by the way, next time, expect serious injuries, because now I got something for you."

Dionne flashed a look at him. "What happened?" she exclaimed. She had been quiet all this time while she tried to discern what was going on between Shehab and Earl.

"I dunno what you're talking about," said Shehab, blanching.

"Yeah, you don't know what I'm talking about," said Earl, lowering his voice to control the impulse to bellow with rage.

"Earl, what happened?" pressed Dionne, grabbing his hand.

"It's all right, baby," said Earl, patting her hand, not patronizingly. "Nothing to get excited about."

Dionne turned her glare toward Shehab. "What'd you do to him?"

"Yeah, what happened?" said a man in the corner.

"I heard some shit," contributed another in the front.

A stir began in the audience.

"Five minutes ago I asked you a question that you still haven't answered," pressed Earl. "Now I know the answer."

"No, you don't," said Shehab, with pretended calm. "I had nothing to do with anything that might've happened to Ignatius."

Somebody in the middle of the hall made a strange sardonic falsetto sound. A guard gave him a dirty look.

"What was that?" said Earl, cupping his hand at his ear and leaning toward the hall area where the sound had come from. "I do believe it was the sound of truth in the surrounding air."

"I'll say this for you," interjected Dionne. "You sure do keep those brutish winos and whiskey-heads in the street employed."

Earl turned to the chuckling audience. "You've just been presented with Shehab's program. Now here's mine. First, we have to address our youth, the seeds to a better world. With the help of the schools and the churches, we have to learn how to write grants for money, not for ourselves, but for supervised after-school programs like homework helpers, how to study, self-organization, choosing the right role models, self-control and taking the future seriously. We have to set up programs for our young women so that they don't get into the demons of trouble that await them. Provide them with the proper social workers, counsellors and mentors…with the serious help of the surrounding community. And keep in mind that that community has a whole host of other problems of its own to deal with which impacts on the youth. Thus, we can build a foundation from which we can then deal with the ills of our society."

A matronly woman near another corner glanced at her watch and raised her hand.

Dionne poked and felt around Earl's back and side until her fingers found a spot, still sore from a savage punch the night before. Earl flinched slightly and she withdrew her hand in horror before she turned her eyes to the guards and then finally brought them to rest on Shehab.

"I dunno what went down between y'all, and I don't wanna know," the matronly woman posed. "What I do wanna know is do we haveta sit through this disgusting spectacle? I like what the teacher said."

The audience exploded in assent.

"I dunno about the rest of y'all, but frankly, the rest of this's turning me off," she went on. "So I'm all for tabling this bu'shit and getting on with the business at hand."

"Yeah," said another. "We heard the brother's program, and we heard yours. I got some stops to make before I hit my bed tonight. I second the brother's nomination."

Shehab continued to lock eyes with Earl. Partly, it seemed, he didn't want to meet Dionne's glare. "Okay," he said finally. "Maybe it's better if I get a mandate."

"You're not going to get a mandate," Earl asserted. "You're going to get a resounding loss,".

"After I win, I'm gonna need your kinda spirit to help me out," conceded Shehab.

Dionne squeezed Earl's hand that was now trembling, as were his knees.

He never realized how firm her grip could be.

They went downstairs to a local coffee shop where, over two cups of coffee, he dolefully told her what had happened with Kaseem, with Washington, with Shehab later that night. He told her about his mugging. (He begged her not to make an issue of it, not because he was afraid, which he was a little, but because he wanted to belittle anything he thought Shehab was involved in. Somehow, in the cockeyed recent events, Shehab had become the symbolic receptacle of all that was wrong in Earl's life and world.) Finally, he told her about his trip south and the reason for it.

She, with her affecting, unblinking eyes, just stared at him, commiseration filling her still face, not even sipping her coffee, not even breathing, it seemed. She looked like a princess of a gold-filled island, and he wanted so much to take her in his arms and go away with her. But he told her if she had any sense, she would lose him as fast as she could. He was not being self-dramatic. He was being all too sincere.

"That what you want me to do?" she asked him.

He hesitated. "Yes, I do. It'd be much easier for both of us."

"How would it be easier for both of us?" she asked, not challengingly.

He didn't answer her. He looked at her and then down, shrugging his shoulders.

She looked down at her still-full cup of coffee and inhaled deeply. "Lord up above, send me the right words to my heart and give me the power to communicate them to this man." She took his hand and leaned close to him. This time, her hand was trembling.

"All right, here goes," she said, her voice lowering. "You laid a lot of heavy stuff on me, and I guess I'm supposed to've recoiled and taken flight from this table. Well, I have news for you. You couldn't've chosen a better way to bring me closer to you. Don't you understand that the more truthful you are, the deeper my feelings for you? Don't you understand that when you think you're being embarrassingly naked, you're becoming more solidly the center of my universe? I don't mean to sound sickeningly mystic. And I know you're at sixes and sevens now. Not the greatest timing. Forgive me."

"Tell me this," he then said. "Would you want somebody like me for a husband?"

It was partly meant as a self-effacing, offhand remark. He was unsure of his responses now, so he was trying anything.

She snorted, quickly smiled, leaned back in her seat and fixed her eyes on him.

"Thought you'd never ask," she responded, her voice a slight tremble.

He peered at her and shifted gears.

"You're not being flip!" he said softly.

"No, I'm not," she said. "I'm talking about what we're talking about. And a few other things. No, you bet your bottom booties I'm not being flip. Not exactly the most romantic proposal, but I'll take it. The other stuff? Hurts that you never shared them. Okay, I understand the whole secrecy business. Still, it hurts. You have to share stuff with me, brother man. I mean it. Important to me. If you wet the bed, you tell me. I'll wear scuba-diving equipment to bed."

Earl looked down and smiled.

"Smile but take me seriously," she went on. Tears came to her eyes. "You hear? Other things. I'd like to meet Anthony someday. Before he's a grandfather would be nice. I'd like to sit down for tea with Ida. Not to pry or take notes but to get to know her. To know her would be to know myself a little more. After all, you and she did produce that marvelous person, and she did love you. Probably still does as I do. As your friend Washington does, and I'd like to meet him also. I know you're vulnerable and tired right now and this's certainly not the right time to lay all this on you, but I'm making my move, appropriate or not."

Earl blinked his eyes as he gaped at her. His coffee was cold so the waitress warmed it for him. She looked at Dionne's cup and walked off.

"Look, brother man," she finally said, sighing. "Maybe it's looked like I've been on your case, because I needed somebody to sharpen my teeth on. Maybe that's my way, wrong or right, and I need to work on that. You don't know how I've prayed every night for a moment like this. I'll stand by you, come running when you call no matter where I am or what I'm doing. And I may come across like a spoiled teenager a lot, but I'm still growing, and I'm still learning.

"Earl, my darling, lemme tell you something, I'm the best thing you have, the best thing that's crossed your path, except Anthony, of course. Ida was probably close before she strayed, and yes, it's not entirely her fault, either. Sugar, here I am. Don't look a gift horse in the mouth."

Earl briefly struggled with himself. "Not the most conventional way to accept a marriage proposal," he finally said, blushing.

"Tonight, we celebrate ... in silence," she concluded. "No sex. You soak in the tub. Lots of alcohol and lots of Epsom salts. And then we'll hold each other and rest."

His return to school was uneventful. The office staff went about their duties, smiling, greeting him, getting ready for the approaching Easter holiday. Ingram stopped at his door early that morning before the children came upstairs, leaned against the doorjamb, and smiled slyly.

"Hope they were biting," he said. "Tell ya, in this racket, you gotta take that day off every now and then."

"How were my classes?" Earl asked.

"Good. No problem. Didn't hear a peep next door. I had to cover one class. They were no problem for me."

Then the bell rang, and Ingram disappeared, much to Earl's relief. Maria smiled when she saw him. "Mr. Chaney, you're back! I'm so glad. We missed you." She walked over to him and patted his shoulder before she took the roll book and proceeded to take the attendance. Officer Spriggs rushed by and gestured to Earl. "Next week," he said and also disappeared. Maria looked at him and shook her head sadly.

The weekend trip to the woods was not postponed. He chose another of his students to take Kaseem's place—Vinny emphatically turned it down—that involved much last-minute scrambling around, the obtaining of consent slips, and numerous phone calls.

It was such a success, thanks largely to Anthony, that the class began immediately to plan for the trip to Stratford and then the Yankees game. Moreover, no administrator had taken him to task for his reactive absence. Everything went so smoothly in fact that Earl became less aware of the profound sense of humiliation still inside him. It was as if Kaseem had never existed.

The time finally came when Kaseem had to go to the bathroom. He held it as long as he could and decided to go during chow. He rushed up to his cell and quickly pulled his trousers down as he shuffled to the toilet like a slave in a silent film. (The cell doors were kept open during the day. Hardly anyone was there.)

He just barely made it and seemed to void a week of food. A female corrections officer glanced at him as she passed by and quickly looked away. He hoped the toilet paper would last him.

Then he heard voices approach the cell. He hurriedly flushed the toilet and wiped himself.

Too late.

Four young men passed by on their way to another cell. "Whoooee!" said one, closing his nose and fanning the air in front of him. "Bottle that up! No wonder we got perestroika! They heard about this new secret weapon!"

The others laughed. One glanced at Kaseem's privates and said, "Damn, brother, I know some bitches got bigger thangs than that on their titties."

"*Knock it off!*" came an approaching authoritative voice. Suddenly, there was at the cell entrance a large black corrections officer whose muscles seemed to bulge through his uniform. "What's the matter? Y'all got nothing else to do with yourselves? You can't let the young man tend to his business without bothering'm? Then you gonna complain we don't give you enough freedom. You all right in here, youngblood?"

Kaseem nodded as he washed his hands. As he listened to the receding footsteps of the others, he strained not to shed one tear, though he wanted to explode.

CHAPTER 25

As she descended the stairs, Julia knew an unpleasant scene was coming up betwen her and her mother. Her mother had always been compliant with her wishes but now, with her spirits and energy so down, she did not know how she would deal with the stalwart, dignified lady whom she so loved waiting for her at the kitchen door, fully dressed to go out.

"Where're you going?" Julia asked her mother who was dressed in a smart, dark brown, Sunday-go-to-meeting suit and corseted, with dark gray hosiery and her hair tied tightly in a bun. It was the day of the trial hearing for Rodney.

"I'm going to the hearing," she answered adamantly.

"No, you're not, Momma," Julia insisted firmly.

"I'm going to my grandson's hearing."

"I'm gonna have to ask you—"

"Save your breath, because I'm refusing your request," Mrs. MacNeil said.

"Momma-"

"That's right. I'm glad you remember who the mother is here. Now I'm going to see my grandson! This discussion is over!"

Julia picked up the suit she had for Rodney to wear, glared at her mother, anxiety flashing over her face, and marched out the door.

Mrs. MacNeil followed her.

Kaseem found himself on a school buslike conveyance that took him to the Bronx County Courthouse. He was shackled to the chair he was in, along with others, and he did not see Fox among them. Security guards watched them like hawks, and there was a slight dankness in the air. He caught a glimpse of Yankee Stadium in the distance, and then he was being taken through a long, dingy corridor at the end of which he could see the silhouettes of his mother, grandmother, and Ezra Horne.

He was taken into a room where the court attendant brought his suit to him. He put it on in front of personnel and other defendants who were putting on their own "appearance clothing."

Outside the room, Julia embraced her son, and then Mrs. MacNeil followed suit. Horne tightened Rodney's tie knot until it was almost pressing his Adam's apple.

"There," Horne said. "I want you to look tight as a drum."

Down the hall, he saw Fox being taken into another room to change. Then Fox came back out and for the first time saw Kaseem. They smiled at each other and then were taken into the court.

The first thing that struck Kaseem when he entered the court were the eyes, glaring at him, some also terrified.

Detective Wenders was there, and so was Officer Spriggs, talking to the court attendant who'd brought Kaseem the suit. Nancy was there, and so were a few others of his victims as well as a few witnesses.

Then he saw her, a slightly portly, pleasant-looking, dirty blonde lady, a cane next to her. God, the lady he'd pushed into the street at the bus stop. On the other side of her was a man who appeared to be her husband, broad-shouldered, graying at the temples, with eyes that bored deep holes into Kaseem, whose eyes looked down as he and Fox were ushered to seats at the front, Horne sitting next to Kaseem and a legal aid counsellor, Richard Romano, sitting next to Fox.

Behind them sat Kaseem's mother and grandmother. There didn't seem to be anybody for Fox, who leaned closely to Kaseem and whispered, "We're fucked."

A man slipped in and sat in the back. It was Fox's father, now sober.

Judge Hyrniak was a short man with white hair and deep lines on his pallid face. His eyebrows pushed down in a permanent frown on two smoldering coals that passed for eyes they couldn't quite conceal. He eyed the young defendants in the room and then sat down at his bench, allowing the court to sit as well.

The room became silent as he looked over the papers in front of him and conferred with the attendant. The assistant district attorney, Amy O'Reilly, a young woman who seemed fresh out of college just months ago, said a few things to the judge, and then he looked at the court.

"The people versus Rodney Wilson and Oscar Roach," he said, somewhat wearily. "I don't want to take up too much time, so let's move things along expeditiously. I've studied the defense's affidavits. Call your first witness."

And the witnesses paraded to the stand, all unhesitatingly identifying Kaseem and Fox as the chain-snatchers. Nancy, by now, was matter-of-fact about it. A few of the victims accused the youths with enraged tears in their eyes, others coldly. A few even showed rage while they were being sworn in.

There was no wavering on the part of any of them, no unsureness. If they all had spears, the projectiles would all have found their marks on the bodies of the two youths. Horne tried his best to shake their testimonies, as did Richard Romano. They tried to punch holes, but there was nowhere to punch. They could do little to cast doubt on the witnesses' reliability. They were swimming against a powerful tide.

Worse, there was no one in that courtroom who didn't know that. And the testifying victims constituted only a small percentage of the total number of victims, many waiving their right and duty to come in and confront Kaseem and Fox, many others simply unknown.

Officer Spriggs and Detective Wenders gave their testimony with their accustomed official preciseness.

Then the portly, dirty blonde lady was led by her husband to the witness stand and sworn in. Her limp was not too bad, but it was noticeable. And she had her cane.

She glared at Kaseem as she identified him. "Why?" she asked.

Judge Hyrniak looked at her. "I must ask you, Mrs. D'Onofrio, not to address the defendants."

She looked down, choking back her tears. "I'm sorry, your honor," she responded.

Her husband stood up. "She has to apologize? She may not walk right on that leg again, and she has to apologize?"

"I'll have to ask you to leave the court, sir," ordered the judge.

"I hope they let you off!" Mr. D'Onofrio shouted to Kaseem as he walked toward the door, the court attendant walking near him but not touching him. "I hope they let you go scot free!"

Mrs. D'Onofrio looked down to her lap and sobbed.

Judge Hyrniak nodded to the court attendant who brought her a glass of water that she refused. "Can you go on?" he asked her.

She nodded and pulled herself together.

"Any further questions, Miss O'Reilly?"

"I've no further questions or witnesses, your honor," said the assistant district attorney.

Fox's father also left the courtroom.

The judge looked at Ezra Horne and Richard Romano, who shook his head. Horne stood up, however, struggled within himself, and then, thinking better of it, sat back down. "No questions, your honor."

The jurist dismissed Mrs. D'Onofrio, who limped out of the courtroom to join her husband while Miss O'Reilly informed him that she rested the people's case.

Because all Horne had were the depositions about Rodney's character before the judge and Richard Romano had nothing, the judge waived any final statements from both counsels and turned his glare toward the two youths. "Stand up, please, Rodney Wilson and Oscar Roach. And I want your eyes on me."

The two youths stood up and looked at him.

"I'm not going to waste anymore of the court's time and the state's money. Let's cut to the quick. Do you have anything to say for yourselves?"

Kaseem was silent. He merely stood at attention and stared at the judge. Not completely with it, Fox looked down at his feet.

"I should think not," said Hyrniak.

"Would it do us any good to say anything?" Fox blurted out, startling Kaseem. Romano tried to hush him up. "You stacked the deck on us. Railroaded us."

"Mr. Romano, I'd suggest you control your client."

Romano, helpless, placed his hand on Fox's shoulder, but Fox shrugged him off.

"What'd you prove?" Fox continued. "Nothing! You get two niggers in front of you, you do that legalistical okeydoke and *boom!* we in the slam."

"One more word out of you, young man," Hyrniak said, "and I will slap a contempt of court charge on you."

"Go ahead! Think I care? Makes me no difference."

"You've got it! Now, from this point on, for every sentence out of your mouth, I will add a year to your time."

"I object, your honor," said Romano.

"You can object till the cows come home. Your client's going to pay for every inappropriate statement he makes in this courtroom."

"You said for me to say something," said Fox, softening.

"That's one."

Fox clammed up.

"Are you finished?"

"Yes."

"Yes, what?"

"Yes, your honor," Fox said reluctantly.

"Now, I'm sentencing you to three to six years at Wyltwick."

Fox looked down.

Judge Hyrniak's eyes turned to Kaseem. "And now Rodney Wilson. Young man, I've been in this business a very long time, seen much more than I care to remember. My experience has made me understand a lot though. True, when I look at Oscar Roach's record and his involvement in these crimes, I'm appalled. The rapacity and viciousness with which he victimized all these good people and God knows how many more makes me sick to my stomach indeed. Perhaps, though, given Oscar's background and circumstances, I can temper my revulsion a little. But when I look at someone like you, Rodney Wilson or Kaseem Abdullah or whatever you're called, my sense of abomination goes to new levels. That your mother and grandmother have to sit through this in this court after all they did for you. Sacrificing a good part of their lives so that you could have a chance at a decent life. Working their hearts out to put you on the correct road. The teachers who put themselves out for you. Your excellent record in school in these last few months. Your award. Why? Why, Rodney Wilson? Was it for the rush you young people're always blathering about? Were you trying to live two lives like *The Scarlet Pimpernel*? No, my friend, you're not *The Scarlet Pimpernel*. You're a thug. I consider you, mister, to be the real evil here. So when I look at someone like you, Rodney Wilson, my skin crawls; a chill runs right up my spine. I'm sentencing you to three to five years in the Otisville Correctional Facility upstate, only because the bounds of judiciary moderation prevent me from sentencing you to more. But you can bet your bottom dollar my eye'll be on you from here on. Your file will occupy a prominent place on my desk. Officers, remove these two from my sight."

Part of Kaseem from some distance watched his friend and him being taken away by the uniformed officers, and part of him looked through the water in his eyes at his mother and grandmother as he passed them.

Julia quietly exclaimed, and her mother squeezed her forearm.

Later, Julia toyed with the handle of her cup and stared at the quarter moon in her thumbnail. The knot in her stomach was a little less now. A faint tremble still lingered in her hands and thighs.

Mrs. MacNeil sniffed as she pulled the tea bag from her cup and laid it down on her saucer.

"Momma," said Julia quietly. "We have to hold up."

"What kinda woman I bring up?" snapped her mother.

"Pretty tough lady. And maybe that was the trouble."

"Oh, don't talk foolishness! What're you gonna do, huh? What're we gonna do? They'll probably feed'm cold food with no nutrition in it. He's a skinny rail as it is. I'll go into his room to pick up his socks." She stopped, and her tears flowed.

"Momma. Your pressure."

Silently, they finished their tea.

"Tomorrow, I'll go to the store. Buy'm a whole new supply of beeveedees. The boy never learned to wipe himself properly." Julia chuckled ruefully to herself. Then a horror came to her. "My God. If any of those animals tries anything with'm in the shower." She placed her cup down. "What'd I do to the boy to make'm do those, do those— I dunno if I can face the morning. I dunno if I want to see what'll face me in the bathroom mirror."

Mrs. MacNeil got up and went to the sink, where she silently washed the few remaining dishes there. She folded the rag and towel and hung them up.

Her daughter regarded her momentarily for any signs of dangerous upset, saw none, and then went to put her cup and saucer into the sink. She kissed her mother and then started out of the kitchen.

"Julia," she heard her mother say quietly while she focused on the chinaware. "I had you out of wedlock, but your father promised to marry me, so I was not fearful. He turned out to be no good of character and vanished to God knows where, and I was urged to give you up for adoption or the people in my village would've washed my face in it. I decided not to and brought you here instead to bring you up. Then you became a mother yourself, and I watched you raise Rodney. Julia, as God is my witness, you were ten times the mother I was. And that's all I have to say on that."

Julia went upstairs to her son's bedroom. She sat on the bed, held a rolled-up martial arts magazine in her hand and stared out of the window at a young birch tree across the street.

Maybe it's for the best, she thought to herself. *Maybe he'll finally learn to wipe himself properly.*

Then she quietly wept.

Chapter 26

With Kaseem's sentence uppermost on his mind, Earl held Dionne's hand as they entered the hall, where they found that the ballot-counting had already begun. A heavyset man from the membership was doing it, overseen by two of the guards.

"We thought we'd start without you," said Shehab, smiling. "You know how long these things take. Give us a head start."

Earl stared at him.

"You have to be kidding," remarked Dionne.

"Of course, you're losing." He turned to the ballot counter. "What're the numbers?"

"Sixty to thirty-five," was the answer.

Shehab turned to Earl and flashed another smile. "I'll tell you this," he said to the stunned teacher. "For somebody who came in late to this and was not that well-known by the people here, you didn't do too bad. Not bad at all."

"Those're very impressive numbers there, bro," said one of the guards.

"You don't believe in propriety, do you?" said Earl, silencing everybody. "Rules. The way things're supposed to be done. That's not for you, huh? You carry your own system with you. Shehab's rules of order."

"Aw, come on. You're not gonna put a pall on all this by not losing gracefully, are you?"

"What was the agreement?" Earl asked. "The votes were to be counted with both candidates present. Was that not the agreement?"

"You can always tell when somebody's losing," added one of the guards. "They start bringing up all kinds of rules and shit."

Shehab signaled him not to say anymore. The hall was filling up with people returning from a break, most of whom had voted, and the ballot count was nearing completion. Shehab had garnered ninety votes to Earl's sixty.

Dionne hugged the teacher, and a few people shook his hand.

He thanked everyone and then asked for a recount.

"Aw, come on, man," shouted someone from the audience. "That'll take all night. I got something to do later. You lost, you lost."

Now uncomfortable, Shehab signaled to the man to calm himself, and they proceeded with the recount, which took another twenty minutes, with Earl studying the ballot counter like an owl studies an unwary mouse. This time, it came to Shehab—eighty-three; Earl—sixty-seven.

"I guess you didn't get that mandate," he said to the newly elected but devastated leader, whose eyes were still avoiding Dionne's smiling face and glaring eyes.

Later that week, the teacher found a large computer-designed greeting card partially outside of its envelope on his desk. It said "We are glad you were in our class, and we will always consider you part of our class." All his official class students had signed it, and Mario's was prominent on the bottom of the card. Even Vinny's signature was scribbled unobtrusively in one corner—no doubt the result of pressure from his classmates—and Mrs. Stanton's signature was even there.

There was no address on the envelope, because no one knew where Kaseem had been sent, so its delivery was left up to Earl Chaney. He showed it to Dionne, who was deeply touched by its sentiment. He himself, though also moved, was still annoyed that such a chore had been put into his lap.

Dionne was quick to catch him up on that. "There's something else that cries for closure in your life."

"Don't start, Dionne," he said. "Please."

"I have to. I'm stripping away obstacles between us. And this's a biggie. It's why you're so peevish."

"I'm not peevish," he asserted, annoyed. "Why would I be peevish?"

"I notice your signature missing from the card," she pointed out.

"It's not my card. It's the kids' card. They made it up, didn't they?"

"This Mrs. Stanton's signature is there."

"They probably asked her," he said.

"Earl. Please. Stay with me on this. It's your card most of all. That's why they left it on your desk. Those kids went ahead and did most of the job for you. You've got to do the rest."

"Which is?"

"You've got to forgive'm. He hurt you, yes. Made you feel like a fool, yes. But you're still his teacher no matter what happened. You've got to teach'm that even what he did can be forgiven. And until you forgive him, you can't forgive yourself...which will stand as an obstacle between us."

Earl stared at her. *When was he ever going to grow up?* he thought.

Compared to the other "joints," The Otisville Correctional Institute wasn't bad. It had lots of open space, large well-organized recreational halls with bar bells, treadmills, free, hanging and wall-mounted punching bags, tables for ping pong, nok-hockey, pool and chess, and basketball hoops. Outside there was a wide field for softball, football, track and soccer. In addition to these, there were handball and racketball courts. It had a good cooking staff and the lounges had computers and TVs. Daily chores were always completed.

Almost every kind of male antisocial acterouter was there—from purse and gold-chain snatchers, burglars, other petty thieves, to drug dealers, rapists and arsonists.

The corrections officers were always alert for trouble, while relaxed in their manner and they seemed to be everywhere. Hence, there was rarely trouble.

Still, Kaseem couldn't let his guard down. There were troublemakers around and the young man could spot them from the look in their eyes and their body movement. He made it a point to stay clear of them whenever they were around.

Inevitably though, one crossed his path one morning.

A squat, pimply baby-faced young man had been constantly watching him. He had uncombed jet black hair, cut short, a pug nose and tiny eyebrows above large eyes. They made Kaseem uneasy whenever they were on him because he knew their owner would soon make a move toward him.

On this morning, though he was concentrated on the outside shrubbery as he leaned against a log fence, he became aware of a tension gripping him He could see, through his peripheral vision, that this person was approaching him. Too late to move away, he turned to face him.

"You from the Bronx, right?" said Kaseem's greeter.

Kaseem hesitantly nodded.

"I'm from Jersey," the other responded, giving Kaseem a pound. "Name's Razor. The man. Wanna ax you a question, if you don't mind. You belong to a gang?"

Kaseem felt irritation starting inside him. "Why you think I belong to a gang?" he asked.

"I ain't assuming. I'm just axing," respondent Razor. He had a tendency to maneuver himself so that he stood directly in front of Kaseem. "Don't get your nose bent all outa shape. I notice you ain't hooked yourself up with nobody here. Better change that. Niggers here start getting all over your case."

"Don't use that word, all right."

"You gonna get all uptight on me. Yall use that word against each other alla time."

"That's different." Confusion mixed with frustration in Kaseem.

"How's it different?" Razor thrust his head forward.

Kaseem started to move away from him. Razor followed him and placed his hand on his arm. "Don't walk away from me when I'm talking to you."

"Take your hand offa me," Kaseem warned.

"I'm putting my hand on you, shithead," responded Razor as he pushed Kaseem on his chest. "There. I just pushed you. What you gonna do about it?"

"Why do you wanna fight? What'd I do to you?"

"You keep to yourself. I don't trust dudes keep to themself."

"Look, get outa my face, hear?" Again, Kaseem started away but this time Razor raced up to him and punched his shoulder.

Now, rage filled Kaseem as he glared at the other. The desire to pile onto Razor and pound him to a pulp filled him. Could he control himself much longer? He began balling up his fists and seriously considering throwing a punch when Razor's eyes moved off him to behind him. A large adult hand came down gently on Kaseem's shoulder.

"Stand aside, son," came an adult voice. Kaseem turned and saw a large white male corrections officer who gently moved him out of his way and stepped to in front of Razor who suddenly had lost his steam.

"Razor, Razor, Razor," the officer sighed. "What am I going to do with you? You're just not getting it"

"He tried to snub me," protested Razor.

"Of course, like all the others," was the man's response.

"He's prejudiced," blurted the squat young man.

"Sure he is," returned the officer, jerking his thumb to behind him. "My office. Wait there for me."

Razor, disgruntled, walked past the corrections officer and Kaseem toward the door. "I'm not good enough for ya, right?" he sneered to Kaseem and then was gone.

"Don't pay any attention to him," said the officer to Kaseem. "You all right?"

Standing like a statue, the young man nodded.

"Call me Greg," the former continued, patting Kaseem on his shoulder. "Hey, come with me."

He pulled Kaseem to a large hanging punching bag and proceeded to put a pair of leather gloves on him. He walked to the other side of the bag and held it. "Ok," he said to the youth. "Let her rip. Let's see what you got."

Kaseem hesitated for a second. Then he threw a straight jab at the bag.

"You gotta do better than that," said Greg.

Kaseem punched the bag a little harder.

"A mosquito's fart can put more force on this bag than that."

The youth grabbed the bag on its sides, bent forward and laughed.

"Think it's funny, eh?" commented Greg. "Well if you don't knock me back on my heels soon, I'm going to start laughing."

Kaseem straightened himself up and began punching with greater force. He began thinking of his mother and grandmother and what he'd done to bring his mother to that office that horrible day. He thought of the pain she must have felt as she pounded on him, pain he'd given her all these years.

He thought of the elderly lady he and Fox had mugged and how she could have been his grandmother. He thought of his father whose faded image now brought to his soul a confused rage.

"Stop!" shouted Gregg. "Take a rest. My god, you almost pounded this bag to pudding."

Kaseem, for the first time, became aware of the throbbing in his knuckles, he was breathing heavily and that his arms had become tired. He sat on a nearby stool.

"Why'd he wanna start a fight with me?" Kaseem asked pleadingly. "I wasn't doing anything to him."

"It wasn't you he was starting a fight with. It was himself. You were just the instrument. You're from the Bronx. You were supposed to beat him up. He feels he's got it coming."

"Huh?" The young man frowned puzzledly.

Greg punched the bag and walked to close to Kaseem. "Razor stole his mom's car, wracked it up and she had him arrested. Then she had a stroke which put her in the hospital. He's been searching for beatings ever since… which got a lot of other kids in trouble. You didn't fall into the trap so my hat's off to you. Speaking of which I have company waiting for me. Take care.'

He gave the young man a light punch on his jaw and was gone.

CHAPTER 27

The school field trip to The Manhasset State Park and the class trips to see *Julius Caesar* at the Stratford Shakespeare Festival in Connecticut and a day Yankee game all worked out just fine.

On the last weekend of the term, Earl finally got himself to drive Anthony up to the Otisville Correctional Facility. It was a beautiful Sunday afternoon. Ida had voiced her objection, but she was outvoted two to one. The drive through what was now a vast panorama of bursting greenery and various blooming flowers, the occasional jolting sight of woodchuck carcasses and the ravens in a funereal dance over them, rolling hills, knolls, hummocks, and wide vistas of farmland seemed to reach to the mostly hidden horizons or the mountain foothills, all covered by plateaus of cows and horses grazing peacefully. The drive took almost two hours altogether.

He walked his son to the doorway of the recreation hall but did not go in himself. He chose to get his bearings outside while Anthony and Kaseem punched each other, made the liberation handshake, and "snapped on" each other, laughing raucously. Kaseem looked healthy and less ill at ease than expected.

Someone tapped Earl on his shoulder. He turned and saw Kaseem's mother and grandmother behind him.

"You came!" she said, awed. "God bless you."

Watching her son and Anthony getting along so famously, her eyes flashed and turned to the teacher. "My goodness gracious, that your son, Mr. Chaney?"

Earl nodded proudly.

"Will you look at that boy, Momma! Spitting image. I just know he's the apple of your eye."

The three went into the large hall to join the two youths. Earl watched Kaseem look at his mother and embrace her ardently. Deeply moved, the teacher noted that she was still taller than he was, but the boy was catching up to her. His grandmother smacked him on his head, and he opened his arms to include her in the triumviral embrace that they held for a number of minutes.

"You bathing regular, boy?" asked Mrs. MacNeil.

"Like a fish in the sea," he answered, and they were silent again.

Then they released, and Kaseem looked somewhat sheepishly at his teacher and his teacher's son. "Well, Mr. Chaney, you finally got the three of us out in the country together." He chuckled self-consciously as the others smiled. "Square business, you were the last person I expected to see up here. You really blew my mind."

"Wasn't that nice of'm?" said his mother as she flicked a speck of lint off her son's pola shirt. "And with's son."

"It's not so bad here," Kaseem started. "I've been keeping my nose clean. Doing a lotta thinking. I'm reading *Julius Caesar* in place of the trip. Nobody bothers me here. They keep things pretty tight. Fox was sent to Wyltwick, which I heard ain't too bad either. I get the willies every now and then, but hey, I'll live with it. I wanna thank y'all for what you did for me and all. And you were right, Mr. Chaney. Mom. Grams. About a lotta things. And I'm sorry for what I did to y'all. If you think the worst of me, I can't blame you.

"Also, Mom, I think someday soon I'd like to be confirmed."

The four people gaped at him.

Could Earl believe him? Well, why at this point would he lie? He decided to push his wonderings to the back of his mind and simply cling to the current pleasantness.

"This is for you," he said, giving Kaseem the card, which the young man read. Obviously deeply affected, his face twitched slightly, and his eyes watered.

He then smiled. "Hey, Mario's name's on this, too. And Mrs. Stanton's." He stared at the card for a moment. Then he looked away. "Can't let these dudes around here see me cry," he said, his voice quavering.

Julia moved to her son and placed her hand on his back.

"I want you to know," said Earl, "that the class did this on their own without me saying anything."

As Earl and Anthony were getting into the car, he offered the two women a lift back to the city.

"No, thank you," Julia said. "We'll catch a cab back to the Otisville bus terminal. We've troubled you enough."

"No trouble. No trouble at all. Are you sure?"

"I'm sure. We'll be fine." She then turned to Anthony. "That's a good father you got there, son. Keep'm well. Fine boy, Mr. Chaney. Fine boy. You take care now."

After Julia said good-bye, her mother and she started toward an empty outside phone to call a taxi. Mrs. MacNeil stood faithfully beside her.

Earl watched them for a moment and then clutched his son's forearm.

"You have much homework?" he asked.

"I did it all. Why?"

"I'm going to keep you out a little longer than usual. We have a restaurant date in the city. There're some special people in my life, and I think it's about time you met them."

Earl glanced again at the two women and then turned on his ignition.